Roscoe Hammer

A Novel
by
Dave Gallemore

First published by Dog Ear Publishing
4011 Vincennes Rd
Indianapolis, IN 46268
www.dogearpublishing.net

ISBN: 978-1-4575-4788-1

This book is printed on acid-free paper.

Printed in the United States of America

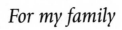
For my family

PROLOGUE

St. Louis, Missouri - 1994

On July 8th, the hottest day of the year, a thirty-two-year-old woman named Mary Lewellen walked into a tavern in the Delmar Loop district, sat down at the bar and asked for a Budweiser draft.

The bartender put the beer on the bar and when Mary reached for it, he looked curiously at the large reddish-brown stain on her right arm.

"It's blood," she explained.

"The bathroom is back there if you need to clean up. Are you all right?" he asked, thinking she might have been injured.

"I'm fine," she said, swallowing. "Why don't you give me a minute or two and then you better call the police."

"Police, why?"

Mary Lewellen, a registered nurse and the mother of two young daughters, then calmly explained that less than an hour earlier, she had stabbed her boyfriend in the heart with a large knife she found in the garage behind the house they shared at 7263 Forsyth Boulevard. He had been sleeping. The blood was his. He was dead.

CHAPTER 1

Mitchell, Missouri – 46 Years Earlier

Roscoe Hammer was a handsome eight-year-old with big blue eyes and a head of rowdy brown hair who lived happily with his family in the tiny town of Mitchell, Missouri in the south-eastern corner of the state. While Roscoe was normal in almost every way, during the school year following his eighth birthday, he discovered something that made him different from his younger brother Andy, and his little sister, Hannah. It was something that made him different from all his friends, and come to think of it, different from anybody he knew in the whole world. Roscoe discovered real magic.

Not the type of magic in the card tricks his Uncle Marvin performed after Thanksgiving dinner each year when the pumpkin pie plates were cleared away. Though always delivered with an inspired flare to the "oohs" and "aahs" of Roscoe and his many cousins, Uncle Marvin's card tricks were just that, tricks.

Neither was it the kind of magic Roscoe had seen performed on television by those flashy, slender men with dark hair and beautiful, leggy helper-ladies. Roscoe had seen these magicians make cars, and huge boulders and once, even a man-eating tiger disappear. But, as his dad had explained while he and Roscoe took in a particularly spellbinding performance on the Ed Sullivan Show, these famous magicians were really illusionists. They made things seem to disappear, or made people look as though they had been cut in half when, in fact, the tiger was still there and the pretty lady was still all in one piece. What Roscoe had seen on the Ed Sullivan television show was

1

really just an advanced version of Uncle Marvin's card tricks. But what Roscoe began to learn that special fall as he and his friends went into the third grade at Masonhall Elementary, the thing that would affect the rest of his life, was that he, unlike anyone else he knew, understood that true magic and life were the same thing.

Roscoe's earliest interest in magic was ignited one day when his father took him to Mitchell's *Ben Franklin Five and Dime* to buy a toy valued at up to one dollar and fifty-eight cents, the then sum total of Roscoe's accumulated wealth, which he had earned, saved and counted over and over again through a full summer of household chores and personal deprivation. He was only five years old going on six at the time, and this was his first shopping experience. He snaked his way up and down the toy aisles slowly, pausing every now and then to carefully touch the merchandise, so as to inspect its quality, or to squint at a price tag. Roscoe's father followed behind him, silent always, the way one might follow behind an archaeologist combing through ancient ruins. Roscoe had financed this trip; he would choose the toy, within reason of course, and he would pay. His father was there for transportation first, and for counsel and calculation only upon request. Those were the agreed upon rules and Roscoe took his time.

Then, suddenly, there it was! He stood wide-eyed, gaping, frozen with wonder. It was the Harry Houdini Deluxe Magic Pak! Not the Beginner's Pak or the Standard Pak...no, indeed it was the DELUXE Pak! At half the size of a shoebox, it promised to contain everything a youngster needed to reprise the world-famous magic of the great Houdini. Roscoe could learn magic, he thought, and dazzle his family, his classmates, even maybe the *older* kids at Masonhall. His popularity would soar. It would be great! And all for the more-than-reasonable price of, oops.... two dollars and twenty cents!

"Two dollars and twenty cents," Roscoe whispered to himself. That was more than he had; more by an amount he couldn't calculate on the spot because his mind was gripped by the prospect that he might not get the Harry Houdini Deluxe Magic Pak after all. "Yipes!"

"Need a little loan?" Roscoe's dad asked with a knowing grin. And just like that, Frank Hammer was promoted from chauffeur to full partner, or as Roscoe's mother Laura would later put it, co-conspirator.

Unfortunately, like so many things from Ben Franklin, the Harry Houdini Deluxe Magic Pak was never so exciting, never so, well, *deluxe*-looking, as it was when first Roscoe spotted it there in the store. At home, under harsh light, the contents seemed cheap, the instruction manual was too complicated, the tricks were more difficult than he had ever imagined. And, Roscoe's pockets were empty. What's worse, at such a tender age he had stumbled for the first time into the vise-grip of that quintessential American transaction, the financed purchase. He had gone into debt. He owed his father sixty-eight cents, plus tax. His indebtedness played on his mind and the more he practiced the Houdini routines, the more frustrated he became. Was he too awkward, too clumsy for magic? Would the audience ever be fooled, for that matter, would there ever *be* an audience? More than once he held his little brother Andy hostage in the bedroom they shared and forced him to watch the ragged routine. Andy was so young he could scarcely speak in complete sentences and even he, having seen the act once or twice, could not be fooled.

Sadly and all too soon, the arsenal of tricks and gadgetry from the Magic Pak were strewn from one end of the Hammer household to the other, victims of Roscoe's discouragement and disinterest. The string of silky scarves that could be made to appear never-ending while being pulled from the magician's pocket, they were lost along with dirty socks, between Roscoe's bed and the wall. The silver interconnected rings that could be mysteriously separated and then, in a blink, looped back together found their way to the bottom of the family clothes hamper. Roscoe's dog Ranger ate the trick dice, which were later "returned" and the Deluxe Pak instruction manual which wasn't. And the counterfeit coin with "heads" on both sides, well, Roscoe lost it down the toilet while....while trying to do too much at once, let's just say.

From this, Roscoe's first introduction to magic, and the fame and celebrity he hoped it would bring, from all of this, scarce little remained. In fact, in just weeks, all Roscoe had to show from the Harry Houdini Deluxe Magic Pak, the only thing he hadn't lost, was one last, lonely artifact, a cheap wooden magic wand, painted half black and half white. Roscoe laid it on his nightstand, the shrine-of-all-things-aspired-to-or-dreamed-of, alongside a newspaper photograph of the New York Yankees. Next to the wand, in Roscoe's own, earliest handwriting was a terse directive to any passerby: "My Magik Wond, Do Not Tuch".

He thought the role of magic in his life was over. But he was wrong, as it had not even really begun.

CHAPTER 2

For a child like Roscoe Hammer, Mitchell, Missouri may have been the best town in the entire world. More a village than a town, its tree-canopied streets curved and had character; they meandered wistfully through the town as though designed by someone absent-minded or lazy, maybe by a drinker.

The commercial portion of Mitchell was only partially captured in the quaint city-center square that Mitchell's four thousand citizens called "downtown". Some of the more important stores and shops were scattered amongst the town's homes, in some cases having been converted from, or set up as convenient extensions of a traditional household. For example, between the Hammer home and Masonhall Elementary, along the path Roscoe traveled each school day, there was a nondescript, white, two-story frame house, the first level of which was Gertie's Grocery Store. Gertie Paulson, a sixty-eight-year-old widow and one of the nicest people Roscoe had ever met, lived upstairs above the market with her older sister, Harriet, who was regarded by most of the citizenry to be slightly disturbed but pretty much harmless. The little grocery, together with a modest life insurance annuity, provided financial sustenance for Gertie and her dependent sister. The friendship of regular customers — half of them children like Roscoe — more than made up for any of the numerous luxuries they did without.

Gertie's inventory was not extensive. Milk, eggs, flour and baking supplies. Fresh chickens from old man Hattan's hatchery and a few good cuts of beef and pork. Cold bottled soda in the summertime. Just the basics. "I'm not out to replace the IGA," Gertie would often say in a voice that was convincing. But what she had, that the IGA didn't have, the thing that mattered most to Roscoe and all the children within walking distance of Gertie's, was perhaps the widest assortment of penny candy in North America, for sure in Missouri.

Each day, before setting out on the six-block journey down Sand Plum Street to Masonhall, Roscoe and his mother would make a quick review of the necessary preparations and cargo: gloves and buckled galoshes in wet or wintry weather, school books and papers, a black plastic pocket comb, and a simple lunch packed the evening before by Mrs. Hammer. Now and then a handkerchief made it in, though Roscoe was not a fan of them.

At Roscoe's request, the contents of his lunch were always kept secret. He liked the surprise each day when he opened his Jet Jackson lunch box to discover a Hostess Cupcake, or Twinkie, or even better, a huge chunk of homemade brownie. For a kid like Roscoe, the surprise was even better than the food.

But there was usually some undeclared cargo as well. Roscoe always kept three or four suitable-for-trading baseball cards in his back pocket; these were the coin of the realm on the playground at Masonhall. And he never left for school without a few pennies for the purchase of Jolly Rogers Firestick candies at Gertie's on his way home. He always had enough for himself and for his frequent companion, Fatty Gilchrist, who never seemed to have any pennies of his own, but whose other favorable traits made him Roscoe's very best friend.

Fatty's nickname was apt. He was short and round, like a minia-ture sumo wrestler. And although he had been so branded by a pack of older teen-aged boys who drove cars, smoked cigarettes and entertained themselves by picking on little kids, Fatty didn't seem to mind it. Why should he, after all? He could make his friends laugh by making funny sounds that appeared to emanate from someone else, like a ventrilo-quist of sorts. He was a better-than-average and mannerly student. And he could hit a baseball farther than anyone in the first three grades at Masonhall, a skill that was particularly critical in his case because he either couldn't or didn't like to run very fast. In about every way you could think of, Fatty was just plain goodhearted and that is what made him Roscoe's best friend and popular with almost everyone.

Roscoe and Fatty became first acquainted because their separate routes to Masonhall Elementary intersected conveniently at Gertie's Grocery. Straight north of there, five full blocks on Sand Plum, was Roscoe's house. To get to Fatty's from the grocery store, you walked east on 11th Street, passing Cobb's Dairy and the Mitchell Public Library. Cobb's was a small but complete commercial dairy where all manner of milk products were processed and packaged for sale to grocers throughout the eastern half of Missouri. For some reason the dairy also operated a small soda fountain in the front of its building where malts, milkshakes and the like were served to customers off the street. Twenty cents there would buy the Fatty Gilchrist favorite, a concoction of sweet cream, soda water and chocolate syrup, all served over shaved ice. The drink was called the Four Hundred and Fatty got his free because his father was the one and only salesman for Cobb's Dairy. Henry Gilchrist was shaped more or less like his son, Fatty, and many in Mitchell believed credit in both cases went to a steady diet of free Four Hundreds.

Up and down Sand Plum, east and west on 11th Street, at Gertie's candy counter, on the playground at Masonhall and on stools at the Cobb's soda fountain, Roscoe and Fatty grew up together in Mitchell, Missouri, the exact place that an obscure social scientist specified — based on geography and population density — to be the very center of the United States. Undeterred by the fact that this honor would not hold up to scientific scrutiny, the town wore the distinction proudly, with several businesses claiming it for themselves. There was Center City Donuts, and Mid-America Plate and Mirror, and the Crossroads Printing Company. If it is natural for youngsters to think of themselves as being at the center of the universe, it was even more so for the children of Mitchell.

"No matter where in the world you are going," Mrs. Sweeney, their third grade teacher, would tell her students romantically, "in Mitchell you are halfway there."

"Doesn't it matter where you start from?" Fatty once asked to the snickers of his classmates. It was a fairly astute question.

"No, Mr. Gilchrist, it does not," she answered sternly, cocking her head just a little to emphasize the point.

Roscoe and Fatty kicked the concept around that afternoon on the way to Gertie's and concluded that Mrs. Sweeney would have made a lousy navigator. But they agreed it really didn't matter; she was just expressing pride in their little town, and on that note she'd get no argument from them. They loved Mitchell, Missouri, no matter where it was halfway to or from. All summer long, the water in the Mitchell public swimming pool served as a clear-blue and cool refuge from heat and humidity. And in the winter, especially around the holidays, predictable snow would fall just so, making perfect white ribbons of the streets and lanes, deep enough for sledding and fun, but not so much as to corrupt the town's gentle, purposeful rhythm. With every springtime pristine, and radiant autumn, the seasons rolled through Mitchell like a lullaby.

This town Mitchell, Roscoe's and Fatty's place, was a perfect place for them and hundreds more like them. It was a town of ornate garden gates, beds of bearded iris, unattended honeysuckle run amok, and unsupervised but safe children. It wasn't the kind of place where bad things would happen.

CHAPTER 3

Fatty's given but seldom used name was Randall, Randall MacArthur Gilchrist. The middle name, MacArthur, was a strictly held secret between Fatty, his immediate family and the only outsider he could really trust, Roscoe. Fatty had an older sister whose name, Beulah, the family could not keep secret. She was shaped much the same as Fatty and their father, and in a cruel and unusual coincidence, a nationally known dairy launched a massive advertising campaign around a female cow spokesperson named.... *Beulah*. Everywhere you turned, there was Beulah, the portly mascot of Hopkins Dairy, pitching chocolate milk, butter, sour cream, whipped cream and cream cheese. It was dreadful. The more Roscoe saw these advertisements, the more it seemed the face of Beulah, the Hopkins cow, took on the subtleties of Beulah Gilchrist's increasingly forlorn visage.

"How sad," Laura Hammer would say each time she came across a photo of Beulah in her *Saturday Evening Post* or *Readers Digest*. "There should be something they can do."

This grizzly confluence of real life and Madison Avenue thrust Fatty into any number of altercations on the schoolyard at Masonhall. The jokes about his sister and the stupid dairy cow were endless, and Fatty would stand for only so much. Though non-violent by nature, he was a pretty good fighter, as witnessed by a few of the Masonhall jokers who took the unkind hilarity too far.

Fatty's basic combat routine was almost ballet-like. He was fat and round, and in the tradition of the great Samurais, he turned this to his advantage. After a little verbal sparring, he would allow his opponent to attempt some kind of takedown. But invariably, their arms could not reach all the way around him which made their grip on the little Tasmanian a point of weakness. At just the right moment, he would drop his weight ever so slightly, and spin his body to the right while extending one of his legs. The offender would chase the spin of Fatty's torso in a failed attempt to maintain his grip and would never notice the extended leg. And of course, the unnoticed leg was the key to this maneuver. Before he knew what had happened, the scoundrel would be flat on his back at the feet of Fatty the Conqueror.

From here, things would get pretty interesting. Once he had them on the ground, with his full heft centered on their chest cavity and their arms pinned beneath his pudgy little legs, Fatty was transformed into the Marque de Sade of schoolyard retribution. He had a whole repertoire of tortures designed to extract a "take it back" without leaving a mark. First there was the spit-drool torture. If the first long string of slimy saliva didn't get them to confess, then for certain the second one would. Nobody wanted two globs of lumpy spittle piled up between their eyes. Or Fatty could just "fart 'em" as he would say. At will, he could squeeze off a raucous, flatulent fog that would incapacitate his prisoner and send innocent bystanders screaming across the playground, eyes watering. Fatty farted Mickey Bartash once and Roscoe was afraid that Mickey had passed out completely.

But the very worst case, the time when Fatty came close to doing some real damage, involved Tommy Corcoran. Corcoran, or "Tommy Corks" as he was known, was two full grades ahead of Roscoe and Fatty at Masonhall and everyone there, including most of the faculty, was afraid of him. He was rumored to have been abandoned in a drainage ditch by his parents at birth, left to grow up in the wild. He was, without a doubt, the biggest bully at Masonhall.

One day, a day Tommy Corcoran would come to regret, he shot his mouth off about Beulah the cow and Fatty's sister and Fatty just sort of snapped. First Fatty hit Tommy with the famous Gilchrist pirouette. He had him pinned to the ground in no time and Tommy was still muttering obscenities the likes of which would have landed Roscoe or Fatty in prison for five years.

"What are you gunna do, Fatso?" Tommy taunted. "You gunna spit on me? I'll drink your slime you fat baby. Go on...go on, I don't care."

Well, Fatty didn't spit on him and he didn't gas him either. What he did staggered even his corner man, Roscoe. Fatty twisted around to his right and with Tommy's arms still pinned down, Fatty whacked him as hard as he could right in the "giblets" as Fatty and Roscoe called them. Tommy gasped and turned bright red. Roscoe gasped. Girls in the crowd turn their eyes away. Fatty himself went into a kind of trance.

Finally, Tommy Corks breathed again and climbed to his feet, gingerly cupping his crotch, as if it would otherwise fall to the ground. He was crying and when he saw all of his old victims in the gallery staring at him, he just turned and ran. He didn't even go back into the classroom after recess. When his teacher asked his whereabouts, some of Tommy's buddies told her he had gotten "the pukes" and went home.

Fatty never really reveled in his victory over Tommy Corks; somehow it actually seemed to make him a little sad. He had vanquished a genuine bad guy, but it didn't change the fact that his poor sister was walking around with a cow's name. It had to be done, but he wasn't that proud of it.

As for Tommy Corcoran, the news got worse before it got better. The next day at school, Tommy was quiet and contrite; other than that, everything was pretty much back to normal. What Roscoe and Fatty learned later though was that from a boy's perspective, things couldn't have been further from normal. It was never reported directly to either of them, but one mother told another mother who told another mother......and finally, Penny Barksdale overheard her mother talking about it and she wrote a note to Roscoe about it. What "it" was, was ghastly. It seems that when Fatty gave Tommy a whack in the giblets, he gasped so hard that one of his testicles *ascended!*

"Ascended!" Fatty whispered to Roscoe with a look of terror on his face. "What does that mean, ascended?"

"It means it went up, I think, but I don't really know," Roscoe answered, still trying to make out part of the note.

"Went up where?" Fatty asked. He was growing more panicked by the second and had unconsciously placed one hand over his lower belly. "Is it just roaming around up there in his stomach? Holly Toledo!"

"I don't know, Fatty, it doesn't say. And it doesn't say if it will ever come back down. What if it just stays......up there?"

"I'm never hittin' a guy down there again," Fatty said. "Never, ever."

A month later word came through a similarly circuitous network that Tommy Corcoran's giblet had dropped back down into position. But in the meantime, poor Fatty had suffered through a rumor that the incident might have made it impossible for Tommy Corks to "make babies". Years later conclusive evidence to the contrary was revealed when Tommy Corcoran and his wife produced Mitchell's only documented case of triplets. Had Fatty been around then, all of Mitchell would have heard a huge sigh of relief. Sadly, he wasn't.

CHAPTER 4

"Pop, explain to me again where my name came from," Roscoe said while he watched his father shaving.

"It came from your great-grandfather. His name was Roscoe too," Frank said, hoping to tie a quick bow on this line of questioning.

"Yeah, I know that part, but where did he get the name?"

"He was born in a small town in Illinois named Roscoe. And in that town there was a factory that manufactured the country's finest claw hammers; it was called Roscoe Hammer. His father, my great-grandpa was a little whacky and he decided that with the last name of Hammer, the coincidence was too great to resist. He named his son Roscoe." He paused briefly to make one last pass with his safety razor. "The first Roscoe Hammer was born in Roscoe, Illinois, home of Roscoe Hammer. There's a little weirdness in every family, son, that's important to remember."

"But why'd you give it to me?" Roscoe begged, with the same inflection one might use when asking why he'd been purposefully infected with tuberculosis.

"Compromise, son, compromise. Your mother insisted that we give you a family name and most of the male names in your family are pretty crummy. Take me for example. Frank isn't my real name, it's Francis."

"I know, it sounds like a girl," Roscoe said flatly.

"Middle name, Marion," Frank added, as if he was telling a ghost story.

"Good grief, Pop, Francis Marion! How did you survive?"

"Barely son. And your grandfather's real name was Romeo, Romeo Marion Hammer. And your grandpa on your mother's side was Clovis and he was a pretty big drinker. We just didn't have much to work with. Roscoe sound better now?" He splashed all the soap off his cheeks, leaned forward to take one last look at his work and then told Roscoe, "So there you have it, Roscoe, Illinois, the home of the Hammers, so to speak."

"Hence, the name," Roscoe said with a quick, perky smile.

"Hence, the name?" his father repeated. "Snappy! Where did you hear that expression?"

"Miss Harriet, down at Gertie's."

"How's that?" Frank asked.

"Well," Roscoe said, "I was down there two days ago and I bought a SlowPoke, and I was eating it, and Miss Harriet comes downstairs and she asks me if it, the SlowPoke, was my favorite thing, you know? I said yeah, I guess so and she asked me why. I thought about it and I said cuz they last so long....they take a long time to eat. And that's when she said it."

"Said what?" Frank asked, straining to keep up with Roscoe's rolling narrative.

"Hence the name!" Roscoe exclaimed. "Get it? Slow...Poke."

"Right, right," his father said, smiling. "Miss Harriet is ah, well, a little different. You know that, don't you?"

"Fatty's Dad says she's a world-class nutcase," Roscoe answered.

"Well, let's just say she's a little different. I think that sounds better, okay? But, 'hence the name', that's a good one. Good for Miss Harriet. And now little man, it is time to get ready for school."

And with that, Frank Hammer pulled his son close to him for a hug, followed by a quick kiss on the top of Roscoe's head, a morning ritual they both loved. "Did you hear that rain last night? Didn't stop till dawn."

"No, I didn't hear it at all," Roscoe said. "*Francis Marion,*" he whispered to himself as he headed down the hallway to his bedroom. "Good grief!"

Two doors down Sand Plum Street, at the tidy home of Jefferson and Althea Woodson, there was an explosion. At least it sounded like an explosion as it came through Roscoe's bedroom window.

Althea was backing her husband's pickup truck, a spotless, ten-year-old, pride-and-joy step-side Chevy out of their tiny one-car garage and discovered a touch too late that she'd forgotten to open the garage door. The door, along with the entire front wall of the garage, came down in a heap on the shiny red truck and all hell broke loose. Roscoe was able to observe this entire calamity from his bedroom window and it made a lasting impression.

Transplanted Mississippians, the Woodsons were large people, she even larger than he, and their natural Southern animation became downright ballet-like as this catastrophe unfolded. Althea screamed for Jesus to help her. A pajama-clad Jefferson – JL to anyone who knew him — came flying blurry-eyed into the driveway and screamed for Jesus to help *him*. Althea made her way out of the rubble and tried to run to JL but he ran *away* from her as if she was on fire or maybe the devil.

"Dear God, what have you done?" he yelled.

"Oh Jesus!" she cried. "Am I bleeding? Oh Jesus!"

"My truck! My truck! Oh my God! What the hell were you doing, Althea?"

"I was going to the grocery, and next thing I knew, the house fell in on me. Oh Jesus. Am I bleeding?" She finally caught up with him and threw herself into his arms crying.

"You're makin' it sound like a earthquake or somethin'. A bomb or somethin'. You ran right through the damned door, Althea. You blasted right through it. Lord Jesus have mercy."

Then suddenly, amidst her sobbing, his softness surfaced.

"Shush now, sugar, it's all right," he said to her. "You ain't bleeding. It's all right, sugar. Damn old truck anyway, it must have lurched on you. It's okay. Shush, now, don't cry no more."

"It did, Jefferson, it lurched on me," she said patting wildly at her red nose. "It lurched and then it all just came crashing down. I could have been crushed like a tomato. Lord have mercy!"

They held each other in silence for a few moments and then, to Roscoe's astonishment, they began to laugh. Softly at first, then graduating to an almost boisterous crescendo that left them both doubled over. Right there in the driveway. Right in the middle of all that debris. They just laughed and laughed. That's the way they were: big, loud, outrageous, funny, soft, mildly profane and loving.

The couple had migrated to Mitchell before Roscoe was born to follow JL's job with the Burlington Northern Railroad and bought the house two doors down from the Hammers. Althea got a good-paying job in the County Clerk's office, and worked there a year or two before something regrettable happened. Nadine Brownbeck, a shameless and unambiguous racist, was elected County Clerk, largely because it had been disclosed one way or another that her predecessor, Althea's boss, had stumbled into an extramarital affair with a young high school English teacher. Being one of only a dozen or so black people in Mitchell at that time, Althea saw Nadine's murky victory as nothing but trouble and decided to quit her job. After all, JL, who worked nights as a rail-yard switchman, had one of the very best jobs in Mitchell and they could get by quite nicely on his wages alone.

From then on, Althea, cooked and cleaned and kept their home in perfect condition, even taking up some of the basic maintenance chores more commonly left the men in those days. And there on Sand Plum Street, from just two doors down, she became Laura Hammer's very best friend. JL came home from work in the morning, at about the same time Frank Hammer was going to work. JL slept, and Frank worked, and their wives shared worries, lemonade, and petty gossip.

Once he was sure Althea Woodson had not killed herself, Roscoe looked down at his dog, Ranger, who had stood faithfully beside him and watched the whole mess. "Whew, that was a close one, boy."

On his way out the door, Roscoe filed a quick news bulletin with his mother and father. "Miss Althea drove the red truck through the garage door, but she's okay," he said. "Me and Ranger saw the whole thing. Bye." Books and lunch box in tow, Roscoe headed out the door and down the street toward a new day that would change his life forever.

CHAPTER 5

*O*nly when you see a living creature draw its last breath, only then can you begin to understand death. Hunters do not understand death; at their hands the dying happens quickly and in the distance. Hunters understand killing. But those who have seen the life go out of a thing, they understand death.

Before there is any sight, there is the sound, the wailing of a half-dead animal. By the time Roscoe can run to the horrific scene, the hunter is gone but the sights and sounds and smell of death are there, in the middle of the street where a small mutt, no more than twenty pounds, drags his crushed hindquarters behind him in sad, manic circles. The dog's back legs and hips are covered in red and yellow blood and through a six-inch gash on his side, an exposed intestine leaks yellowish and brown waste. He yelps and yelps and pulls his own death behind him in circles. His mouth and nose ooze blood and mucous and vomit and his eyes, his sad yellow eyes bulge with pain. Roscoe's face is frozen but his hands tremble like an old man's and a throbbing lump pushes on the top of his throat. He wants to help the little dog but he cannot move. Somehow he knows there can be no helping here on death's edge. The circling gets slower; the circles grow smaller. The broken animal has less and less breath to offer each cry, until there is no sound. And then, while Roscoe trembles and cries, the poor dog collapses. His wet, yellow eyes turn toward Roscoe and reach out like the hands of a beggar. The dog knows he is alone. One last, quick flash of terror sparks across his eyes and then they glaze and life leaves him. Roscoe feels like he can almost see the life leave this little mutt. And he feels smaller somehow, as though all of life has become instantly, microscopically smaller.

Still sobbing, Roscoe turns and runs. He stumbles over the curb and falls into a spirea bush. He gathers himself and runs again, as fast as he has ever run. He runs and runs and cries. At the edge of the Masonhall school-yard, he falls to his knees and vomits.

Imogene Sweeney, Roscoe's third-grade teacher, was the first to see him. She was perhaps the school's most famous disciplinarian. Serving as Principal when four sixth-grade boys were caught in the boiler room smoking unfiltered Pall Malls, Imogene prosecuted the perpetrators and expelled them for six weeks in a case that was there-after known as the Masonhall Massacre. The whole episode soured her on administration and she voluntarily retreated to the classroom and third-grade misdemeanors. Even this tough veteran, upon hear-ing Roscoe's story, was moved nearly to tears. She put her arm around him and took him straight away to the school nurse's office.

"Lay down on the cot until you feel better, Roscoe," she said softly. "The school nurse should be in soon. Just tell her what you told me."

"Yes, ma'am," Roscoe answered. "I should be fine in a few min-utes."

"No hurry. Close your eyes and rest a bit."

A gentle breeze came through the window and Roscoe began to feel the knot in his throat relax. His shoulders surrendered into the fresh white linen on the cot and he drifted off.

In half-sleep, Roscoe's mind went to his own dog, Ranger, an eighty-five-pound Bluetick Coonhound that had never seen a rac-coon. Ranger was adopted by the Hammers as a puppy and had grown up alongside Roscoe. He was gentle with children, but too big for the house, where, to Laura Hammer's growing dismay, he occa-sionally urinated behind the divan. His long, floppy ears and drool-dripping dewlap endeared him to Roscoe, Andy, and especially, little Hannah, but he had driven a wedge between the Hammer's and their next door neighbor, the widow Morris, by treeing her aging Himalayan a half-dozen times. He soiled the rugs. He dug through the garbage pail. He howled at almost everything and sniffed house guests indelicately. Ranger, who slept with Roscoe every night, was a good dog on thin ice and Roscoe knew it. He had overheard his mother discuss with his father the idea of giving Ranger to old man Hattan who operated a hatchery two miles south of town. Hattan knew that a Bluetick would ignore the poultry but police the kind of varmints that steal eggs and kill chickens.

"I'm always looking for a good coonhound," he told Laura upon hearing her complain about Ranger's misbehavior. "Tell your boy the dog would have a good home here. I'd even throw in a couple of big roasting hens."

"I'll keep that in mind, Mr. Hattan," Laura said politely. What she really wanted was to accept his offer that very minute. But she didn't. Ranger was part of the Hammer family, at least for the time being.

When Roscoe was aroused, it was to an unfamiliar sound. It came through the window, carried from a distance it seemed by the day's breeze. Cher-clip. Cher-clip. Cher-clip, clip, clip. The sound, in perfect rhythm, came from somewhere past Masonhall's empty playground, somewhere across the adjacent street. Cher-clip. Cher-clip. Cher-clip. It came from behind a large forsythia, wide and unkempt and green in this late season. It came from a terrifying man Roscoe had seen only once before in his life, a hedge-clipper wielding hulk, Mitchell's own monster, Crazy George Mabry.

Mabry was a sixty-five-year-old stump of a man who wandered Mitchell's neighborhoods trimming bushes for widow ladies and elderly homeowners and terrifying the town's children with his malevolent gaze and angry muttering. His balding head sat atop a short neck and rounded slouching shoulders and at every bend and fold in his thick body, at the waist, the knees and especially the elbows and neckline, there was a dark ring of sweat and filth. His eyes were buried deep behind thick wire-rimmed glasses and his two-day beard made his whole face look grey and dead. He wore khaki colored trousers and a matching shirt with the sleeves rolled into a tight wad at the elbow which made his massive forearms bulge like smoked hams. His trousers were cuffed just above the high tops of his Wolverine work boots and when he walked, his body swayed from side to side as much as it moved forward, giving the appearance of stalking. All of this combined with his incessant, deep-throated mumbling, kept children and most adults a safe distance away.

Despite his menacing demeanor, George had little trouble finding work. He did not rake leaves and he did not mow grass. He trimmed bushes and hedges and nothing more. His work was greatly admired and he took payment only in cash. He kept a modest passbook account at the Mitchell Savings and Loan where the fussy tellers cringed to see him come into the lobby with his occasional deposit. As soon as he was gone, they would rush to the ladies washroom and complain of his smell and engage in petty chit-chat about the inexhaustible stockpile of George Mabry rumors.

Some said George had no proper home or rented room, but lived alone in a lean-to shack on the banks of Shale Creek, just outside town. Some said he peeked through windows now and then, but there was no real proof. Some said that he had once thrown a full brick through the picture window of the Jessup house when undertaker Walt Jessup, believing George had made an improper comment to his wife, refused to pay for an afternoon's trimming work. For the brick-launching episode there were conflicting stories but enough evidence to occasion one of George's many nights in the Mitchell jail. He found himself in the jail every two or three months and each time, when released, he would find that the Mitchell police had relieved him of any pocket money that hadn't made it to the Savings and Loan. And the town's children told wild, grizzly stories about George. One oft-repeated yarn had him killing and dismembering a dog with his trimmers. "Yeaaaaah," the most imaginative in the group would invariably add, "and I heard he ate the thing."

In fact, nobody really knew where George slept at night, nobody knew what he ate, and nobody knew the subject of his constant muttering. In truth, little was known about George Mabry. He trimmed and pruned like an artist, but he was just the town's half-wit. "Don't look at him," a dutiful parent would admonish. "Best not stare. Don't talk to him. Just keep away from him." Cher-clip. Cher-clip. Cher-clip, clip, clip.

"Mr. Hammer, are you feeling better?" It Mrs. McKenzie, the school nurse. Roscoe hadn't noticed her when she came into the room.

"Ah, yes, yes ma'am, better," he answered, struggling to focus.

"It sounds as though you had quite a morning, young man," she said, craning around to try and make eye contact.

Something was going on across the street, near the forsythia where he had seen Crazy George. A flashy blue car pulled alongside the curb and stopped. An arm hung out of the driver's window and there were tattoos on the arm and there was a cigarette in the hand at the end of the arm. Someone on the passenger side jumped out, shouted at Mabry and then threw a gunny sack toward George, landing it right at his feet.

"Are you all right, Roscoe?" nurse McKenzie asked. "What are you looking at over there?"

"Oh...nothing ma'am," Roscoe answered. His eyes were glued on Mabry, who was on his knees, peering into the gunny sack.

"Oh, I see," the nurse said, finally catching sight of scene across the street. "That's old George Mabry. You stay away from him. And, you need to go back to Mrs. Sweeney's classroom now, our Principal is making an announcement this morning and you need to be present."

"Yes, ma'am," Roscoe said, still fixed on the silent drama playing out across the street.

"Now, Mr. Hammer!"

"Okay, yes ma'am," He stole one last glance. Cigarette smoke curled from the window of the blue car as it pulled away and Roscoe thought he heard the people inside laugh, though he couldn't be sure. He saw George Mabry's head drop as he closed the sack; he was still on his knees when Roscoe left the room and headed for Mrs. Sweeney's class. As he climbed the stairs Roscoe wondered why Mitchell's monster was on his knees.

CHAPTER 6

With one eye on his mother, his little sister Hannah, and Gertie Paulson – all gathered together at the front counter – Andy Hammer made his way carefully to the small newsstand in the back of Gertie's where customers could find a few Marvel comics, the current edition of the St. Louis Globe Democrat, the Mitchell Courier, and a half-dozen well-known periodicals. Amongst the latter was an issue of National Geographic that Andy found most curious in its manner of display. On the magazine cover he could see only the magazine's title and the face and shoulders of an African lady carrying a large pot on top of her head. The rest of the cover and, importantly, the rest of the African lady was covered by a piece of scrap cardboard that had been trimmed to reveal just what it did and nothing more.

Andy was about to do what any five-year-old boy confronted by this kind of mystery would do when she spoke.

"I remember you." It was Miss Harriet and her words hit Andy in the back as if having been shot from a pistol. He jumped and spun around, his feet nearly leaving the floor.

"Huh?"

"I remember you, you're the handsome young courier who came to the telephone company office from time to time. All of us girls were older but we secretly wished that you would take us dancing at Gaslight."

"Dancing? Huh? I'm Andy Hammer. I can't dance."

"Oh, I know that," she said, tossing her head back and smiling. "That's now, but I'm talking about back then."

Harriet Merchant was an old maid with an opaque past and a reputation for undocumented memories. Nobody, except perhaps her sister Gertie , really knew any better, but her dreamy recollections were hard to pin down, even for her contemporaries there in Mitchell. Once in a while someone would ask Gertie about one of Harriet's more farfetched yarns. Finding these interrogations intrusive, she would consistently reply that her sister's meanderings were simply a mild case of dementia and should be of no concern or interest to anyone. Her sister, Gertie was convinced, would surely parish before going completely bats and in the meantime her memories or fabrications, take your pick, weren't hurting anybody.

"I'm only five years old," Andy answered. "I don't have a 'back then'."

"Yes, I know. And your tiny sister, Hannah. She is darling, isn't she?"

"I guess so..."

"What are you looking at back here?" Harriet asked. "Are you looking at that magazine?" She pointed to the one.

"No."

"Are you sure? The one with the cardboard?"

"Nope."

"Oh, I see. I thought you might be curious about the cardboard."

"Why's it there? The cardboard?" Andy asked, trying to make the inquiry seem casual.

"Because behind it, the lady's breasts are exposed."

Andy's head snapped around in the direction of his mother who was still chatting with Gertie. He knew what breasts were, but just barely.

"Oh, breasts. How come?"

"Because it is hot in Africa and women don't wear shirts."

"Sometimes my sister doesn't wear a shirt."

"This is a little different."

"Guess so." He badly wanted to look behind the cardboard.

"Andy," Laura Hammer's voice rang out. "Time to go. Hannah is getting fussy. Did you find a comic?"

Andy's little head snapped again. "No ma'am, no ma'am, but I'm ready." He had wasted his time looking at part of a naked woman from another continent. And talking to kooky Miss Harriet about a "back then" he never had.

He headed in the direction of the front counter where Gertie who had been holding Hannah was returning her to Laura. From behind him, Harriet spoke again.

"Your brother Roscoe saw it," she said, almost in passing.

"Huh?" Andy said. He kept walking.

"He saw the little dog die. Today. Then he ran. He was crying."

"Come on Andy," his mother said. "Go get in the wagon."

"Okay momma." He was looking over his shoulder at Harriet as he, his mother, and Hannah left the little store. Laura loaded Hannah, Andy and a few groceries in the Red Flyer and off they headed, north on Sand Plum, with Andy wondering what in the world Harriet was talking about. He didn't like the idea of his big brother crying.

Back in Mrs. Sweeney's classroom, Roscoe noticed right away that Fatty wasn't there. In the pandemonium of the morning he had run right past their normal meeting place. Fatty's sick, he thought. But he'd been at the Hammer house for most of the previous two days and he looked all right then. As usual, he was clowning around and eating everything in sight, but he didn't look sick to Roscoe. Oh well, he was about to miss out on a tiny bit of unusual excitement at Masonhall, an official Principal's announcement.

Principal Gray was just that, grey. Her hair was grey, her skin and eyes were grey and, fittingly, her clothes were grey. They hung on her the way bedsheets hang over summer-house furniture in the off-season. She looked to be one hundred years old and when she spoke her head shook such that some of the white powder she used on her hair dissipated. To Roscoe it looked like her head had been on fire and was now smoldering.

"Young men and young ladies," she began carefully, "I have some bad news today. One of your classmates, Mr. Randall Gilchrist, has come down with the measles." The silence that filled the room was first broken by a little redhead named Hattie who was rumored to be sweet on Fatty.

"Are the measles real bad? Is Fatty going to be okay?"

"Randall will be just fine young lady. The measles create a good deal of discomfort, and it is indeed a highly contagious disease. But a complete recovery is virtually assured."

She sounded like someone carefully reporting the news on the radio. *Discomfort. Complete recovery. Virtually assured.* What was she saying? Was there a chance Fatty was going to die and she just didn't want to spit it out right there in front of his entire class? No, she said *Randall will be just fine*. She wouldn't lie about that. She could get in big trouble for lying. Roscoe's mind was spinning. It was scarcely nine o'clock and he'd seen and heard more than he could handle. At the very moment he wondered to himself what could be next, grey Mrs. Gray told him.

"This is just one of four cases reported here at Masonhall, and there have been similar outbreaks at McKinley and Lincoln Elementary and two undiagnosed but suspected cases in our Junior High School. Our county health officials have conferred with the school board and all agree that school across the Mitchell school system should be suspended for one week in an effort to stem the spread of the disease. You will be dismissed immediately and we have prepared an informational flier for you to take home to your parents. Thank you for your attention. If your parents have questions, they can reach our school nurse by telephone during normal classroom hours."

"Children," Mrs. Sweeney said, "if you have no questions for me or Mrs. Gray, you are dismissed. Please pick up a flier on your way out."

Suspended, for a full week. Fatty was sick, no doubt experiencing "discomfort". But Roscoe had been granted a one-week pardon and was trying hard not to look on this development as a twisted bit of good news. As it would turn out, the news could not have been worse.

CHAPTER 7

T he flow of news in a place like Mitchell is mysteriously effective; the salient facts related to the measles outbreak somehow beat Roscoe home. He came through the door and found is mother on the telephone arranging an appointment for Hannah with Dr. Porter. There was worry in her voice.

"Thank you," she said to someone on the other end of the line. "We'll be there shortly." She hung up and turned to Roscoe. Before he could speak, she did. "Take off your shirt, I need to look at your stomach."

"How did you know about it, momma?" he asked, pulling shirt over his head.

"They notified the officers of PTA." She studied his stomach with her eyes and her hands. "I don't see anything yet. Do you feel all right?"

"Yeah, why? Do you think I'll get 'em, the measles?"

"I don't know Roscoe, but Fatty's been here a lot and the measles are pretty contagious. So far Andy looks clear, but Hannah is running a fever. I'm taking her in to Dr. Porter." As she moved quickly through the house preparing to leave, Roscoe followed behind her.

"Are they bad, momma, the measles? Don't you just get kind of a rash?" He had read the flier.

"Yes, for you or Andy, that's right. You will be sick for a few days if you get them. That's all. But for a toddler, for Hannah, it's differ-ent. You have to be more careful. It can get out of hand."

"Out of hand. What do you mean?"

"She could get real sick, that's why I have to take her to Dr. Porter, to make sure that doesn't happen. Don't worry."

"Momma, I saw something real terrible today that I need to tell you about."

"Okay Roscoe, but not now, I can't listen right now. I have to get your little sister ready. I want you to stay with Andy. You can tell me when I get home. Now go entertain your brother, please, okay?"

"Yes, momma," he said, doing his best to not be frightened by his mother's obvious anxiety. "Andy, where are you? Let's watch the TV."

Only a few minutes later, Laura came into the living room with a sleepy Hannah on her hip. Andy and Roscoe were on the floor watching an old army movie on the family's Motorola.

"Andy, you mind your brother while mommy's gone. Roscoe, you keep an eye on him. And be careful with the TV, you know how your dad is about that thing."

"Okay momma," Roscoe answered, his eyes still glued to the phony combat scene unfolding there in the living room. "Bye."

"Oh, yes, I almost forgot. After your movie, Roscoe, I want you and Andy to walk down to Gertie's for me. I forgot to get milk this morning and we need some for supper. I left enough money for a quart on the kitchen table. There's enough for a few pieces of candy, too, but not too much. Maybe you could pull Andy in the wagon, he likes that."

"Do I have to?"

"Roscoe Hammer."

"Yes, ma'am. Okay. Bye."

No sooner than Laura and Hannah were out the door, Andy decided he didn't like the combat movie. He wanted Roscoe to play Slap-jack. But every time they played Slap-jack, even if Roscoe tried to lose, he would somehow win and that usually resulted in a pro-longed crying jag from his little brother. The morning was going badly.

"Andy, how about this? " Roscoe said in his best grown-up voice. "How about you go look at your books for just a little while and then I'll pull you in the wagon down to Gertie's and we'll get the milk and candy? How's that sound?" Andy sensed there was a catch.

"How long do I have to look at my books?"

"Just a little while. My movie will be over pretty soon."

"The whole movie? That's too long. The whole thing?"

"Andy, that's it, that's our plan. I watch my movie, you look at your books *without* talking to me, and then I pull you in the wagon down to Gertie's. That is our plan. Now go on."

In what seemed like no time at all, the Americans defeated the Japs and Roscoe was loading his little brother in the wagon. Pulling the wagon with Andy or Hannah in it was easy for Laura or Frank, but for Roscoe, it took all he had and it was awkward. He walked sideways part of the time and backwards part of the time. He could pull it by putting both arms behind his back but it hurt his shoulders. He didn't see why Andy couldn't just walk. What did they think he was, a mule?

"Hey Roscoe, today Miss Harriet said she knew me from some time that was before I was even born."

"She's nutty," Roscoe said.

"She said you saw a dog get killed or something and that you cried."

Roscoe stopped and spoke with his back turned to Andy. "What did she say?"

"That a little dog died and you saw it. Why did we stop? Did you cry, Roscoe?"

"I don't know what she's talking about. Like I said, she's nutty."

"So you didn't cry?" That was the part Andy cared about.

"No. Now let's drop it, okay?"

"Okay."

When they got to Gertie's, Andy announced that he would wait outside in the wagon. When Roscoe asked why, Andy circled his index finger alongside his temple making the universal "crazy" gesture. For perhaps the first time in the entire day, Roscoe laughed.

"What kind of candy do you want?" he asked Andy.

"Gunball."

"You mean gum-ball. *Gum*...ball, not gunball."

"Yep," Andy chirped back flatly. "One red, one blue."

"Never mind," Roscoe said. "I'm not getting you a gum-ball. They're too big. You'll choke to death and I'll be in trouble for life. I'll get you something else."

28

Roscoe was in and out of Gertie's in no time. He got the milk, got the candy, made a little polite small-talk with Gertie and dodged Harriet altogether. He got back outdoors to Andy in less than five minutes, precisely the amount of time it took Andy to decide he needed to pee.

"I gotta go," he told Roscoe flatly.

"Now? Here? Are you sure?" He was almost three years older than Andy and he'd never used the toilet at Gertie's. "Can't you wait?"

"No, Roscoe, I gotta go. If I don't I might pee my britches. You gotta take me in."

"All right," Roscoe said with a sigh. "Come on, hurry up."

Back inside Gertie's, the boys found Buster Odom, an officer on the Mitchell police force, looking for the perfect apple. This stumped Roscoe; he'd been in the store not five minutes earlier and hadn't seen Buster. Maybe he had come through the back door, he thought to himself.

"Hello boys," Buster said with a kind of formal and quick nod that people in authority use. "You out for the measles situation?"

"Yes, sir," Roscoe answered.

"Is that your gun?" Andy asked, pointing at Buster's holstered service revolver. Roscoe gave him a stern look.

"Yes, son, it is. Smith and Wesson."

"You ever shoot anybody with it?"

"Shut up Andy," Roscoe said, pulling his brother by the arm toward the back where the bathroom was located.

"Nope. Sure haven't. Hope I never have to," Buster offered as the two boys walked by. "You two behave now."

When they got to the restroom and Roscoe pulled the door open, they knew right away where Buster had been. It hit the boys like mustard gas, staggering them both.

"There you go," Roscoe said, stepping back from the door and turning his head away. "You said you had to pee. Go on."

"I can't go in there," Andy whispered. "I can't!"

"Well, there isn't anywhere else to go, so you gotta go in if you're going to go."

"Oh, man," Andy said, pacing. "Fine. Geez!" Andy drew a deep breath, held it and went in. With the door closed behind him, his words were muffled but discernible. "Whoa! Holy Toledo!"

Without looking, Roscoe could sense that Buster had heard Andy's outcry and banged on the door. "Hurry up in there." He turned and smiled awkwardly at the officer. Buster looked at him with suspicion, as though he'd fooled a polygraph machine.

"Everything all right back there?" he asked.

"Yes, sir, officer, we're fine," Roscoe replied. "Let's go Andy."

Roscoe got Andy loaded in the wagon and took off.

"Officer Odom could hear you when you were in there. It was embarrassing!"

"He didn't flush good," Andy countered. "Looked like a black rat. Huge!"

"Geez Andy, shut up! Hang on to the milk. Geez."

As Roscoe and Andy came within about two blocks of home, the fancy, mysterious blue car that Roscoe had seen earlier in the day pulled alongside them on Sand Plum and the person attached to the arm with tattoos stuck his head out and spoke.

"Hello boys," he said, dragging out the words. Roscoe sensed danger and tried not to look at him. He kept walking.

"Don't say anything," Roscoe whispered to Andy. "And don't look."

"Hey kid, I'm talking to you," the driver said, clearly addressing himself now to Roscoe. "Stop!" Roscoe obeyed and turned slowly, fearfully in the direction of the shiny blue coupe.

His instincts were perfect. The shiny blue Mercury and the voice belonged to a young man named Bobby Cato, the son of a mean and vulgar Scot named Wilyem Cato. Old man Cato was a notorious whiskey drinker who lived in a ramshackle farmhouse two miles out of town and who made sport of beating Bobby's mother till she'd had enough and ran off with a vacuum cleaner salesman from the Ozarks. The night she and her hillbilly boyfriend stole away, she set the Cato barn on fire in hopes of creating a lasting memory for Wilyem. He swigged Jack Daniels and laughed while it burned to the ground. He redirected his violence to Bobby until, at about age sixteen, Bobby learned to hit back, first out of desperation and in defense, later for the fun of it.

George Mabry's reputation for malevolence was the product of rumor, speculation, and imagination. Bobby Cato's was well-documented, widely known. After a year of sport boxing with his drunken father, Bobby robbed a Rexall drug store, was convicted and sentenced to ten years in Harrington State prison. He served seven of the ten and was released with an even greater appetite for violence than he had before entering. He held a no-count, part-time job pumping gas at Doak Posey's Phillips 66 station. Posey paid him a minimum wage but gave him free use of the station's repair bay, including the hydraulic lift and the mechanic's tools, a fringe benefit that permitted a low-life like Bobby to keep his blue Mercury looking and running like a million bucks.

People wondered, rightly so, why Doak would hire Bobby, with his blemished past and all. The answer was actually pretty simple. Doak didn't want a kid working the station in his absence, and there were no able-bodied adults in Mitchell who'd pump gas for five dollars a day. There was one other reason: Doak may have been the only person in Mitchell, including the police, who wasn't afraid of Bobby Cato. Though twenty years senior to Cato, at six-and-a-half feet tall and two-hundred and eighty pounds, Doak was a massive, muscled titan. He looked quite literally like the strongman from Ringling Brothers. The second repair bay in his garage was equipped as a crude gymnasium of sorts with barbells and other exercise paraphernalia where Doak worked to a full sweat almost every day. Bobby was permitted to use the barbells too, but he didn't. He was built tight and thin like a jack rabbit, and he'd had all the idle exercise he wanted at Harrington.

Doak was quiet and kindly, always respectful and friendly to customers. He had never married, and when he was away from the station, he kept to himself. His only flamboyance was a massive Indian ring made of sterling silver and turquoise and a wide matching bracelet. Old men in Mitchell snickered at Doak's jewelry, but never where he could hear them. Bobby didn't dare snicker. When Doak hired him, he told Bobby that if there was ever any trouble of any kind, he would not involve the police and Bobby knew exactly what he meant.

"What do you want?" Roscoe asked Bobby, his voice shaking a little.

"I want to talk to you, you little snot-wipe, that's what." He stopped the car, got out and walked up on the sidewalk beside Roscoe and Andy who crouched behind his brother.

"Talk about what?" Roscoe asked, his eyes darting around trying to avoid contact with Cato's.

"I heard you got a Bluetick Coonhound, a male. My female at the farm will be coming into heat soon and I thought we might mate 'em. You'd be entitled to a pup out of the deal."

Roscoe didn't know Bobby but he knew strangers could be dangerous and this one was more dangerous than most. He could smell danger in the stale cigarette smoke on his breath; he could see it on his venous, tattooed arms. Bobby Cato was a guy to get away from.

"Ah, I don't think so," Roscoe said.

"Why not? Your dog too good for my dog?"

" No, I just don't think so."

"What's he got in that bag?" Cato asked, pointing to Andy.

"Nothing. Just some milk."

"Milk, huh? Sounds good." He grabbed the bag out of Andy's hands, pulled out the quart bottle and pushed the cap off with his thumb.

"Hey," Andy screamed. "That's our milk!"

"A-huh," Bobby said, gulping from the bottle. "Good, too. Cold."

"Give it back," Roscoe said, trembling. "It's ours."

"Yeah, it's ours," Andy said, inspired by his big brother's bravery.

Cato wiped his mouth and then turned the bottle upside down. "Lookie there. It spilt, didn't it boys? I'm real sorry 'bout that. I am for sure sorry."

"Get away from those boys and get on out of here!" Althea Woodson's voice boomed from her front porch where she stood in a defiant pose with her hands on her hips. "Get on out." Roscoe was as once startled and relieved.

"Hmmm, what have we got now?" Cato sneered. "A neighborly rescue is it?"

"Roscoe, Andy, you boys come on up here with me," Althea instructed. "Come on now. Leave the wagon there. And you, Bobby Cato, you go on your way. Leave us."

"This is no business of yours, lady," Cato barked angrily. "Go back in your house." Roscoe and Andy made their way quickly to the porch where they stood behind their protector.

"Go on Bobby Cato, before I call the police."

"Go on and call 'em, Aunt Jemima. I know 'em all. Don't matter to me. I ain't done nothin'." Bobby sauntered back to his idling Mercury, slid into the driver's seat and took a minute to light a smoke. "Boys, I'll see you some other time, okie dokie?" He exhaled, threw his head back smugly and squealed away.

Having heard the ruckus, JL Woodson came through the front screen door pulling his shirt on. "What is going on out here? Althea, you boys, what's the trouble?" He'd been sleeping all afternoon and was groggy. "Who was that?" he asked, pointing toward the Mercury, now in the distance.

"It was that no-good Bobby Cato, that's who," Althea answered. "He was scaring these boys. I want you to report him to the police, JL, I do."

"Did he hurt you boys? Are you all right?"

"Yes, sir," Roscoe said. "We're all right. He was just bothering me about my dog, Ranger."

"And he took our milk," Andy added quickly. "He drank some and then spilled it all out."

"Your dog, your milk?" JL rubbed his head.

"That scoundrel was threatening these boys, scaring their pants off, and I want you to report it. He has no business around here. He is dangerous, JL, he's been in the penitentiary."

"Althea!" JL Interrupted, casting his eyes toward the boys in an effort to hush is wife. "I'll call, but it likely won't do any good. But I'll call."

"Boys, you come on in and have supper with me and JL," Althea said, opening the screen door. "Your momma called and she and your daddy won't be home for a while."

"Why?" Roscoe asked quickly. "Is something wrong? Is Hannah okay?"

"Don't worry Roscoe. They'll all be home shortly after suppertime. Doctor Porter just needed a little more time with little Hannah, that's all. We're having red potatoes, fried corn and pork steaks. Come on in."

Andy was none the wiser but Roscoe sensed something was being withheld. A wave of worry rushed over him. He could hear his mother's voice in his head. *It can get out of hand.*

CHAPTER 8

For two days Hannah's fever would not break. It would ebb and then spike again, over and over, but it would not break. And Roscoe saw his mother and father gradually descend into fear and despair. They wrapped her in a damp cotton sheet and took turns walking her around the house. They fed her ice chips and rocked her. They kept a cold compress on her forehead and held her close, whispering prayers and encouragement into her tiny ear. But the fever would not break.

Hannah ate almost nothing; one or two saltine crackers every two hours would trigger diarrhea so painful she cried. Then she would fall asleep. Her beautiful, rosy cheeks were flush one minute and sallow the next. Her eyes drooped, lazy and grey. Roscoe performed little routines that had always made his baby sister laugh but now she just stared at him, too weak to react. Finally, Frank and Laura resorted to putting Hannah in the bathtub filled with cool water; she screamed until she almost choked. Roscoe and Andy went to the front porch to escape the sound.

When Roscoe tried to talk with Laura or Frank about Hannah's condition, when he made inquiries, they were abrupt and dismissive, their fear masquerading as anger and blame. They whispered to each other secretly about what might need be done next. Roscoe worried that Fatty would never be welcome in their home again. He worried that his mother and father might collapse. He worried most about his baby sister.

By the second night, Hannah's fever still had not broken and she lay fitfully dozing in her crib. When Andy was asleep and Frank and

Laura, both exhausted, had fallen asleep in the living room, Roscoe took his magic wand and went into Hannah's nursery and stood silently beside her crib. She was adorable to him. Her hair was a gentle mix of gold and auburn; her eyes, closed now, were sea green. Her little nose was funny and her mouth was the most perfect Roscoe had ever seen.

There, alone and in the dark, Roscoe secretly, silently tried to will his baby sister back to health. The magic wand? What could it hurt, he thought? He would pray, he would stand guard, he would try to perform magic. He would do anything to bring her back, to make her the happy toddler she had been. Ranger came into the nursery and stood beside Roscoe who put one hand on his faithful dog's head and whispered to him the sadness and fear he felt. They stood together in the dark and tears came down Roscoe's cheeks. He squeezed the wand as hard as he could.

The next morning, Laura found Roscoe and Ranger asleep on the floor in Hannah's nursery, where they used her stuffed animals for pillows. And she found Hannah in her crib, her bedding and her bedclothes soaked. Her hair was matted with sweat, but her eyes were open and bright. Her coloring was normal. She smiled at Laura. The fever had broken.

Crying with joy, Laura woke Roscoe, dispatched him to wake Andy, and took her daughter downstairs to Frank who held his daughter to his chest as he had the day she was born. The fever had broken and relief began to course through the Hammer family. Roscoe placed the wand back on his nightstand and looked at it in a way he never had before. Had it worked, he wondered? Could it have possibly worked? He looked at Ranger who, as usual, looked dumbfounded. Somehow, the dog seemed to know Hannah was better and that was all that mattered.

While Hannah sat happily on the divan drinking orange juice and watching Bugs Bunny on the Motorola, the rest of the family began to stagger back toward a normal routine. Frank, who had been off the job for two days, shaved and got ready for work. Laura stood for a moment at the kitchen window, pulled her shoulders back slowly and smiled. Then she attacked the stack of dirty dishes piled in the sink, started a pot of coffee and put two eggs in a pot to boil. A soft egg and toast for Hannah, she thought, would be just about right. Not too much too soon, just a little nourishment. The fever has broken, she's better, but we mustn't get ahead of ourselves. Just a little nourishment. Exhale, finally.

Andy and Roscoe had a short, celebratory pillow fight in the bedroom, then got dressed, brushed their teeth went downstairs to the kitchen with griddle cakes and bacon in mind. Their father readily agreed to the menu and Laura went right to work; her family needed a meal. She boiled the eggs, fried bacon to perfection, made flapjacks, marshaled Roscoe and Andy to set the kitchen table, poured a cup of coffee for Frank, and somehow almost never took her eyes off Hannah. Hannah, her adorable, blond-headed survivor, her radiant angel, looked up and smiled at her mommy. Laura felt a quick catch in the back of her throat and choked back a tear. "Breakfast's ready," she bubbled. "Come on boys, let's eat. I'll get Hannah."

The tiny kitchen table, heaped with hotcakes, bacon, eggs and all, snapped everyone into place like a giant magnet. The two boys sat straight-backed in their chairs, ready to attack the abundance while Frank positioned Hannah's highchair.

"Go on boys, help yourselves," Laura said as she slid Hannah into the highchair. She and Frank sat down and cast each other a sunny glance. Things were better. Everyone ate.

When Frank had excused himself from the table, and Andy had staked a claim on his favorite position in front of the television, Laura began to clear the table.

Hannah was still chewing on her dry toast and Roscoe was happy to sit and watch her. For the first time in two days his mind darted back through some of the dramatic events he'd not had a chance to share: the little dog, Crazy George Mabry, the encounter with Bobby Cato. Maybe now he would have a chance to tell his mom how much life had changed in three days.

"I saw a little dog die in the street," he said. "It was really sad."

"You saw what?" Laura asked turning toward her son. "What little dog? Where?"

"Laura, have you seen my wallet?" Frank shouted from the top of the stairs.

"It's down here on the counter," she replied.

"How about my car keys?"

"On the way to school," Roscoe interjected. "He got hit by a car."

"Just a minute, Roscoe," Laura said. "No, Frank, I don't see your keys. They must be up there somewhere."

Somehow oblivious to this mangled, three-way conversation, little Hannah made a slurping sound as she sucked the last of her orange juice from the bottom of her baby cup. Standing behind Hannah, Laura heard the sound and started toward the fridge.

"Does my little Hannah need some more?" Laura asked, opening the refrigerator door. Hannah had learned to talk in short, broken sentences, but she didn't answer. She did not turn her head. She didn't move at all. Laura froze for a moment then took the glass bottle of juice out, closed the door and turned slowly to Hannah. "Hannah," she repeated cautiously, this time a little louder. "Do you want some more? Hannah?"

Hannah sat quietly holding her empty glass in one hand and a piece of toast in the other, gazing at Roscoe. He glanced up at Laura and saw the terror sweep across her face. "Hannah!" she repeated, even louder. Still, Hannah did not answer and did not turn toward Laura. What Roscoe could see with certainty from his vantage point — the thing Laura could not see but knew too well — was that his baby sister had not heard her mother.

"Mommy," Roscoe said, plaintively, "I don't think she heard you..."

Laura trembled, her mind spun, she was dizzy, she could not draw a deep breath and her stomach rolled. She dropped the glass bottle of juice and it shattered. Hannah did not flinch. Laura slumped to the floor, cutting her knees on the broken glass.

"Frank!" Laura screamed. "Come quick!"

CHAPTER 9

Hugging the southwest boundary of Mitchell and loosely following the meandering path of Shale Creek was Harmony Park, a glorious testament to former mayor Ralph Harmon who people said had personally planted more than one hundred of the park's trees. "My shovel, my hands, God's dirt," he would say each new spring. Harmon loved the park and was rumored to have pilfered from every city department's budget to support its splendor.

Two gravel through-roads ran along either side of the park and between them there were a half-dozen picnic shelters that looked like Lincoln Log cabins without walls. These structures were supported by four native-stone columns and anchored by a large-mouthed stone fireplace at one end. The roofs were of natural cedar shake shingles and the gables were painted freshly each year in forest green. Mayor Harmon had come upon such shelters while vacationing in the mountains of Colorado and decided in characteristically autocratic fashion to import the design, declaring when questioned about it, "My constituents deserve a little taste of the Rockies!" The local newspaper reported that each shelter was built at the imponderable cost of three thousand dollars, but the Mayor refused to release any official accounting. "Nobody ever asked me how much money came out of my own pocket for those hundred trees!" rang his defiant rebuttal.

To the south and west of the park, beyond the Mitchell city limits, lay open farmland, and to the north, separating the park from public baseball fields and the rodeo grounds, were the elevated tracks of the Burlington Northern. At the easterly most end of the park there was a dam on Shale Creek that created a round bay with a small island in its middle. This bay, Donut Bay officially, was the only wintertime ice skating venue in town. Raucous hockey games were common there once the ice was safely frozen, and in the springtime and summer, weekends found the little bay surrounded by children shoulder to shoulder, fishing for perch and crappie with cane poles and corks. This time of year, in the fall, ducks and geese reluctant to begin their migration roamed freely, looking for picnic scraps and pooping all over.

The Shale Creek dam, often referred to as the low water dam, was constructed at such a level as to allow a two or three-inch stream of water to flow over it when weather conditions were normal. The water fell about fifteen feet into a shallow pool where Shale Creek reconstituted itself for its run out of town and into the next county. Because this pool was well below eye-level for anyone around the bay or in the park, a negligent street superintendent once permitted his crews to dump large chunks of concrete and asphalt into the pool below the dam. Sharp, jagged corners of stone protruded from the shallow pool and made any effort to scale down the banks very risky. Thus, the area below the dam was strictly off-limits to children. In fact, the only people who frequented it were Mexicans who worked on the Burlington Northern track crew and often spent their lunchtime fishing for carp and drum and other trash fish that gathered in the rocky pool below the dam. No one would eat such fish, but the Mexicans would grind them up and use the resulting mash as a cheap and effective fertilizer for their tomato gardens. This mash was also the base ingredient in a putrid concoction simply and aptly known as stink bait, a lumpy, slimy compound that catfish could not resist.

Rickety green wooden benches were scattered helter-skelter around the bay, placed there mainly for the benefit of elderly park patrons and young mothers. One of the benches would become something of a church pew for Roscoe over the next weeks and months, a place for him to privately try and pull back together the remnants of his unraveling life, a place to worry out of sight, a place where all alone he could hear the sound of his own sad heart pounding, a place to say short, plain prayers.

Harmony Park was a long walk or short bicycle ride from Roscoe's house and in late afternoon when school was out, he could normally have Donut Bay all to himself. In his second retreat there following news of Hannah's deafness, Roscoe took the magic wand and threw it in anger as far as he could over the dam, presumably to the rocky slosh below. The wand had betrayed and tricked him, suggesting first that the most dire conditions could be reversed, then giving way to an outcome more tragic than anything Roscoe had imagined. Laura and Frank knew the possible side-effects of Hannah's case of "hard measles" and the protracted fever, including nerve damage and hearing loss. This accounted for the desperation Roscoe had witnessed through those three awful days. But he knew nothing of these side-effects, and when he learned what had happened to his baby sister, he was devastated.

He was sitting on the bench with his hands together in his lap and his joyless eyes scanning slowly across the bay when a deep, scratchy voice came from behind him. "This yours?"

Startled, Roscoe turned quickly and saw George Mabry holding his magic wand. "This yours?" George asked again, gesturing with the wand.

"It was, yeah," Roscoe answered slowly, still taken aback by this sudden appearance of Mitchell's monster.

"What is it?" Mabry asked.

"It's a magic wand, a sort of toy. Where'd you find it?"

"I was down below the dam eating chicken and it came flying down there. What'd you say it was?"

"A magic wand, like someone might do magic tricks with. I didn't mean to throw it at you down there. I just didn't want it anymore. I didn't know anybody was down there. I better get going." Being within arm's reach of Crazy George made Roscoe nervous. He scooted to the end of the bench and then stood up. "I better get going," he said again.

"Wait," George said, licking his fingers. "You want some chicken? I got some more down there."

"No, thank-you," Roscoe answered, careful to give his reply a polite inflection. "My momma will be making our supper soon." He wanted Mabry to know that people were expecting him.

"Wait," George said. "Mind if I sit?"

"Nope, I mean no sir," Roscoe said.

"You sit too, just for a bit," George said flatly. Roscoe couldn't tell if it was an invitation or the beginning of a kidnapping; he decided to play it safe and took a position so far at the end of the bench half his backside went unsupported. "You 'fraid of me?"

"Yes, a little bit," Roscoe answered weakly.

"Little bit or a lot?" George asked with a slight smile that Roscoe, looking straight ahead, didn't see.

"A lot." Why lie, Roscoe thought.

"No need," George said. "I ain't never hurt no little kid, never ever. Ain't never hurt hardly no one other than a couple of fellas that done it to me first, or hurt some other person. Never a kid though. Nope."

A little unsure how to reply, Roscoe finally said simply, "That's good."

"I know what people say 'bout me," George said, looking straight forward, as if he was addressing himself to more than just Roscoe. "I know they say things, bad things. But they's wrong. You heard things 'bout me, ain't you?"

"Yes." Roscoe was growing anxious again. "I should be going home now, Mr. Mabry."

"*Mr. Mabry,*" George repeated proudly. "Not too many young'ns call me that. No siree. What you heard about me, son?"

"I heard you threw a brick through Mr. Jessup's picture window," Roscoe said, looking away from George. "I heard that."

"It's true, I done it. But I done it cuz he owed me ten dollars for some hard work I done for him and he wouldn't pay cuz he said I ogled his wife who I never ever saw, not ever, and when I said he should pay me he throws the brick at me first and he hits me right here, right on my knee. I thought he broke my leg at first, it got all swolled up and left me hobbling for more than a week. Anyhow, when he hit me with the brick, I said, well to hell with you undertaker, and I throwed the brick right back at him and he ducks and it went right through his picture window. Well, glass came crashin' down and old Jessup he screams like a woman and starts running in circles sayin' he's going to call the police."

"What happened then?" Roscoe was taken in by the story and his guard had come down.

"He done it. He called the police. By then I'd run off but they found me and throwed me right in the pokey, swolled up leg and all." George, who had taken some excitement in recounting the incident, stopped and a look of vague sadness and confusion crossed his face. "Later on he come around and told me that his wife was confused, that another fella had been givin' her the eye, not me like she said before. He give me the ten dollars which I took cuz it was owed me all along. I asked him to square it away with the police and he said he would but I don't think he ever did nothin' 'bout it."

"Geez," Roscoe said. "That's not right."

"No, it ain't. And you can see how folks just boil all that down to old Crazy George throw'd a brick through the undertaker's window, just like that was all there was to it." He stopped for a moment and picked back up the trail. "What else you heard?"

"Nothing really," Roscoe answered. "Nothing much."

George knew better but thought it best to move on. "Why'd you throw this thing away?" he asked, gesturing again with the wand.

The sadness that had been there before George came along returned.

"Because my baby sister got sick and I thought I could help her get well with it. But I couldn't. It's just a crummy toy. It didn't help her at all."

"What sickness she got?" George asked.

"It was the measles. She's over it now but she had a real high fever for three days and it hurt her ears and now she can't hear. They say she might not ever be able to hear and that since she hasn't completely learned to talk, when she does it will sound funny and she'll have troubles."

"That's real sad, Roscoe," George said with genuine empathy.

"How'd you know my name?" Roscoe asked, a little suspicious again.

"I know nearly everybody 'round Mitchell. I go all around town and I hear people talk 'bout things, 'bout folks and I remember names purdy good. That's all. Does your baby sister know she can't hear?"

Roscoe thought for a moment; it was a question that hadn't occurred to him. "I guess so," he said, cocking his head to think. "I mean she could hear before so she must know. But she's not even two so it's hard to asked her about things, especially complicated things. I'm positive she knows though."

"And she ain't never going to get better?" George asked.

"Doc Porter talked to special doctors all the way to Saint Louis. They say probably not. But they might not know for absolute sure."

"Doctors ain't always that smart," George said, trying awkwardly to extend his new little pal some comfort. "Maybe they's wrong."

"I gotta go," Roscoe said, dropping his chin sadly. "My momma and dad will be waiting." This time George did not object, but Roscoe didn't stand up. He just continued to stare across the bay, motionless. "And my family is a wreck," he said in a defeated voice that trailed off at the end.

"Is that right?" George replied.

"My momma just walks around, sort of like a ghost, never talking to me or my dad or my little brother. She just looks at Hannah and talks to her in whispers. Or she just looks out the window. She does that a lot."

"She's real sad, I bet," George said.

Like George had done earlier, Roscoe was now speaking to a larger, imaginary audience, to invisible listeners across the bay. "Sometimes she fixes our meal and puts it on the table and then she goes off in the bedroom and doesn't even eat with us. I ask my dad about it and he just rubs his face and says she will get better, my momma that is, but she doesn't. She just keeps looking out the window. Once or twice our neighbor, Mrs. Althea Woodson, she had to come down to our house and help take care of us because momma just stayed in her bedroom for a day or two — never came out."

"I got an idea for you," George said, trying to sound upbeat. "Maybe you should get her a plant or somethin'. Maybe a nice plant."

"A plant?" Roscoe asked with a hint of skepticism. "You think a plant would help? I thought that stupid wand would help. And you think a *plant* would help. Geez, we must both be crazy."

"I ain't smart, but I ain't stupid either. I know some things. And I can tell that certain things sometimes make people feel better when they's sad. Good weather can do that. And plants can do that. I ain't crazy. I know about plants."

"I'm sorry," Roscoe said, knowing that he had hurt George's feelings. "I didn't mean anything, really. You might be right, a plant might help my momma. What kind do you think? What kind of plant?"

"Maybe a Christmas cactus or somethin' like that. Somethin' with blooms, even in wintertime. It'll be winter for you know it."

"Good idea, Mr. Mabry, thanks," Roscoe said. "Maybe I can save my allowance a couple of weeks."

"No need," George said, digging in his pocket. "Here you go, here's two bucks. That should get you dern near any kind of plant." Roscoe hesitated. "Go on, son, take it."

"I can't take your money, Mr. Mabry."

"Ain't mine but for 'bout an hour. Before that it was Mrs. Murphy's whose bushes I trimmed up beautiful this mornin'. I ain't gonna miss somethin' I had only an hour or so. Now go on, get your momma a plant."

"O....K," Roscoe said hesitantly. "I guess. Thanks, Mr. Mabry."

"And not a word about the money comin' from Crazy George, right?"

"Yes, sir." Roscoe stood to leave.

"One more thing, Roscoe," George said, pausing to put the question just right. "You seen my little dog die in the street the other day, ain't that so? The day after it rained hard all night till daybreak?"

"Yes, sir, I did. How did you know?"

"Someone told me. You wanted to help my little dog, I know you did. And I know it made you sad."

"I did want to help him, but I didn't know what to do, he was so hurt. I just cried and ran as hard as I could. And when I got to the schoolyard I fell down crying and puked so hard I thought my eyeball might pop out. I never saw anything die before. Do you know who ran over him?"

"Not for sure, nope. Got an idea, but don't know for sure. If I find out for sure, then me and them might have some trouble between us. That little dog and me was pals for more than ten years, we were. You didn't see who done it, did you?"

"Whoever did it was gone before I got there. I didn't see 'em. I wish I could have helped your dog, Mr. Mabry."

"I know you do. And I know it was a hard thing for you to see. Would be for any man, much less a boy like yourself. You best run on home now. Remember, Christmas cactus, give that a try. A nice full one."

"Good bye, Mr. Mabry, and thanks."

Roscoe was twenty yards away when George stopped him one more time. "His name was Satchel. That was my little dog's name. I bought him a little collar and name tag at Woolworth's. Satchel." Then, waving the wand, he added, "I'll keep this for ya." Roscoe waved to his new friend one last time and made his way toward Sand Plum Street. The air was cool and light and he felt like running.

CHAPTER 10

Doak Posey's 66 Station was located just across Main Street from Pud's, a pool hall and tavern owned by a short, round, hairy man named Merle Pudman. Pud, as he was known to the patrons, was a perfectly detached proprietor and saloon-keeper, indifferent to all manner of behavior, except that which might result in property damage. The place served only bottled beer and common bar food from a long skinny bar in the front with the back two-thirds of the joint used up by two regulation snooker tables. At Pud's you could drink regular beer, or mix it with tomato juice if that was your taste, you could shoot pool, play dominoes and gamble a little. You could not break the furniture or puke in the toilet; if you did, Pud would chase you off with a shillelagh he kept handy behind the bar. Women did not go into Pud's, which made things simpler.

Pud's place was conveniently located for Doak who drank at least one and never more than two bottles of beer every day of the year. He came in each day between three and four and took a stool near the end of the long bar. In a silent ritual most comfortable to both of them, Pud would pop the top off a Schlitz and set it on the bar in front of Doak who would nod a polite, unspoken thank-you. No money changed hands because Doak was one of only a handful of regulars allowed to run a tab. Pud's credit standards were strict.

"Heeey Doak..." The drunken voice came from somewhere in the back, near the snooker tables. "How's my boy doin' for ya over at the station? If he don't do right, just pop him one. Tell him his old man said so."

Doak turned slowly, reluctantly and found the slurring voice. It was Wilyem Cato, seated alone in the back where the dirty shafts of sunlight that splashed the front of the saloon couldn't find him. He was a small, caved-in looking man, with wrinkled yellow skin and thin, yellow-grey hair. He was unshaven for a day or two at least and his eyes drooped down as though he was talking to the table-top where there was a half-empty bottle of Pabst. "You gotta keep him....lined out, if you know what I mean."

Doak did not respond to Wilyem, but looked at Pud who shrugged dismissively. Cato was as regular as his wallet would permit, which was influenced mightily by the meager but consistent wages Doak paid his son Bobby. There was no love between father and son, but Bobby was willing to buy his beer, at least within reason. The house they shared, shack that it was, was in the old man's name, and alcohol, Bobby figured, kept him manageable.

"Come on back here, Doak, have a beer with me," Wilyem said, getting louder. His head seemed slightly unbalanced atop his skinny neck. "I'll give you some pointers."

Doak rose finally and began walking back in the direction of the drunken voice. Doak walked like a hangman, slow and steady, without any discernible reluctance or enthusiasm. When he got to the table, he stood silently towering over Cato who rolled his head back, pulled his eyes up and spoke.

"Sit down here, I'll give you some pointers 'bout my boy," he mumbled.

"Don't need any pointers, Cato. Bobby and me understand each other pretty well," Doak said with a decided air of disapproval.

"Come on, now, sit down a minute. How's he doing for ya? He doin' all right?"

"All right so far," Doak said, annoyed. "Since you ask though — you being a concerned parent and all — I'd tell you that Buster Odom is across the street right now talking to Bobby about a complaint he got on your boy. Nothing too serious I don't think, but you know I don't want anybody around who's trouble, you know what I mean Wilyem. Maybe you could remind young Bobby of that."

"What complaint?" Cato asked angrily.

"He scared some young boys is all Buster told me. I didn't want any details. Enjoy your beer, Cato." Doak pushed his chair back and stood to leave.

"The hell you say. Who filed this complaint, anyhow?" Cato asked, sounding slightly less drunk.

"JL Woodson, according to Buster. Good man. Not a trouble-maker."

"The railroader?" Cato asked. "He got boys?"

"Nope, it was some other boys. Woodson just told Buster about it, that's all."

"Can I buy you a beer, Doak?" Cato asked, hoping for more information.

"No pointers, Cato, and no beer. I buy my own. Now quit hol-lering. You're bothering Pud's clientele."

"Sumbitch boy-kisser," Cato muttered under his breath as Doak walked away.

Back at the bar, Doak took the last swig of Schlitz.

"Nuther?" Pud asked.

"Nope," Doak answered, gestured subtly toward Cato. "Stinks up the ambiance. Bad for business."

"You want me to run him off?" Pud asked, sounding eager.

"Naw, got to go back to work. Don't bother."

Across the street, Doak saw Buster's patrol car at the pump, with him behind the wheel. Bobby ran a wet chamois through the hand-ringer then held it by two corners and snapped the thing out cracking it like a bull-whip. He was wiping down Buster's windshield when Doak came on him from behind. Doak wrapped his big right hand around Bobby neck and squeezed just enough to cause Bobby to stiffen with pain. He rested his other arm on the hood of the patrol car and leaned in to address Buster.

"Everything okay here, Officer?" Doak asked with friendly, mock politeness. "Did you find my employee here, young Bobby, did you find him cooperative, and respectful?"

"I think we're all lined out, Doak," Buster said with a slow smile.

Doak kept a tight grip on Bobby's neck and used it to turn his head slightly toward him. "I'm glad to hear you and the officer are all squared away, Bobby. That's real good." He released Bobby's neck and motioned for him to finish the windshield. "Thanks for coming in Buster. Appreciate the business."

"Welcome, Doak. See you next time," Buster said to Posey. Then, to Cato as he finished the windshield and hung the hose back on the pump, "Stay out of trouble, Bobby."

"Always do," Bobby grumbled as Buster started the patrol car and pulled away. He stepped away from the pump, tried to crane the tight pain out of his neck, lit a cigarette and threw the dead match into the street.

CHAPTER 11

A Christmas Cactus has no thorns. Rather it has long, narrow, lime-green leaves that appear to be delicately formed by several smaller connected leaves the shape of large tear drops. On a healthy plant there are dozens of these leaves all about the same size, all extending far enough to droop, giving the cactus the look of a fern. During the holidays and into the early part of deep winter, tiny pink blossoms appear at the end of all the cactus's leaves where they live until March or April. All of this had to be explained to Fatty who accompanied Roscoe to the florist shop in the town square and who was more than a little curious as to why Roscoe wanted this particular plant.

"I've never heard of this cactus thing," Fatty said. "What made you choose it anyway?" Roscoe's secret financing was sufficient to get a really large plant, and he and his friend took turns carrying it. When it was Fatty's turn, he carried it on his head which made him look pretty ridiculous.

"I read about it in a book," Roscoe said, lying weakly. "I liked the idea that it has flowers during the wintertime. I'm pretty sure my mom will really like it a lot."

"Well, it might look good at Christmas, but right now it's ugly and heavy if you ask me." It was cool, but Fatty's forehead and lip had moistened under the weight of the Christmas Cactus. "Heavy and ugly," Fatty laughed. "Like me!"

"You're not ugly," Roscoe replied. "Penny Barksdale said you look like Roy Rogers in the face."

"You big liar," Fatty said, trying not to look flattered by Roscoe's report.

"No, really, she said that."

"Oh well, what does Penny know, anyhow? Here," he said, handing the plant to Roscoe, "you lug it a while." As they made the exchange, a familiar voice came from across the street.

"What are you yo-yos doing?" The question and the voice were cheerful. It was Tommy Corks, headed the other direction. "Where ya going?"

Tommy and Fatty had patched things up some time ago, and each respected the other, though it flowed disproportionately from Tommy, having once been so thoroughly vanquished by the his younger opponent. He ran across the street to join them.

"We're headed to Gertie's to get some foil and ribbon for this plant," Roscoe explained. "It's for my mom."

"How come?" Tommy asked.

"She's been kinda sad because my little sister, Hannah, got the measles and got real sick and it hurt her hearing."

"Where'd she get the measles from? She's just a baby isn't she?"

"Probably from me," Fatty offered sadly. "I had 'em and I was over at their house a lot."

"You don't know it was you, Fatty," Roscoe said. "It could have been anybody."

"I suppose," Fatty said reluctantly, dropping his head a little.

"She going to get her hearing back?" Tommy Corks asked.

"Maybe not," Roscoe said. "But nobody knows for sure."

"Well, I'm a believer in miracles," Tommy said, gazing down at his own groin to make his point. "You know what I mean?"

"Everything still okay down there?" Fatty asked, awkwardly looking for the right phrasing, but glad to get off the subject of Hannah and the measles. "You still all right?"

"Never been better," Tommy said with a big grin. "You know what I mean?"

"Oh yeah, sure," Fatty said, casting a puzzled glance in Roscoe's direction. Neither of them had any idea what Tommy meant, but they sure weren't going say so.

"Yeah, absolutely," Roscoe said with a shrug that Fatty could see but Tommy could not.

And with that, Tommy paused, looked up and panned the horizon as though he'd lost track of his own story. "Well, anyhow, I gotta go. See you yo-yos later."

Roscoe and Fatty were both speechless, left only to wave weakly and wonder about the subtext of Tommy's anatomical report. They looked at each other for a moment; Fatty spoke first. "Weird," was all he said.

"Yeah," said Roscoe, and then they walked on toward Gertie's. At about the time the store was in sight, Roscoe who looked as though he'd been contemplating something stopped and turned to Fatty. "You want to know something even weirder than Tommy's story?"

"Yeah, what?" Fatty replied eagerly.

"The Christmas cactus wasn't really my idea. I'd never heard of it until two days ago."

"What's so weird about that, I never heard of one either? Who told you about it?"

"That's the weird part." Roscoe leaned closer. "It's just between you and me, Okay?"

"Yeah, yeah, what is it?"

"George Mabry told me about the Christmas cactus. It was his idea."

"Crazy George? Are you lying?" Fatty took a step backwards. "Crazy George Mabry! I don't believe you."

"I'm not lying. I saw him in the park, by Donut Bay. He was eating chicken."

"What were you doing there, in the park?" Fatty asked.

"Just sitting on the bench, alone. Alone, I thought anyway. He came up behind me. Scared the poop out of me at first."

"Do your mom and dad know?"

"No," Roscoe said emphatically. "And I don't want 'em to. They've got enough stuff to be thinking about without getting all worked up about George Mabry. You can't tell anyone, right? You said it would be between just us."

"Okay," Fatty said, rubbing his head nervously. "But you better watch out. That old guy is crazy you know? There's a reason people are afraid of him."

"I know. And I really was scared. I even thought about just running, but that seemed kinda stupid. After a few minutes, he seemed all right to me, not really crazy at all. I asked him about that story about Mr. Jessup and the brick through the window and all, and he had a completely different version of it. And it pretty much made sense, at least to me. And he didn't have any reason to lie to me, if you think about."

"I don't want to think about it," Fatty replied. "I'd have crapped myself for sure."

Roscoe started to walk again.

"Anyway, I told him about my momma being sad over Hannah's hearing and all, and he suggested a plant. He suggested this very plant," Roscoe said, gesturing with the cactus. "I promised him I wouldn't tell, but he gave me the two bucks to buy it with."

"No way! You lie!" Fatty exclaimed.

"Nope, it's true. Now remember, not a word to Gertie or your mom or dad, or anyone."

As usual, Roscoe and Fatty were warmly received by Gertie. "Ah, my favorite two vagabonds are here. What brings you handsome young men around? My goodness, what a lovely Christmas cactus. What might be the occasion?"

"Hi Miss Gertie," Rosoce replied. "It's a present for my momma, on account of her being down in the dumps lately."

"Oh, yes," Gertie said. "I'm so sorry about Hannah. Please let your momma know that we're praying for improvement in her condition, the little angel. God's purpose in these matters will someday be revealed. Tell her we're praying."

"Yes ma'am, I will."

"I'm afraid I gave 'em to her," Fatty said. It was the second time he had said it out loud, and he looked as though he might cry.

"It could have been anyone, Fatty," Roscoe said. "Don't look at it that way. It's not your fault. It's not anyone's fault."

"Roscoe's right, Randall, it isn't anyone's fault," Gertie added. "God's purpose in these matters will be revealed in time. Don't blame yourself."

"Yes ma'am," Fatty said faintly.

"May I tell you boys something about the Christmas cactus?" Gertie said, thinking it best to change the subject.

"Sure," Roscoe answered.

"Well, most any plant will benefit greatly from a spot in the window that affords it morning sun. Like most people, the sun is at its best in the morning. The Christmas cactus, though, in the weeks and months leading up to the holidays, requires darkness to prepare for blooming, ten hours of darkness per day, at least."

"Oh no," Roscoe said. "Are you kidding me, I got my momma a plant that we need to keep in the dark? I'm going to take it back."

"No, no, Roscoe, don't do that. The blossoms that it produces in the holiday and deep winter months make it well worth it. Sometimes they bloom all way into spring. Your momma will be very happy with it, trust me."

"But for a while, it can be out, in the sunlight somewhere?"

"Yes, that's right."

"Okay," Roscoe said, still a little skeptical. "I was hoping that maybe you had some fancy foil or a ribbon or something that would dress it up a little. The old black pot it's in was all they had at the florist place." Then, on second-thought, he added, "Well, what I mean is that all I had left after buying it was fifteen cents and they didn't have anything that cheap. Do you?"

"No, and I'd give it to you if I had foil and ribbon, but I think maybe I could do you even better." Roscoe and Fatty were alert. "Out back, behind the store, that old shack, you've seen it, haven't you? Well, that used to be Mr. Paulson's potting shed. There must be a hundred old pots out there, some of them a lot nicer than that. Anything you find out there you can have for free."

"Really?" Roscoe asked eagerly.

"We could use your change for candy," Fatty whispered.

"Yes, free," Gertie repeated. "Mr. Paulson would be delighted." She reached below the counter and got an old padlock key. "Here," she said handing it to Roscoe. "Just be careful out there. Nobody's been in it since he passed. You might see a few spiders, or even a raccoon. Just be careful."

"Yes, ma'am," Roscoe said. "Thanks a lot, Miss Gertie."

From Gertie's back stoop, the old potting shed was scarcely discernible. It was shrouded in reckless, twisted honeysuckle vines and its roof was caked with thick green moss. The shack's siding was of vertical pine boards, cracked and splintered and with only a hint of old white paint blistered and faded to grey. The earth seemed to reach up around it, giving it more the look of a mineshaft entrance than a shed and the narrow path leading to its door, hacked from honeysuckle, was only wide enough for the boys to pass in single file. Roscoe led and Fatty followed, toting the cactus.

"Spooky, huh?" Fatty said.

"Naw," Roscoe answered. "It's just an old shed. Just watch out for spiders."

"I hate spiders. You ever seen a tarantula? They have fur on them for crying out loud. I read in a book that a tarantula can kill a cow!" Fatty said, craning around, trying to see in front of Roscoe.

"No tarantulas in Missouri, Fatty," Roscoe said, inserting the old key into the rusty padlock.

"Oh yeah? Sure, no tarantulas. Who told you that, your new buddy, Crazy George?"

The old door creaked as Roscoe pulled it open, and a wave of musky air rolled out at the boys, taking their breath away and causing them to squint. The tiny room was full of shadows and shards of dingy light leaking through the gaps and cracks in the shed's siding and roof. As well, there was one single window divided into four dirty panes of glass on the front that let in a wider swath of smokey sunlight. Roscoe left the door open and, all in all, there was just enough light to make out the contents of the place.

One wall had been covered with burlap in an apparent effort to make the shack more weather-tight, and against that wall there was a long, narrow table cluttered at one end with empty seed packets, seedling trays and an assortment of ancient, rusted gardening hand tools. Stacked on the other end were flower pots, a dozen or more, most of them terra cotta orange with white watermark rings, but some faded red and blue and yellow; the sight of them made Roscoe hopeful.

Fatty put the cactus on the potting table and pointed at the opposite wall. "Hey," he said, "look at that." He was pointing at a large map of the world, with curled corners and faded colors, pinned to the wall with brown thumbtacks.

"Maybe Gertie's husband was an explorer," Roscoe said.

"And look, even more pots!" Fatty exclaimed, pointing at motley assortment at least as large as Gertie had promised stacked precariously on the floor and up the back wall of the shed. The different stacks appeared so haphazard that the selection of any one pot might bring the whole hodgepodge crashing down. "How you gonna pick?"

Against the back wall, in the darkest corner of the room, there stood a tall, empty bookcase. Roscoe tilted his head and squinted his eyes. "What's that back there?" he asked, pointing at the bookcase.

"A bookcase," Fatty said matter-of-factly.

"No, behind it, what's that?"

Now Fatty craned his neck and leaned in the direction to get a better look. "I dunno. Is it a door? It kind of looks like a door."

Roscoe took two steps toward the bookcase for a better look. "It is a door. There's a padlock on it. Look. What do you think is in there?" he asked, sensing they had come upon an honest-to-goodness mystery.

"Who cares?" Fatty asked, growing tired of the shed and its dusty clutter.

"Don't you want to know?" Roscoe replied, trying to sound dramatic. "I'm going to try the key on that lock." And he did, but without success. "Rats. Different lock and key, I guess."

"Come on Roscoe, pick out a pot and let's get outta here," Fatty said plaintively. "I gotta get home pretty soon or my mom will be all over me."

"You go on, I want to take some time picking out the right one. I'll see you tomorrow."

"Can I have a dime for some candy?"

"Jeez, Fatty. Here's a nickel. I'm keeping the dime for a soda. See ya."

Fatty was glad to get out of the shed and, strangely, Roscoe was happy enough to be left alone there, surrounded by pots and relics, an old mariner's map of the world, and a mysterious hidden door. It was oddly pleasing to him to be where the past was piled high in every corner, where his eight-year-old imagination could run free, where he could envision people and times gone by better than they were, more daring and interesting than they were, larger and smaller than they had really been. It reminded him of being secretly alone in his grandfather's attic where he spent two hours looking at his own father's military uniforms and photographs of him with the crew he bravely commanded. And alone now, in the shadowy quiet of the shed, his troubles, his family's troubles, seemed less hopeless. Gertie's words came back to him: *God's purpose in these matters will someday be revealed.* He wondered if he was strong enough to move the bookcase.

CHAPTER 12

After hard rains in Mitchell and to the north, Shale creek would run with vigor, but usually not for long, maybe a day or two. And so, George Mabry thought the time was right. Time to let Satchel go on his way most naturally. He stood by the Shale, below the dam and one hundred yards down-creek and thought about what he wanted to say.

The dog was still in the bloody flour sack. He saw no reason to move his friend from one thing to another; he was gone, after all, and George understood that in a more fundamental way than most people would. George understood being gone, passing. He lived in the world of nature, of life and death and decay and renewal; he knew intuitively that Satchel was on his way to something else. But he was sad, to be sure, sadder than he had been in many, many years. He drew a long breath and then spoke.

"I think it's time to float the Shale, Satchel. By-God, I'll surely miss you, just like I already do, only maybe worse as winter comes on. In winter, when there was no work and the wind would blow cold as hell, you and me, we hunkered together, by a stick fire, we would. And I told you stories and you listened just like you could hear. And I would make up what I thought your answers would be and sure as hell some of 'em were doozies and there we'd be, you and me, by the fire."

Here George paused, and shuffled, and moved in a circle, as if the next part was the hardest for him. "I s'pose you're wondering, as you would be right to do, why some sumbitch would do this to a little fella like you. You wasn't a biter or a barker or any kind of trouble-maker. The plain answer is that I don't know. I know you haven't never done anything to deserve it, but — and I hate to say this out loud – I s'pose I have, and maybe they done this to you to get back at me. I hope not, but I know I've done some things and I know maybe I got something comin', but it shoulda come to me, direct, not to you."

George lifted the bag, looked inside again, and then twisted the top shut.

"So, I guess Satchel, here at the last I'd say I'm sorry cuz I'm thinking right now that somehow I brought this on. I'm going to be hoping that what's next for you is as good as you deserve, which is plenty good. I sort of wish I could ride with you. I'm a little tired and would enjoy your company from now till my own end."

George laid the flour sack in the Shale creek and watched it roll gently toward Arkansas. He wiped his eyes with a filthy handkerchief.

CHAPTER 13

Roscoe was angling around looking for the leverage he needed to lift one end of the heavy bookcase when Gertie came into the shed behind him. "What are you doing over there, Roscoe?"

Startled, he turned quickly. "Oh. Nothing. I was just trying to see what was in there, through that door behind the bookcase."

"Nothing as interesting as you likely imagined. Just Mr. Paulson's old mowing machine and some garden fertilizers and chemicals and whatnot that he thought better kept locked away. I don't even recall where he kept the key. We'll break in one of these days and have a look. Did you find a pot that you like?"

"Yes, ma'am," he said, pointing to a blue one on the long table behind her.

"Ah, yes, blue. That should look very nice with the pink blossoms, I think."

"Was that Mr. Paulson's map, there on the wall?"

"Well, I suppose it was, though I don't remember. He probably imagined himself on sweeping adventures, magnificent journeys." Then smiling, she said, "Younger men, with growing families and obligations, they have too little time for imagination. But older men, men like Mr. Paulson in his later years, they have time on their hands." She stepped closer to the map. "They look at maps like this one and dream." Then she turned away from the map with a hint of sadness in her eyes. "You should probably take your blue pot and run along, now, your momma will be looking for you. She's going to like the cactus very much." She turned back toward the map while Roscoe slipped the black cactus container into the blue pot and stepped through the door. He had the uneasy sense that he had saddened Gertie and turned to speak.

"Thank you again, Miss Gertie. I didn't mean make you sad by asking about the map."

"You have a good heart, Roscoe Hammer. It wasn't you, it's this shed, it was one of his favorite places and reminds me of him. It wasn't you at all. Now run along."

On the walk home, he felt good, like he had done the right thing in buying the plant and he had said the right thing when the sadness came over Gertie. Good – not happy, as there was still too much trouble for that — just good, solid, like maybe he was back on the right track.

At home Roscoe came through the door with his chest out and the plant in both hands. He found his mother and father in the kitchen. Laura was at the sink, washing vegetables, and Frank was at the kitchen table.

"Hi, Pop," Roscoe said cheerfully. "Why are you home early?"

"Oh, no reason really. Your momma and I needed to talk about some things, that's all."

"What things?" Roscoe asked, sensing trouble.

Laura turned and dried her hands with a dish towel. Surprised, she asked, "Where did you get that plant, Roscoe?"

"I bought it for you, momma," he said proudly, sitting the cactus on the table. "Miss Gertie gave me the pot."

"How sweet of you, son," Laura replied. "A Christmas cactus, one of my very favorite plants. But why?"

"I just thought that with Hannah's measles and all, you had been pretty sad and that a plant might help you feel better. It should bloom by Christmas time."

A silence filled the room. Laura had been genuinely touched by Roscoe's gift, but his explanation embarrassed her, or made her angry, it was hard to tell. She turned away, back toward the sink. "Thank you, Roscoe, that was very thoughtful. We'll have to find a sunny spot for it," she added, with little conviction. "A sunny spot."

"Actually, momma," Roscoe said eagerly, "that's an interesting thing about it. After a while we'll need a dark spot for it so it can get ready to bloom. That's what I learned about it."

For a moment nobody spoke and Roscoe's eyes lost their earlier brightness. Finally, Frank broke the silence. "That was a very nice thing for you to do, Roscoe. I'm proud of you."

"What things?" Roscoe asked his father. "You said you had to talk about some things? What things?"

"Nothing for you to worry about, son."

"What things?" Roscoe asked again, this time louder.

Laura turned, looked at Frank and then answered. "Your little sister and I are going to Saint Louis for a short while. Your daddy and I were discussing the plans."

"Saint Louis? For what? For how long?"

"Calm down, Roscoe," Laura said. "There is a place there, a school, a school for deaf children and their parents. They will help Hannah there. They will help her begin to learn how to talk and how to recognize sign language. Do you know what sign language is?"

"Yes, I know what it is! She's only one! She's too little for school." His face was red now and he was almost shouting.

"She's not too little for this kind of school. She will go back many times as she gets older, but the doctors say it is important to start as soon as possible. It is a school for me too. I will learn sign language and I'll teach it to you and Andy and your father. This time we'll only be away a week or so, not long at all."

"This time? What do you mean? How often are you going to go away?" Roscoe asked, growing more and more desperate.

Andy came into the room. "What's wrong with Roscoe?" he asked, directing the question to Laura.

"Nothing is wrong. Go back in the other room and keep an eye on Hannah."

"Go on son," Frank added.

"How often, momma? I have a right to know." Roscoe shouted.

"I always have to go in the other room," Andy complained.

"Andy, now," Frank commanded. "Roscoe, I want you to calm down."

"The truth is I don't know how often, Roscoe," Laura offered, struggling to remain composed. "But it is important. There's no other way."

"But what about us? What about me and Andy? What are we going to do?" he asked, now fighting back tears.

"What do you mean?" Laura asked. "Your father will be here with you. You'll be fine. It's only for a few days."

"He has to work! We won't be fine! He'll send us down to Mrs. Woodson's."

"Roscoe! Stop this. You are being selfish!" Laura said firmly, growing angry. "Your sister needs this; we must go. You need to understand that she is not going to get her hearing back. Your sister is going to be...she *is*...handicapped. Do you know what that means? It means when she plays outdoors like you and Andy, she won't be able to hear her friends. When she crosses the street, she won't be able to hear the cars. When she speaks, it will sound different and other children will make fun."

"Yes, momma, I know and it makes me sad too," he said weakly.

"Her life will never be like yours. If you want to be a ball player, then maybe you can. What if she wants to be a ballerina, what should I tell her? What if she wants to play the piano? That's what it means, young man. Maybe you should think about that before...."

"Momma, I know! I know! Stop!"

"Laura! I think that's enough," Frank said, seeing complete hopelessness in his son's red eyes.

That's enough. It was all he said. Roscoe wanted him to tell his mother that he and Andy needed her too. That his life had changed too, in ways none of them knew, and he wanted to talk about it and have them listen. He wanted his father to tell his mother that her despair and melancholia was crippling their family. He wanted his father to tell his mother that Roscoe had given her a plant as a gift and she shouldn't scream and tell him he was selfish. He wasn't selfish, he was eight years old. But his father said none of those things. *That's enough*. Nothing more. Laura went to the living room where she heard Hannah crying and Roscoe, wiping his eyes, turned away from his father.

"Are you all right?" Frank asked.

"Yes, sir. I need to go feed Ranger." The feeling that he was on the right track was gone.

Roscoe filled Ranger's bowl with Purina Dog Chow and watched his big sloppy friend enjoy the day's only meal. How, Roscoe wondered, do dogs seem to always be happy? If he could figure it out somehow, then he could be happy again, the way he had been just days before. And why, he wondered, could his mother have been mean to him? Didn't she know how much he loved his baby sister? In his mind, Roscoe posed these as silent questions for Ranger, who, at the moment, seemed smart and happy and unaffected by the calamity all around him. And of course, there came from Ranger no answers, only an occasional pause in the chomping and a vacant, peaceful glance back at Roscoe as if to be sure his master was still there, at his post. Watching Ranger eat didn't make Roscoe happy, but it calmed him somehow; it slowed his heart down.

"This will all get better in time." The voice, his father's voice, came from behind him. "She will come back to us."

"Who will?" Roscoe asked, thinking he meant Hannah.

"Your mother, she will come back."

"I guess so," Roscoe said flatly, not wishing to provoke discussion or disagreement.

"We will be okay, Roscoe, we will."

"Yes, sir."

"Supper will be on soon. We're having pork chops," Frank offered, craning around to get a peek at his son's face.

"I'm not really very hungry, Dad. Could I be excused from supper?" Roscoe asked, turning away. "I found the key to Miss Gertie's potting shed in my pocket; I think I should return it. Maybe I'll be hungry by the time I get back. Would that be okay?" He was trying to be properly respectful, but it didn't really matter what his father said, he wasn't eating, he'd made up his mind and that was that.

"If you don't feel like eating right now, why don't you go up to your room and rest for a little bit while I eat dinner with the family. Then, I'll walk down to Gertie's with you. Maybe we can talk some more. How does that sound?"

"Yes, sir," Roscoe said. "Holler when you're ready."

CHAPTER 14

"Don't be mad at your mother, Roscoe, please." The request came halfway into the walk to Gertie's after a prolonged silence.

"I'm not mad," Roscoe said. They both knew he was lying.

"You can talk to me," his father offered gently.

Roscoe wanted to tell him that he was mad at him too, at least that was part of it, but he didn't, opting for a broader, more general reply. "I'm mad because things are all messed up for our family. Just a little while ago everything was great and then Hannah got sick and now everything is......crazy. I keep trying to help make it better and nothing works."

"I'm proud of what you've tried to do, son, but you can't make it better all by yourself. It's going to take time. But we'll get through it. I promise you."

"Dad, do you think Hannah will get her hearing back?" Roscoe asked directly, cutting off any obvious escape route.

"I think she might, yes, at least partly," Frank answered quickly, sensing that something more cautious, more reflective, something more his norm would not be helpful. "But I think your mother is right, we can't count on that. We have to prepare for the possibility that she might not. We have to prepare for the worst and hope for something better."

"Why do you say that, Dad? Why do we have to prepare for the worst?" Roscoe asked. It seemed to him his father was headed back to the middle of the road where he had always done his best work.

"So that if the worst comes about, we won't get blind-sided."

"Didn't that already happen, Dad?" Roscoe asked. It wasn't really a question. He was through talking.

Gertie's market was within sight when JL Woodson's red Chevy truck rumbled up the street behind them. He tooted the horn and pulled over alongside Frank and Roscoe. The light had grown dim just before dark and a shapeless puff of exhaust curled up behind the truck; he rolled down the window. "Evening gentlemen," he said. "Where might y'all be heading on such a nice night?"

"Just a quick walk down to Gertie's. You doing all right?" Frank answered.

"Doin' fine, thank you. On my way to work."

"You have that thing running a little louder than normal don't you?" Frank asked, nodding at the red pickup.

"Hit a possum or raccoon the other mornin' in the middle of that downpour. Never even saw the thing. Knocked the muffler loose I think. I'm goin' to have to have Doak Posey take a look at it. Repairs from Althea's attack on the garage door have to come first though. The muffler makes it sound powerful, don't you think? I kinda like it, truth told." JL saw Roscoe look away and took the chance to lean slightly in Frank's direction. "I need to have a quick word with you sometime, just you and me, whenever we can."

"Roscoe," Frank said, "why don't you run that key on up to Gertie's. I'm going to talk to Mr. Woodson for a minute. I imagine she's closed up for the evening; just leave the key in her delivery box on the back stoop. Try to be quiet, you don't want to scare her or Harriet. I'll wait here for you."

Roscoe took off, plenty glad to be free from talk with his father, or anyone else for that matter. It was becoming too easy for him to be alone.

From several yards away he could tell that the store was dark, closed up as Frank had suspected. Light shown in the windows on the second floor, where sheer curtains were drawn and silhouettes floated lazily across. It was Gertie and Harriet, slowly making ready for bed.

He walked a wide circle around the building, making certain to stay out of the light thrown from the upper windows, and headed toward the back stoop. As he approached, he caught in the periphery a glimpse of something peculiar, a dim wisp of light coming from the dirty window of the potting shed. He stopped and turned and squinted, wondering first if maybe it was just a reflection, a light from somewhere else reflecting just right. He took two cautious steps toward the shed and he could see well enough then to be sure; there was a light inside the potting shed, and it danced a little as if made by a flame. He moved closer still, stepping carefully so as not to make even the slightest sound. He crouched down and worked his was to a silent position just below the windowsill, where he paused and drew a deep breath. Suddenly the light in the windows above the store went out, startling him. Now there was darkness all around, except for the glimmer from inside the shed. He rose slowly and peeked through the dirty glass. The light wasn't coming from the main part of the potting shed. The bookshelf had been moved, and the door behind it was ajar, and it was from there that a skinny, dancing shaft of light floated. And now he could hear whistling, faint and soft, but happy, like an old cowboy camp song. And the whistling too came from behind the mysterious door he had asked Gertie about that very day, the door behind the bookcase too heavy for him to budge. Then, he saw the door move, slowly it opened wider and in a split second, he knew that the source of the whistling, the owner of the light within was about to step out, out where he could see Roscoe peering through the window. He turned and ran, scrambled really, on all fours like a cub bear, trying to stay low and out of sight. Then, when it seemed safe, he stood and ran flat out. In seconds, he was around the house and back to the street's edge when he turned back for a look. The light in the shed was gone, swallowed up by the honeysuckle and the darkness.

Roscoe did his best to catch his breath and compose himself as he walked back toward his father, where JL Woodson was just pulling away. The campfire song played in his head and frightened him as he walked.

"Did you put it in her delivery box?" Frank asked as Roscoe approached.

"No, huh-uh. It was dark, and the lights upstairs went out and it was a little spooky back there. And I didn't want to make a noise and scare 'em, like you said."

"That's all right, it can wait until tomorrow. You can give it to Gertie herself tomorrow."

"Yeah," Roscoe answered, feigning a modest smile, "that's right, tomorrow."

On the way home, Frank tried to casually introduce the subject of his side-bar conversation with JL. "Mr. Woodson was telling me about the episode with Bobby Cato."

"Yeah," Roscoe answered, unsure how much information JL had shared.

"Did he scare you and Andy?"

"Me a little maybe, not Andy. Sometimes Andy doesn't get it, you know?"

Frank smiled. "Yes, I know, it's one of the benefits of being a five-year-old."

"He was a creep. Took our milk," Roscoe reported plainly.

"That's what JL told me. You did the right thing by avoiding a conflict with him. I'm glad Althea was there."

"What's wrong with him?" Roscoe asked.

Frank paused, then said, "He's a young guy who's had a rough life and it's made him mean, real mean."

"Miss Althea said he's been in jail. Did you know that, Dad?"

"Yes, I knew," Frank answered. Then, he stopped, and motioned for Roscoe to stop and turn toward him. He squatted down so as to meet his son at eye level. "I want you to promise me that you'll do everything you can to stay away from Bobby Cato. And if he bothers you again, I want you to come straight to me. I'll take it up with the police. This guy is nobody to mess with, Roscoe, do you understand? It's important."

"I understand, Dad, I promise. What did he do to get put in jail?"

"He robbed a drug store here in town. It was before you were born." What Frank intentionally omitted from his report was the fact that Bobby had pistol-whipped a young female clerk in the course of the robbery, leaving her blind in one eye. That, he felt, was more information than his eight-year-old son needed.

"Okay," Roscoe said, and they walked on.

Twice each day for the next three in a row, Roscoe made it a point to walk past Gertie's place. On each pass he angled for a new vantage point from which he might catch a glimpse of movement or light in the old shed. But there was none to be seen, just the old shed, dark and shrouded in honeysuckle, surrounded by weeds, no light, no motion. And with each pass his imaginings about the secret section of the shed and its inhabitant would swing from the plausible, even probable, to the fantastic. It could have been Gertie herself. It might have been only Harriet in the silhouettes above the store and Gertie was in the shed reminiscing about her days with Mr. Paulson. Or, might it have been a thief or squatter? Or someone hiding out, hiding from the police or an enemy? Roscoe didn't disclose his experience to anyone, except of course, Fatty.

"Why did you run? Why didn't you wait to get a good look?" Fatty asked when Roscoe brought him into his confidence.

"I didn't want him, or *it*, or whatever, to see *me*. I was just outside the window, only a couple feet away," Roscoe argued, sensing all the while that Fatty was right, he should have stayed for a better look-see.

Possessing a polished flare for dramatic speculation, Fatty quickly offered up his own theory. "I think it was the ghost of old man Paulson. Had to be. She said he liked messing around out in that shed, right?"

"A ghost! Don't tell me you believe in that kind of crapola?" Roscoe replied, using a word he had only become comfortable using now that he was in the third grade.

"Yeah, I do, I'll admit it. Bet you do too for real."

"Do not. Ghosts are crapola. Period. I think it was Miss Gertie."

"I thought you said you saw her in the window upstairs?" Fatty came back, arguing his case.

"So, I must have been wrong; it was probably just Harriet."

"So if it was just Gertie, why'd you run away? Answer me that one," Fatty replied throwing out his chest.

"Cuz I didn't know it was her then! I didn't have time to think about it."

"See," Fatty went on, "your story just doesn't add up. You're going in circles, Roscoe. I'm telling you it was the old man's ghost."

"Shut up, stupid. Ghosts equal crapola."

"Okay, but I'm just saying...." Fatty trailed on, reluctantly letting the debate fade.

Roscoe secretly remained quite intrigued — and scared too — by the mysterious shed sighting, but a more immediate problem was competing for his time and attention. He changed the subject.

"Ranger ran off again," he said to Fatty blankly. "He's been gone two full days now."

"Ranger? Huh?" Fatty was still pondering the ghost of Henry Paulson.

"He's done it before, but not for a long time."

"Will he come home, you think?" Fatty asked, catching up.

"Always has, but I'm worried. One time he came back all scratched up like he'd been in a fight with a mountain lion. I'm going to have to start looking for him in my spare time. I'm worried."

"Awe, he'll show up I bet. He's gotta eat, right?"

"There's another possibility that's got me worried, too," Roscoe said, putting both hands behind his head. "My mom might have hustled him out to old man Hattan's before she left for Saint Louis with Hannah and not told me. She was getting pretty fed up with his pissing in the house."

"Without even telling you? Geez, that would be real low-down, specially for a mom. Geezola, I hope you're wrong about that one," Fatty said, shaking his head in disbelief. "Did you ask your dad?"

"Yeah," Roscoe answered. "He said she didn't, but I don't think he really knows for sure, you know? I mean, she might not have told him either." He paused for a moment then collected his thoughts and went on. "Anyway, I gotta start looking for him. Keep and eye out, will ya? I'm going to use my bike; I can cover more ground that way. Just what I needed, huh?"

Fatty, who had a more advanced command of the profane, wrapped things up with an attribution to his father. "You been in what my old man calls a regular shit storm."

"Yeah, well, I gotta go. See ya later."

"Yeah, later. Good luck, buddy. I'll be lookin' round."

CHAPTER 15

R oscoe stood at the top of the bank, just a few feet from the dam in Harmony Park. Looking down he could see George Mabry's shoulders and the back of his head. He was standing in tall weeds, looking away from the creek beneath the dam when Roscoe called to him. "Hello, Mr. Mabry?" he shouted loud enough to be heard over the sound of the cascading water. Mabry strained to turn his head without turning his body. He couldn't see Roscoe, but recognized his voice.

"Yeah, boy, it's me. Taking a piss. Give me a minute; I'll be up."

"Sorry, no hurry," Roscoe shouted back.

When Mabry was done, he shook and wiggled, zipped his khaki trousers awkwardly and climbed up the bank where he found Roscoe politely looking away. "What are you up to, boy?" Mabry asked between heavy breaths.

"I'm out looking for my dog, Ranger. He ran off, two days ago. He's a big sloppy coonhound. He'll come if you call his name. He's run off before, but never for more than a day or so. I was hoping to find you here to ask if you'd look for him around town," Roscoe said hopefully.

"I ain't seen him, but I'll look." Just then, in the distance from the south, came a series of three or four pops. Roscoe and Mabry both turned to the sound.

"What was that?" Roscoe asked.

"Dove hunters. Down south. Season opened yesterday. Been hearing it all day long."

"Hunters, huh?" Roscoe replied, his mind racing to find some possible connection to Ranger's disappearance. "Shotguns?" he asked.

"Yep, shotguns. Ever fired one?" George asked.

"No," Roscoe answered. "Have you?"

"No sir," Mabry replied. "No shotguns, but I got me a gun, a pistol."

"You do?"

"Yes, sir, I do. Found it when I was doing some work for an old gal whose dead now. She was a widow and when I showed it to her she said she didn't know where it come from and I could take it for my own. Three bullets in the cylinder. Never fired it."

"What did you do with it?" Roscoe asked, with a young boy's natural curiosity about guns.

"Nothin'," Mabry replied flatly. "I keep it wrapped up in a yellow rag and stowed in an old coffee can." Then came another series of pops and again, they both turned. "Sure couldn't shoot no flying dove with it, that's for sure. Probably couldn't even hit that big tree over there. But I got it, anyhow, just in case."

Roscoe had gone to his favorite bench and after scanning the southern horizon once more, George walked over and joined his young friend.

"No guess where your dog went off to?" George asked.

"Nope. But I'm worried my momma might have given him to Mr. Hattan. They had talked about him going out there to the hatchery where he wouldn't be pissing in our house and causing trouble. I'm worried she might have snuck him out there before she went to Saint Louis with my baby sister."

"You reckon?" George asked. "I wouldn't think she'd do that."

"I don't know," Roscoe answered sadly. "I hope not, but I don't know."

"Hey," George replied, with forced cheerfulness, "did that Christmas cactus make your momma feel better? Did it work out good?"

"I'm not sure. She liked it okay, I guess, but we had a big fight."

"Cuz of the plant? I don't get it."

"No, just because of everything that has been going on with my family, with Hannah and all." Then, sensing George's disappointment, he added, "But the plant was a good idea, it really was."

"I'll look hard for Ranger, boy, I will, I promise. We'll find him."

Roscoe paused for a moment then squinted his eyes a little and posed a questioned he was afraid to ask. "Do you think that Bobby Cato could have stolen Ranger? You know he wanted to mate him up with his coonhound."

"Maybe," George relied. "He's no count. I thought hard about it and I reckon he killed my little Satchel. I got no proof of it, but he and one of his no good buddies brought him to me in a flour sack. They throwed him right up where I was standing and laughed like goddamn hyenas, pardon my language. There's no tellin' what that fella would do. I don't mind asking him 'bout Ranger if you want me to. Him and me are gonna square off sometime soon anyhow, on account of Satchel. You want me to?"

"I don't think so," Roscoe replied slowly, recalling his father's admonition. "I promised my dad I would stay clear of Cato and even though it would be you asking him, you'd be doing it on my account. If I figure out that he really might have taken Ranger, I'll tell my dad. That's what I promised him."

"If you say so. But if you change your mind, you just give me the word."

"Yes, sir, I will. I'd be grateful if you'd keep an eye out for Ranger, like you said."

"I surely will," George answered, trying to sound hopeful.

Two days later, Roscoe awoke to find Ranger asleep on the front porch. Roscoe knew where he had been and he knew who had rescued him.

CHAPTER 16

W inter came early that year, and it came with conviction. The old ones in Mitchell went indoors to stay, and children like Roscoe, walking to school each day against the bitter wind would walk backwards off and on to keep their faces from freezing. Everyone, young and old alike, wore thick gloves, layer upon layer of clothing, topped by heavy, hooded parkas or long woolen overcoats.

Except Bobby Cato. Bobby learned in prison that heavy clothing could be used against you. He once saw a gang gather around a suspected snitch in the yard. There was a fracas and after a while the disinterested guards fired some warning shots. The gang dispersed, and what was left was the snitch, with his coat sleeves pulled over his hands and tied in a knot and the body of his coat pulled up over his head. He had been kicked to death. The impression was indelible.

And so, as was normal, when he came through the door at Doak Posey's station, he was wearing a light-weight chambray jacket and shivering.

"Morning Doak," Bobby said, pouring himself a cup of thick black, steaming coffee. "Are you putting motor oil in this stuff, Doak? Jeez! Oh well. Say, Doak I got a good litter of pups comin' and I'd be happy for you to have one. I figure they're going to be worth fifty bucks each and I'd let you have one for only twenty. How about it?"

"Come in here Bobby, I need to talk to you."

Bobby stepped slowly into the tiny office. "Yeah?"

"Sit down, Bobby, with your coffee. I want you to be comfortable. I've made a decision I need to tell you about. It's a kind of mathematical decision," Doak said.

"Yeah?" Bobby answered, his eyes darting around nervously.

"That's right. I want to take you through the math."

Bobby squirmed as Doak continued. "Number one: the good officer Buster Odom was in here the other day and we got to talking. And some way or another, the incident between you and those young boys came up. And Buster told me something I hadn't known until then. He told me they were the Hammer boys, Frank Hammer's sons."

"Yeah, so?" Bobby said defensively.

"Well, Frank Hammer and me have been friends a long time. He's a good man, and he's a good customer. So that's number one — you messed with some boys that I care something about." He paused a moment then went on. "Then there's number two: Kooky old George Mabry was by here the other day and he said that he had summoned all his considerable investigative powers and determined that you 'borrowed' the oldest Hammer boy's hound for purposes of that litter of pup-hounds you were talking about — 'borrowed' without asking, according to George."

"That crazy old buzzard don't know what he's talking about," Cato came back.

"I agree with you that George's credibility isn't, well, it isn't a hundred percent. But you know, Bobby, I somehow think he's figured this one out, I really do."

"He ain't figured out shit!"

"Then there's number three," Doak calmly went on. "I know you've been closing this place early. Pud calls me every time you do."

"With no business comin' in here, what am I supposed to do?" Bobby argued.

"Do what you're paid to do, that's what. Close at closing time, which is established by me, the owner of this place, not you, some sorry ex-con who I was crazy enough to hire," Doak said flatly. "What's even worse than you closing early on no authority at all, you been putting a full shift on your time sheets. Which means, Bobby Cato, you've been stealing from me."

"This is all bunk," Bobby said, "bunk cooked up by a kid and an old half-wit."

"Pud is no kid and he's no half-wit, and neither am I!" Doak paused for moment and then continued. "And there you are, Bobby, one, two, three. So, do you know what one plus two plus three equals? Do you?"

"Huh?" Bobby answered.

"One plus two plus three. Basic mathematics. What does it equal?"

"Six?" Bobby said, feeling stupid.

"No!" Doak answered. "Wrong! One plus two plus three equals I have decided to fire your no-good ass. That's what it equals. Now if that seems too personal for you, look at it this way, what I've really decided is that I was stupid to hire you in the first place and so what I intend to do is un-hire you. Think of it as me rectifying my own mistake."

"You son-of-a bitch," Bobby started.

"You see Bobby, there's another example of your lack of good judgement," Doak replied. "You are right enough; my mother was indeed an unpleasant, ill-tempered person, maybe the most profane woman I've ever known. Myself, I didn't care for her one bit; dare say I was relieved to see her go. But I do not know why you'd want to bring her into all of this. I'm going to tell myself that this is an emotional day for you and I'm going to look past this... miscalculation of yours. But be clear about this Bobby, if in the next few days I should see anything unusual around here, a broken window, the chamois tubs turned over, spit on the sidewalk, any thing like that, then I'm going to find you. Not even the slightest provocation will I be able to ignore, Bobby Cato, you remember that. Now get out of here."

Bobby stood, silently turned and walked out. Once out the door he lit a cigarette, exhaled a huge cloud of smoke and decided that one way or another, this wasn't done. There would be some blood come from this — his or somebody else's. That's what made Bobby so dangerous, he pretty much didn't care which.

The afternoon of that very same day, the day of Bobby Cato's unceremonious dismissal from Doak Posey's Phillips 66, found Fatty Gilchrist on his bicycle running a routine errand for his mother on a route that took him straight down Main Street, right in front of Doak's station and Pud's directly across. At about that point, had one been observing from a distance but within earshot, it would seem that something akin to a sonic boom blew Fatty and his bicycle clean off the street and into the boxwoods that circled the one-hundred-year-old oak in front of the Memorial Auditorium right next to Doak Posey's place. While Fatty struggled mightily to untangle himself from his bike and the boxwoods, Doak Posey came out of Pud's looking like something at once near-tragic and funny had happened. Quickly, Doak saw Fatty out of the corner of his eye.

"You all right?" Doak asked, approaching.

"What happened?" Fatty replied. "I'm caught up in the sprocket on my bike."

Once there, Doak could tell that Fatty had fallen victim to two things at once. No doubt the boom startled him, maybe it was even enough to knock him off the street, but at just about the same moment he had gotten his jean cuff caught in the machinery of his bicycle. It was this two-dimensional calamity that threw him off the street and into the bushes. Doak helped him up and, with the bicycle still awkwardly attached to his pant leg, led Fatty the twenty yards or so to the repair pit in his station.

"Sit down there and I'll get you undone from that thing," Doak said.

While Doak popped the joint in Fatty's bicycle chain that held the thing together, Fatty asked again about the sonic boom. It turns out, according to a fairly calm recounting by Doak, that it was a shotgun blast that sent Fatty careening into the bushes.

With the chain popped, Fatty's pant leg came loose.

"Is it torn?" Fatty asked, hoping beyond hope that is was not.

"Looks okay to me, boy," Doak answered. He studied the label on the jeans for a minute. "Nice jeans. No damage done."

"They're almost new," Fatty answered. "My mom just got 'em for me. I'm not crazy about them because they've got that double padding in the knees, you know? But what are you going to do? My mom was happy to get me some new ones so I'd hate if they were messed up. You know?"

"I'd say they are made for big tough guys," Doak said. "You come back tomorrow and I'll have that chain back on for you. Why are you riding a bike in this cold anyhow?"

"I'd rather eat a bug than walk," Fatty said. "As long as there's no snow or ice." He paused for a moment then asked again, "Were did that boom come from?"

The boom, it turns out, was completely coincidental. Doak had been at Pud's and in the course of normal conversation had asked if Pud had any kind of security beyond the stick he kept behind the bar. Well, Pud motioned proudly to Pony Ladezma, Pud's sole employee who fried burgers and dogs on the grill at the end of the bar. Pony pulled an eighteen inch, sawed off, double-barreled shot gun out from under the bar and thumped it down, barrel up on the bar. Pony's dramatics, it turns out, were a little extreme, and the force of his presentation on top of the bar caused the thing to go off, blowing a six-inch hole in Pud's ceiling. As one might imagine, Pud went into a conniption, yelling broken, profane Spanish at Pony. And, across the street, Fatty Gilchrist, at just the wrong place and time, went head over heals into the bushes.

Doak smoothed the cuff of Fatty's jean and reminded him, "Come back tomorrow to get your bike. You sure you're okay?"

"I'm fine, Mr. Posey," Fatty said. He noticed the bracelet on Doak's wrist. "Where did you get that, Mr. Posey? I like it."

"It was given to me by a friend. A good friend," Doak said.

"It looks good, and it matches your ring."

"The friend who gave it to me lives in Colorado."

"Oh yeah, Colorado? I've always wanted to go there."

"He's a man," Doak said. "My friend is a man."

And just like that, Doak Posey decided to release one of Mitchell's biggest secrets. It was as if he was returning a fish too small to keep to the shallow water at the edge of Shale Creek. He gently let it go. It's funny how people decide when it's time to do that.

CHAPTER 17

On December 6th, on a bitter winter night, a young apprentice switchman in the Neosho yards, one hundred miles southwest of Mitchell, switched six cars off southbound Burlington Northern number 109. When he uncoupled the cars, a man's arm, severed near the shoulder fell out onto the track bed. In the call back to Mitchell where the cars originated, the young man, a boy really, could barely speak. With the cold and the mutilation and the blood, he explained, it was hard to tell, but it might have been a negro's arm. He just couldn't say. What should he do? Should the arm be preserved? Soon enough, in Mitchell, they had the answers.

At first light, with Roscoe just between sleep and wake, two men in long grey overcoats and Sunday hats were on the porch at the Woodson house. The sound that awakened Roscoe was the worst he had ever heard, worse than anything he would hear until years later when, outside a courtroom, he heard the cries of a mother whose son was sentenced to twenty years in the penitentiary. The sound this day came from Althea Woodson whose heart had been forever broken.

Shortly after the call from Neosho, the yard manager in Mitchell found JL dead in a pool of his own blood. He had scratched his way fifty yards across the gravel yard, and died slowly and alone in the cold and darkness. Althea's cry sounded deep, like that of an animal whose young had been taken. Roscoe's eyes cleared just in time to see her collapse in the arms of one of the grey men.

JL Woodson's death unleashed a torrent of activity, the likes of which Mitchell had never seen. His kin, all negroes of course, and all from Mississippi, from Yazoo City and all the surrounding little towns, they all came north in a caravan. There were eight vehicles in all, sedans and trucks of all makes, models, but of the same vintage— barely highway worthy. Among them there was a panel van with the words 'Rice Brothers Plaster and Painting' printed in blue and fading on the side. All tolled, more than thirty-five family members came to pay their respects. Aunts, great aunts, cousins, nieces and nephews, an uncle, and a brother, and the Pastor Robert Earl Woodson of The Path to Grace Baptist Church of Yazoo City, Mississippi, they all came. By agreement reached in advance, Pastor Robert would share the pulpit with the rector of St. Agnes Episcopal in conducting his brothers funeral service. It was a pairing that would later be likened to a delta blues guitarist playing alongside a classical cellist.

When they arrived, JL's and Althea's kin filled to capacity the only motor hotel in town, the Siesta Motel, a string of five low-slung, pink stucco cabins arranged around an old fountain that hadn't operated in twenty years. Each cabin came with a double bed, a kitchenette of sorts, television and telephone service, and bath towels for two, accommodations that were taxed by the average occupancy created by Mitchell's newest visitors. At four to five per cabin, there was still over-flow, and the good women of St. Agnes made arrangements for the remaining family to sleep on cots in Fellowship Hall of St. Agnes, which was in the basement of the church. Bath linens were provided so that the guests could wash up in the adjoining bathrooms, and modest meals were served by members of the altar guild at normal times of the day. For three days, Mitchell was alive with more negro people than it had ever seen before or has seen since; white folks were friendly, accommodating, and more than slightly agog.

JL's sudden death created a new, only slightly discernible crack in the relationship between Laura Hammer and the rest of her family, a fissure regrettably most noticeable between her and her husband. She went, as anyone might have expected, immediately to the side of her friend Althea, supporting her in every possible way. In advance of the Mississippi entourage, Laura accompanied Althea to the funeral home to make all of the arrangements. Together they decided that a make-shift prothesis, the arm from a mannequin borrowed from the local JC Penny should be used to downplay the gruesome nature of JL's death. And, according to railroad tradition, they decided that his switchman's lantern should accompany him in the casket. While the lantern-to-light-the-way symbolism was vaguely uncomfortable to most Episcopalians, JL was clearly more railroader that he was church-goer, and so, that was that. And, finally, at his other side, there would be a King James version of the Holy Bible. Althea's thinking was that he had made so little use of the book above ground, that it might come in handy, even entertaining, in the afterlife. Lest everything be decided by some over-sized and overly emotional committee — who the by the way would not be paying the freight — this was all agreed to before the Mississippi delegation hit town. Credit to the ever-caring, cool-headed, and budget-conscious Laura.

But, Frank, Roscoe, and to a lesser degree, Andy, all felt the tug. Hannah and the travels to St. Louis had taken their toll. And so had the sadness, the darkness, the undercurrent of animosity toward anyone who seemed to have dodged the kind of problems that had beset the Hammer family. Years later, Roscoe would remember a time, which could have been here, near the death of JL Woodson, or maybe a little later, when his mother took him aside and asked a question he would never forget. *If you had to live with either me or your father, what would you want?* To an eight-year-old, she might as well have asked who would he choose to have die, his mother or his father? The question was searing, crushing, unforgettable. What was forgettable, was his answer, which in later years he truly could not remember. Which means, of course, it was some mumbling version or another of "I don't know". And who could blame the kid?

And now, there was a new family member, Althea, with a deep loss, who needed Laura's care. And the others, the family members who were keeping up appearances, they could get by for a while. With Frank, this logic was wearing thin. He wanted his wife back; more than that, his children needed their mother back.

A day before the service, Laura hosted a dinner for some selected members of Althea's family who had made the trip north. Among them was one of only a few young people in the entourage from Mississippi. His name was Jermaine; he was fourteen years old and he was Althea's nephew, by way of her sister, Margaret, who couldn't make the trip on account of being in Birmingham, where her daughter was in the very midst of having a baby. Strangely, Jermaine and his aunt Althea had never met. By virtue of being older, not to mention a negro and from the South, Jermaine was more than a curiosity to Roscoe. When the dinner table was cleared, he decided to try and learn more.

"Did you know your uncle, Mr. Woodson?" Roscoe asked.

"No. Only what my momma told me about him, that's all," Jermaine answered. "Why, did you know him? I mean, good?"

"Yep," Roscoe said. "Our families have been friends for a long, long time."

"So, did you know he was married before, before my aunt?"

"Married before? No, I didn't know that. Neither did my momma. Or anybody here in town. Before?"

"It doesn't matter. But he was. But so what, right?"

"I guess....but...well, I guess so." Roscoe paused to calculate.

"All I really know about is my aunt Althea, and she's the best. That's all I care about. I hope she moves back home with us."

"Why?" Roscoe asked, genuinely confused. "What's wrong with here?"

"Everybody likes to be where they are like most everybody else. The South ain't got much, except one thing, lots of black people. If you are a negro, and you want to be around other black people, then Mississippi is the place for you. People always want to know why negroes stay in the South where there's no work and things are so sorry. It's cause there are more negroes in the South. And, the weather is warm. What's so hard about that to figure out?"

"My momma says you are a casket bearer for Mr. Woodson," Roscoe said, deciding to change the subject.

"Yep. Me, your daddy, and four others," Jermaine said. "Between you and me, some of the others are kind of feeble. I've never done it before and I hope we don't drop him."

Noticing the conversation between the two boys, Frank Hammer then asked Jermaine if he was involved in athletics.

"No sir, I am not, and I suspect I am the only boy my age in Mississippi who isn't. I do play the piano, though, and I am, if I say so myself, not too bad. You mind?" he asked, pointing toward the upright piano in the Hammer living room.

"Oh please do," said Laura Hammer, who had always wanted something important played on her piano.

Jermaine then went in to a medley of *Swinging on a Star, Rum and Coca Cola,* and aptly enough, *Baby it's Cold Outside,* all of which the group adored. Adored is too modest a word. He was phenomenal, performing with the polish and ease of a seasoned professional musician. No one in Mitchell had heard anything like him. And, as it turns out, he had never had any formal musical training. He literally played by ear. You call out the tune, and if he had heard it, he could play it. Right there, on the spot.

While Jermaine was in the middle of his second number, Roscoe noticed a young girl, maybe six or seven years old, in the living room playing with Hannah. He was captivated by Jermaine's playing, but couldn't resist going to his younger sister and her new playmate.

"What is your name?" Roscoe asked.

"Maevella," she answered, unsure how to take this new, bigger person.

"Hannah seems to like you. My name is Roscoe."

"Is she your baby sister?" Maevella asked.

"Yes."

"She can't hear. Did you know that?"

"Yes."

"Can I help her?"

"Only the way you are. She loves to play with those toys."

Then, from the parlor, Roscoe heard his mothers voice, "Roscoe, Jermaine is playing the piano. It is remarkable. Please come listen."

"I can hear from in hear," Roscoe said. "I'm watching Hannah and Maevella play."

That brought Laura, and with a slight fury.

"Jermaine is playing like a professional musician, and you can't come listen? Why do you embarrass us this way?"

"I was watching them play with toys, that's all. I didn't mean to embarrass you. Why are you so mad?" Roscoe asked, exasperated.

"I'm disappointed, Roscoe, not mad," she said as she turned and left the room. Roscoe went back to wondering what made him such a bad son, or was it a *disappointing* son, and what made a virtual stranger like Jermaine so suddenly perfect. It was a question that occupied his mind long after all the guests were gone and everyone in the Hammer household was in bed. He asked Ranger about it and got his usual answer.

The next day, at about seven in the morning, Pastor Robert Earl Woodson was looking for somewhere to shave. The bathroom in unit 5 at the Siesta Motel was unavailable to him because his wife, Nadine, was horribly cramped up on the toilet suffering from God knows what.

"Yankee food, I guess," Robert said to his nephew in unit 3. "Or maybe stress, or travel. Who knows? It's awful though; been going on all night. I hope she can make it through the service."

"Clifton, your Uncle Robert Earl needs the bathroom. Hurry up in there," Robert's nephew said to his young son.

"I am using the toilet, daddy," the answer came back. "Give me a minute."

Robert Earl began to think out loud. He told his nephew, John Ray, that he didn't know what exactly pulled families apart. It was not the basic needs, food, shelter, the love of folks near you, it wasn't those things that caused it. It was the pursuit of something more, something better, something loftier that did it.

"JL was my younger brother and he came here to follow his job, which was a good job with the Burlington Northern. But when they closed the yards in Yazoo, they told him they would find him something there in Mississippi, maybe not quite as good, but something. But he came up here instead. I think he came because he thought they would appreciate him more, on account of the sacrifice of moving and all. He thought maybe he'd be promoted to some higher position, which of course never happened. But he made a good life for himself and Althea, and he visited us down home as often as he could, especially when Momma was alive. But as time went on, he and I, we knew each other less and less."

"Clifton!" John Ray shouted. "Your great uncle needs to shave."

"And what about your daddy, my older brother? What, sweet Jesus, was he thinking, moving all the way out to California. He said there were high-paying jobs out there in the aircraft business, building airplanes and all. And they had around-the-clock sunshine. He wanted to get in on the aerospace field. Well, you tell me, John Ray, who the hell wants to fly on an airplane built by a negro from Mississippi who never even made it through the eighth grade? Would you fly on such a plane? I sure would not. And now, there he is without a pot to piss in and no money to even come bury his little brother."

"Uncle Robert," John Ray replied, "daddy's on relief and has been for near on five years. He's had one leg cut off and he's in a wheelchair and in a home. He can't come to Missouri to a funeral. Lot's of things are his fault...but not that. Clifton, your great-uncle needs to shave!"

"You are right John Ray, I suppose," Robert conceded. "But, you wake up one day and somebody has died and your family is strung from hell to Christmas. It kind of corners you, if you know what I mean."

At about that moment, Roscoe showed up at the door of John Ray's unit with a basket of cinnamon rolls. Freshly baked, he explained, by his mother Laura, for the folks at the Siesta Motel who couldn't take part in the breakfast prepared by the ladies of St. Agnes for those who occupied Fellowship Hall.

"Yes, sir, young man," John Ray said enthusiastically. "Those look real good."

"Who is there?" Pastor Robert Earl asked from the bathroom.

"It's me, sir, Roscoe Hammer. I've come with cinnamon rolls."

"Where is your momma?" asked Clifton, who was halfway through his first cinnamon roll. "How did you get here?"

"She went to the market for some orange juice and dropped me off here. She'll be back soon."

"Who is it Clifton?" Robert asked, from the bathroom.

"It's the Hammer boy, uncle Robert. He's got cinnamon rolls."

"Boy, you, the Hammer boy, come here where I can talk to you."

Cautiously, Roscoe stepped toward the bathroom door. The pastor Robert Earl was a good-sized man, and in his undershirt, with shaving cream on his face, he looked to Roscoe even larger than that. He had a large belly, but bulging arm muscles as well, and his neck was thick and strong. His head was bald, smoothly so, but the cream on his face covered a coarse, dense beard. When he moved the razor against his face, he seemed like someone who knew what he was doing.

"Yes, sir?" Roscoe said cautiously.

"First, boy, be sure and tell your momma how much we appreciate the cinnamon rolls and all the hospitality. Will you do that for me?"

"Yes, sir," Roscoe said.

Robert Earl took a moment and cleaned the safety razor, splashing it wilding in the sink. "Do you know, boy, what you will experience today?"

"No sir, I do not," Roscoe answered, with greater certainty than he had felt in a long time. He had never been to a funeral.

"Today you will witness a great battle, an epic battle between death and despair on one hand and life and love and joy on the other. That is what you will see."

"Yes, sir," Roscoe answered, without knowing exactly what to think.

"It will be a battle, young man, and I pastor on the side of love and life and joy. And, we need all our soldiers, our warriors, on our side. Can we count on you?"

"Huh?" Roscoe said, unclear as to what he was being asked to do.

"Will you stand for life and love and joy, against death and despair? Will you stand with us, young man?"

"I will!" declared Roscoe, with a resolve he had never, ever felt.

"Good. Now young Roscoe, that is your name isn't it, now, please do not take cinnamon rolls to unit 5. Miss Nadine is sick as she can be, with the cramps and all, and she certainly would not be interested in a cinnamon roll this morning."

"Yes, sir, I do understand. I will not bother her. And I will stand with you sir. I will."

CHAPTER 18

T he sanctuary of St. Agnes was a large domed room with twenty-five rows of pews on each side. The altar was raised four feet above the sanctuary floor and was shaped as a proscenium arch, about twenty-five or thirty feet across. At one end was a large cavity for the organ player and at the other end was a sort of secondary pulpit where lay readers and soloists and the such would participate in the service. To the rear, at even a higher grade, were three rows of seats for the St. Agnes choir.

On this day, all the members of JL's family and friends from Mississippi were seated together in reserved pews on one side of the aisle. It was a sea of black faces, save one, Laura Hammer, who sat to the right of Althea and held her hand from time to time. On Althea's left was her sister who held her left hand when it seemed useful. The casket bearers were seated together, just behind the friends and family section of the sanctuary; again, there were four negro men plus Frank Hammer. Jermaine was seated in the organ pit where he would later perform.

Andy and Hannah, and, temporarily Roscoe, were assigned to the church nursery. But Roscoe, and Fatty who had been similarly confined, decided that they were a little too old for such a set up, and escaped to the far corner of the sanctuary balcony where they could see just about everything without being seen. It was a position the two of them often occupied during normal Sunday services at St. Agnes.

The service started with an abbreviated version of the funeral liturgy taken from the Episcopal Church's Book of Common Prayer and was conducted by the Right Reverend Joseph Gleason, Rector of St. Agnes. The abbreviation, fashioned by Pastor Gleason himself, was a courtesy to the out-of-town Baptists whose day it was after all. Still, the service was plenty Episcopalian in that there was a good amount of sitting, standing, kneeling, special prayer and responsive readings, which left the Mississippians floundering around, trying to figure out what pseudo-catholic hocus-pocus might be coming next. At times the ceremony was dreadfully herky-jerky. But finally, due in large measure to the steady hand of brother Gleason, the St. Agnes congregation and their guests from the Delta made it through and put a bow on this segment of the service with a standard Episcopalian funeral hymn, followed by a more than slightly audible sigh of relief.

And then Robert Earl Woodson took to the altar. Or stage, as it was. He moved from one end of the altar to the other with a walk full of power and purpose. At each junction, at one end or the other, or occasionally behind the actual pulpit in the center, at each of these stops he would pause theatrically and speak in a baritone voice that vibrated the sanctuary walls like a timpani drum.

First, in slow measure, he told the story of a young JL Woodson. A boy who had grown up in the Delta South, working like a grown man from age ten. A young man who had excelled at athletics, football in particular, and whose talents had earned him the chance to attend Troy State University, just south of Montgomery, Alabama. He would be the very first in his family to go away to college; what greater burden could one bear? An injury would unwind the financial support that sent him to Alabama, and so he came back, where the old ones said he belonged all along, to south Mississippi. And there he was idle for too long, until he somehow found the Burlington Northern Railroad. They hired him on the track crew, the lowliest of jobs offered. He worked with whites and coloreds and Mexicans who brought vodka and lemonade in mason jars for their noon-time drink. They repaired track, hour upon hour, day upon day.

Finally, he had the opportunity to test for switchman and with a more-than-acceptable score, his name went on a waiting list. And he waited. And he waited.

When the day came, when he was made switchman in the Yazoo yards, he took his mamma and daddy to dinner, all they could eat, at Billie Jean's Catfish Hut on the south edge. Pastor Robert, still moving, remembered the day, and then paused. It was time for a hymn.

And after the hymn, Brother Robert Earl became, well...more animated. Still he moved from one end of the altar to the other, and with certainty and purpose, as before. But now, now, he seemed determined to lift the congregation up from a solemn, sad remembrance, to something better, something higher.

"But, brothers and sisters, I tell you now, our brother JL is not in the box you see before you," he said, pointing to the flag-draped coffin below the pulpit. "That is not him."

"Then who is it?" Fatty whispered to Roscoe.

"Shhh! He's making some kind of point," Roscoe said.

"No," went on Pastor Woodson, "that is only what he left behind. My brother, your brother, he is on his way to something better. A better place. That box is empty!"

By the reactions he observed, even at his age, Roscoe could tell that the Pastor's point wasn't coming across perfectly. After all, *the box*, as he called it, wasn't empty, and most of Mitchell and all of the folks from Mississippi knew it. It contained, at a minimum, a railroad lantern, a bible, the embalmed body of JL Woodson and a mannequin's arm from JC Penny. Something may have gone on to a better place, but there was still a box full of something else.

Which the pallbearers, young and old, weak and strong, found out as they lifted JL and took him down the aisle to the back of the sanctuary. While they did, the congregation, lead by Pastor Robert Earl, began what seemed an earthy version of the Episcopalian's responsive verse. Suddenly, spiritual outbursts, prayers, supplications came spontaneously from the crowd. And when they did, Pastor Robert followed as he should.

Receive our brother. Thank you Lord Jesus.

Spare him harsh judgement. Thank you Lord Jesus.

And as these extemporaneous prayers came forth, those in the congregation who had nothing to say began to hum and clap softly, giving a gentle rhythm and tone to the proceedings.

Make a place for him at your table. Thank you Lord Jesus.

There were moans and other sounds of sadness. There were large women sweating and cooling themselves with fans. There were babies, only a few, screaming as though they had been abandoned. But the entire affair had such a sway to it, a tempo, a beat. At one point, Roscoe looked down and saw Fatty marking time with his index finger. He was being swept up. He was a crusader.

Cradle him in your arms, oh Lord. Let him rest, Lord Jesus.

And then they took him out. The pallbearers took JL Woodson down the aisle, to the back of the church and out to the waiting hearse. Along the way, at the back of the sanctuary they passed by one person who had been there largely unnoticed.

"Look," Fatty whispered to Roscoe. "Back there, it's George Mabry. What's he doing here?"

"Now follow us, brothers and sisters, all who can," Pastor Robert called out. "Follow us to the gravesite where we will give JL a glorious send off. Thanks be to all who cannot join in, and thanks be to God Almighty."

Roscoe rode to the cemetery with his mother and father in the Hammer family Olds 88, while Andy and Hannah stayed back in the St. Agnes nursery. On the way, his mother raised the question of George Mabry's appearance at the service.

"Did you see that crazy old coot?" she asked Frank. "What was he doing there?"

"I don't have any idea. Maybe he and JL knew each other some-how."

"Impossible. JL would never have anything to do with that awful man, never. Althea wouldn't have allowed it."

"Maybe Althea didn't know," Frank offered, hoping to bring the discussion to some sort of graceful close.

Roscoe had heard enough and he experienced some kind of involuntary impulse, a need to speak up on George's behalf. "George Mabry is not crazy. He is my friend. He has been my friend for pretty long now. He's smarter and nicer than most people know."

"What did you say, young man?" Laura asked. "George Mabry is not your friend and I think..."

"Is too, momma. He is a nice man. He gave me money to buy you the Christmas cactus. It was his idea. And he rescued Ranger. And he has been my friend when I was sad about Hannah."

"That's enough, Roscoe!" Laura said, turning around for the first time. "Who do you think you are speaking to, Roscoe Hammer?" Then she turned to her husband. "What has come over him, Frank?"

They had reached the cemetery and rather than answer, Frank chose to appear pre-occupied with properly parking the car. To his way of thinking, the discussion — perhaps too generous a word — could wait. Neither he nor Laura could hear it, but in the back seat, Roscoe had begun to gently cry.

Frank took his place with the other pallbearers behind the hearse. Laura quickly found Althea and the two of them started up a slight hill toward the gravesite, arm in arm. Neither Frank nor Laura noticed that Roscoe stayed back in the car, out of the cold mist that hung over Prairie Lawn Cemetery. At the top of the hill a white canopy had been erected to keep the winter drizzle off the friends and family who slowly formed a half-circle behind the grave. It also protected a young blond violinist, a prodigy of sorts, whose mother was a member of the St. Agnes Altar Guild, and who played Amazing Grace softly as the pallbearers made their way toward the grave. Althea was now standing directly behind the gravesite, with her best friend and neighbor at her side.

On the way up the hill, Frank Hammer, a practical man, began to think in practical terms. There were two strapping young, uniformed men from the funeral home walking conspicuously alongside the pallbearers, suggesting that there was at least a chance someone might falter. Frank found himself trying to guess who the weakest link in the chain was. But then what difference would it make, he thought? If we drop JL, he'll be back down in the road before these two bodyguards can do anything about it. Just let us get him to the grave!

And, thank God, they did. They got him up the hill and onto the contraption that cradles the casket until the time comes to lower it into the grave. The violin music stopped and Pastor Robert Earl Woodson positioned himself at the foot of the casket.

At the bottom of the hill, with Fatty now at his side, Roscoe stood outside the car and looked up toward the gravesite through the dreary mist and fog. Everyone above stood perfectly still, except for men who, from time to time, would look down on the women beside them to see if they needed comfort. Althea Woodson looked drained, defeated. Sadness hung from the trees and Roscoe wondered if the forces of death and despair were winning. It seemed they were.

"Where do you think you go? When you die, I mean. What do you think?" Fatty asked Roscoe.

"I don't know," Roscoe answered. "To heaven I hope. But I probably won't."

"How come?" Fatty asked.

"Because I hate my mother. If that won't keep you out of heaven, I don't know what will," Roscoe answered.

"I think everybody hates their mom some times," Fatty said trying to sound encouraging. "I know I thought I was going to hell when I punched Tommy in the nuts that time." Roscoe made no response and Fatty was happy to let the conversation fade.

"Here, at the end of his journey," Pastor Robert Earl began, "my beloved brother would have me be brief. Brevity came so naturally to him. But to an old Baptist preacher, it comes so hard. But because I know he would want it, today I will be brief. And to that end, I will allow him to speak for himself the way he would if it was possible. If my brother could, he would say that he was a simple man, ordinary in almost every way. He would say that he had made mistakes and had made his apologies, had asked forgiveness and mended fences where he could. He would take no credit for the one thousand or more acts of generosity and kindness — credit that was undeniably due him. If he had the chance to speak directly to his maker, which I suppose he has by now, I believe he would ask to be judged not on past acts, good or bad, but rather on the basis of the man he was on the very day and in the very moment he was taken. He would say, and rightly so, that none of us is the person we were a lifetime ago, a week ago, a minute ago. We are who we are right this very blessed second. Just as I am, Lord, he would say, take me just as I am."

As Roscoe climbed in the back seat, people started down the hill toward their cars. A big negro lady sang in a beautiful voice, a voice that seemed to float on the sound of a soft and perfect violin:

> Just as I am without one plea,
> But that thy blood was shed for me,
> And that thou did bid'st me come to Thee,
> Oh Lamb of God, I come! I come!

Frank slid into the front seat and gestured to Roscoe behind him. "Come up front with me, son. Your mother is riding back to the church with Althea."

Roscoe loved riding up front with his dad and he moved quickly. As they pulled away, he looked back up the hill and thought he saw JLWoodson disappearing into his grave. He had been to his first funeral and didn't much like it.

Back at St. Agnes, the tide began to turn. There was waiting in Fellowship Hall a feast unlike any other that had been prepared for a funeral. The good ladies of St. Agnes had outdone themselves. There was roasted and pulled pork with fingerling potatoes. There was sweet corn and pepper relish. There were two or three versions of meatloaf, one particularly suspicious, and there were boiled potatoes with butter and parsley. There were candied carrots cooked in butter and brown sugar. And one lady who had actually come from the South made collard greens and pinto beans seasoned with bacon and ham; the stuff vanished in no time at all. Of course, there were cakes and pies too numerous to mention. And, along with all of this, the vestry of St. Agnes had voted to permit the serving of red wine. The vote carried, despite the objection of Iris Mickey, who only conceded after the other members accepted her amendment. The wine, she insisted, should be watered down, cut by half. Ironically, this was precisely the recipe the church used for the preparation of communion wine. The wine served at JL Woodson's funeral luncheon was, at least by St. Agnes standards, holy.

People ate, laughed, and greeted one another as though it had been years. How could one death bring so many together? And why? How could loss be such an occasion for communion? Death it seems reminds us of what we will miss before we do. And so we shake hands, and hug, and even dance together — because someday we will die, just like JL Woodson.

Late in the afternoon, almost evening, Roscoe was back at home, resting on his bed when he heard laughter. He sat up on the edge of his bed and looked out the window. All of the cars and trucks from Mississippi were lined up on the street in front of the Woodson house. And all of the family members were on the porch, hugging and kissing Althea. They were saying good-bye, on their way back home. And they were strangely happy. He thought about how many unusual things he had seen out his window, just by being a neighbor of the Woodsons. A man dies, his family travels farther than it ever has from home, and they come together, first in sadness, and then with love and laughter. How could that be? The forces of life and love and joy had won the day. Death and despair would have to wait.

"I forgot to give you something," Frank Hammer said to his son. "I picked this up on sale the other day. I thought you might like it." Frank handed Roscoe a tattered paperback book entitled "The Art of Magic".

"Thanks Dad. I'll read it, all of it, I promise. I'm tired right now, though."

"Your first funeral, right?"

"Yes, sir."

"You did great," Frank said. "By the way, the Reverend Robert Earl told me he liked your name. He said it sounded like someone who knows what he's doing."

"But I don't know how to do anything," Roscoe said.

"Not yet, maybe, but someday son, you will. I promise."

Frank kissed his son and left him alone. Roscoe opened the book his father had given him and read.

Magic is the art of the unseen and relies on a prevalent misconception. We walk through our days, most of us believing that what we can see is reality, and what we know is the truth. But magic and life continue to teach a lesson, a lesson to which we are strangely resistant. Again and again we are reminded that reality is always, always more than we can see. And no matter how much we know, we can never know the whole truth. And why are we reluctant to learn this? Because to do so is to accept the fact that we will forever be at least slightly bewildered. We will find ourselves perpetually asking that old question which is central to magic and life: How did that happen?

Roscoe fell asleep and didn't wake up until morning.

CHAPTER 19

Roscoe was coming up the basement stairs when he heard his mother and father whispering. He had been in the basement watering the Christmas cactus. He had taken it there a month earlier, moving it from its original spot on the living room coffee table. No one had noticed it was gone.

"They don't know how it happened," Frank said. "George was nearly dead."

The words stopped Roscoe on the stairs. He stood quietly in the dark, halfway up, listening carefully.

"They figure Cato beat him to a pulp. Used a tree branch on him. Size of a baseball bat, they said. Then there were shots fired. And Benny Ybarra and one of his fishing buddies heard the shots and came running. The found George unconscious and they found Cato on the rocks below the dam with a hole in his head."

"Good Lord," Laura said, "what in God's name? Did Mabry shoot him?"

"Couldn't have," Frank said. "George was almost dead when the shots were fired. It couldn't have happened that way. Buster Odom already ruled that out. He couldn't even find a gun."

"Where's Mabry now?" Laura asked.

"County hospital," Frank said. "He lost an eye, but they think he will pull through."

Roscoe had heard enough. He cleared the steps and burst into the kitchen, red-faced, afraid. "What happened to George Mabry? I heard you talking."

"Roscoe, George has been hurt. Pretty badly," Frank answered trying appear calm. "He's in the hospital, but they think he's going to be all right."

"Roscoe...," Laura started.

"I want to go see him. At the hospital. I want to see George," Roscoe said.

"I'm not sure that's a good idea," Laura said.

"I want to see my friend."

"I'll take you," Frank said. Laura was puzzled but silent. "I'll take you tomorrow."

In the car, on the way to the hospital, Frank tried to prepare his son. First, he wanted Roscoe to know that George was in bad shape and that how he would look might startle him. There would be bruises and cuts with stitches, and a patch over one eye.

"What happened to his eye?" Roscoe asked, trying to act grown-up.

The eye was injured, his father explained, injured beyond repair. A patch would always be over what had been George's eye.

And, Frank wanted Roscoe to know that George would likely be confused and woozy on account of taking some pretty bad bangs on the head. In short, Frank wanted his son to be ready to find almost anything in that hospital room short of a corpse.

And there was something else requiring preparation.

"Officer Odom talked to me today," Frank started slowly, "and he would like to talk to you about all of this in the next day or two."

"Me?" Roscoe asked. "Why me? I don't know anything."

"Well, you've kind of been George's friend lately and he thinks you might have heard him say something that would shine a light on all of this. I told him it was real unlikely, but we'd do our duty."

"Okay, I guess, but jeez. How could I know anything about this? Will you be with me?"

"All the way, buddy, all the way," Frank said with a reassuring smile.

At the hospital, Frank asked Roscoe if he wanted him to go into George's room with him.

"I'll be fine," Roscoe said bravely, knowing that he just might not be.

Young boys are not normally staggered. They are awake, running, jumping, bouncing around, or they are lazy or asleep. But not staggered. Well, on this day, Roscoe was. Staggered. Slack-jawed. Dizzy. He found his way to the small chair alongside George's bed quickly.

"George," he whispered. "Are you all right? Are you awake?"

"Roscoe...boy....hello there." George's words came slowly as if he needed time to put ample breath behind them. "You...came...to see...old George?"

"I had to," Roscoe answered. "I heard you got a terrible beating from Bobby Cato. I had to come see you. I'm pulling for you George. I want you to know that."

"I do. Truly...I do. And I'll be...just...fine, in time," George said, his one good eye rolling. "Pirate," he whispered.

"Huh?" Roscoe responded. "Pirate?"

"The...patch. Like a....pirate, huh?"

"Oh, yeah," Roscoe said with a smile. "You'll look like a pirate."

George closed his eye as if he needed to rest and Roscoe gazed at the crucifix on the wall at the head of the bed. How had it happened, he wondered?

After a while, George's eye rolled open. "You still here?" he asked.

"Do you believe in God, George?" Roscoe asked, he eyes still fixed on the crucifix.

"I imagine you'd....call...me a believer, yep. Why...do you...ask?"

"Do you think he watches over us?" Roscoe asked.

"I think he wants...us...to watch....over each other. That's what I....figure."

Then George closed his eye again and Roscoe sat quietly watching him sleep and listening to him snore. He looked calm and comfortable and more, well, more groomed than normal. He awoke once more, only long enough for Roscoe to ask a last question.

"George," Roscoe asked, "where do you live?"

"Why, boy...thought you...knew. Right...here...in Mitchell... Miss..ouri, that's where."

CHAPTER 20

R oscoe was on his knees, using a screwdriver he found in his dad's workshop on a loose board on the back of the potting shed when she spoke.

"Please don't do that," she said. Her voice, deep and slightly dangerous, startled Roscoe so that he dropped the screwdriver and the board pinched his finger. "It's cold enough in there without prying boards away. Shouldn't we just go inside, through the door, and see what you came here to see?"

The voice belonged to Harriet. She was dressed in a long white dress with a heavy grey shawl over her shoulders. Her silver hair was pulled back tight in a bun, and her deep blue eyes shown bright. Once Roscoe looked right at her, she seemed calm and kind.

"Ma'am?" Roscoe answered, scrambling to stand up.

"You've been here before, I know. I think it is time we go in to see what you came here to see."

"Yes, ma'am."

Inside the shed, Roscoe's questions began to find answers.

There was a cot, with bedding military tight and tidy. There were Wolverine boots at the foot. A kerosene stove for heat, and an oil lamp for light. A simple throw rug alongside the cot. A footlocker for clothing. A crate at the end of the cot with a Steinbeck novel and a magic wand — Roscoe's magic wand — on it. And there was one old tattered, ratty chair, for reading one might suppose. Harriet sat in the chair with Roscoe on the cot.

"Is this where George Mabry lives?" Roscoe asked plainly.

"Yes, it is," Harriet answered in kind. "You are now the fourth living person on this earth to know that."

"Huh?" Roscoe replied.

"What you now know, has only been known by me, George himself of course, my sister Gertie, and JL Woodson, with whom I feel certain the secret is safe. And now, you too know — as so badly you wished."

"I don't understand," Roscoe said. "How did he come to live here? Why is it a secret?"

"I will explain that to you, young Roscoe. But first, you must tell me what else you came here today to see or find. Tell me the truth and then I will answer all your questions." She looked deep into him and he could tell somehow that he was safe.

"I wanted to see if the gun George told me about was still here. Bobby Cato was shot with a gun. Officer Odom told my dad that there was no way George could have done it, but I couldn't help it....I wanted to know if the gun was here."

"The gun is not here. We will get to that in time. First, though, I want you to know some things," Harriet said calmly. Then she began.

The story Harriet told was the story of her life. She moved quickly through it, because over the years, she had lost track of some of the details. It was a life, a life with rough edges; fine details wouldn't change that.

She had grown up in Mitchell, with her older brother Robert and her younger sister Gertie. Her father was a banker and a state senator. He was known to almost everyone in Mitchell as "the senator" ; even his own children called him that. It was a title he treasured. The senator greatly favored his son and made no effort to hide it.

When Harriet was fourteen, her mother, whom she adored, and her brother were killed in an automobile accident. Her heart was broken. She and her younger sister were left to be raised by a man who grew more distant and bitter with each passing day. He hired a wretched woman named Beatrice to help with the household chores and to instruct his daughters in all the womanly areas. During his trips away to Jefferson City, Beatrice was surrogate mother, father, disciplinarian, and spy.

As her father grew more and more cold and detached, Harriet, even by her own measure, became more rebellious and defiant. She looked for opportunities to confront him, often telling herself that she was doing so to protect her younger sister from his cruelty.

Great, colossal arguments with Beatrice became regular, and upon one of his returns from Jeff City, Beatrice reported to the senator that Harriet had been nipping the bourbon in his study. When Beatrice confronted her with this, Harriet told Beatrice that she looked like a man, a hairy hillbilly man, and needed to mind her own damned business. A physical altercation ensued during which Harriet had "torn great gobs of hair right out of Beatrice's scalp".

That very day, the senator decided that Harriet should go away to a school in St. Louis, Madeline's School for Girls. Madeline's boarding school advertised itself to the wealthy as a place for "young women needing special attention". The tuition was breath-taking, even for a man like the senator. And it came with conditions that were non-negotiable. The school took in a girls who suffered from a broad range of self-destructive behavioral problems and the administration had unabridged authority when it came to the manner and amount of discipline needed to reform a particular student. Importantly, the school was also given complete authority to administer medications that could help return the student to "an attitude and manner of accepted civility". In short, in return for thousands of dollars, the school could beat or drug a girl into submission, however it saw fit. Harriet was given the benefit of all that Madeline's had to offer. And every night, she fell asleep in a dormitory to the moaning, crying, and profane muttering of young girls who were unwanted and afraid.

"I came home to Mitchell dull-minded and detached," Harriet said. "I had learned to arrange a perfect place-setting. I had learned to interact properly with the help, though by then we had no help. I had learned even the basics of ballroom dancing. I did very little of what I'd be taught to do. In fact, I did very little at all. And that which I did, I did without a whiff of enthusiasm. While other girls my age were out drinking whisky sours bought for them by hopeful young men, I was at home in dim light trying to muster the will to get through *The Saturday Evening Post*. I was near dead."

It took time, but slowly, the effects of Madeline's started to fade. The discipline, which in Harriet's case had been harsh and abundant, slipped away first. But the medications, the experimental concoctions of the staff psychiatrist, those lingered longer, and caused some permanent damage.

"My little sister, Gertie, saved me," Harriet said. "She nursed me back to some degree of health. Our roles were reversed; she took care of me. And along the way, when there were whispers and stares, she didn't mind taking one of the town's gossips down a notch. And she knew how to do that, believe me."

Finally, the senator died.

"I am ashamed to say that I prayed for that day," Harriet said. "But then again, I prayed for many things back then that did not happen. Maybe my prayers had nothing to do with his demise."

By then Gertie and Harriet were able to care for themselves and manage their own affairs. After a suspicious and unseemly allocation to Beatrice — who, by the way, vanished almost immediately — there was a comfortable inheritance for the sisters to share. They used a large percentage of the money to buy the house that would become Gertie's Grocery.

After a few years, Gertie met and married Henry Paulson. Paulson was a devoted husband and a kind brother-in-law. When he and Gertie went for weekend drives through the countryside, Harriet was always invited and usually went along. Now and then all three dined together at one of Mitchell's restaurants. In those days, they were, by almost any measure, a very happy threesome.

"As time went by," Harriet continued, "I seemed to get better and better. But still my mind would wander. Even in my happiest moments, it would meander back to Madeline's or life with the senator. To this day, it is hard for me to remain fixed on something. Hard to tell a long story as I'm struggling to do now."

But eventually, Harriet regained enough confidence and ambition to apply for and take on a job as an operator for the telephone company. It gave her spending money that she could call her own and at least a semblance of a social life. She made friends. She, and a few of these lady friends played cards together, enjoyed an occasional cocktail, and progressed to "old maid" status together.

One summer Henry Paulson was working in his beloved tomato patch when he suffered a massive heart attack. He died almost instantly. It took months for the sadness to lift, but when it did, Gertie and Harriet reasoned that they would need someone to look after the lawn and Henry's considerable and beloved plantings. George Mabry, odd as he was, seemed the best choice.

"And so why does George live here?" Roscoe interjected.

"I see you have a nose for the story, young Roscoe," Harriet said. "He lives here because I, with my sister's consent, invited him to, that's why."

George did excellent work for the sisters and he took payment in-kind from the grocery store. For many years this arrangement held well. George would show up at just the right time in the spring and would work regularly through fall. Then he would mysteriously slip away for winter. There were never any questions asked. Gradually, ever so gradually — because each was more skeptical of the other than were even the town's people — Harriet and George began to notice each other. One hot day, Harriet worked up the courage to take George some lemonade. He gulped it down and thanked her in his own awkward but sincere way. He told Harriet that he liked working there more than any of the other places he worked in all of Mitchell. He was no smiler, but he smiled at Harriet. From then on she took him lemonade or iced tea almost every day.

"I tell you this, Roscoe, with a little detail," Harriet said, "only so that you may know one thing."

"What is that?" Roscoe asked.

"Over the years — and I mean many years —I came to love George Mabry. And he grew to love me, I think. Please be clear about this: Our relationship, mine and George's, is as proper as it can be. There never has been, nor will there ever be any courtship. No wedding bells. We are decades beyond that. But to be plain about it, in all my years, I have never known true affection from any man other than George Mabry. If I could choose my way of dying, it would be by any manner so long as I die in his arms. I would do anything for George Mabry. And so finally, as cold weather began to come on one year, I — we really — invited George to stay here for the winter. Here in this shed. And he has been here since. He comes in after dark and leaves just before light, and that way, it's nobody's business. Which is how he, how we, like it."

"Why did Mr. Woodson know?" Roscoe asked.

It was chance only, Harriet explained. George left the shed in the dark before dawn and JL drove home at about the same time. One day JL saw George coming out of the shed, and that was that.

"George tracked JL down and tried to explain, but George is not great with words, and I suspect it came out sounding, well, peculiar," Harriet said. "But do you want to know what old JL said back?"

"What?" Roscoe asked.

"He said that just because a man sees something and thinks he knows something, that doesn't mean he should go around talking about it. And even if what he knows is true, he's not in any position to judge. And so, JL said he didn't make any judgements and he didn't make any suppositions. That's all he said. And with that he became someone George admired greatly. That's why he was at his service."

"Is George's gun here? You said we would get to that."

"No, it isn't here. Look over there," she said pointing, "the coffee can with the yellow rag. It's empty."

Roscoe drew a deep breath and asked *the* question, "Did George shoot Bobby Cato in Harmony Park?"

"No."

"Then where is his gun?"

"It is in the tall grass by the train trestle in the park."

"How do you know?"

"Because I put it there."

"I don't understand," Roscoe said, with fear creeping into his voice. "Why did you put it there?"

Roscoe gripped the edge of the cot tightly with both hands. His knees ached and quivered. His mouth was dry, his breathing shallow.

Harriet stood and turned away from Roscoe, as if what she had to say next made it hard to look at his innocent face and frightened eyes. After a moment, she started.

"A few days ago, I heard George and Bobby Cato arguing. I heard it out my window. They were just up the street on the sidewalk," she said, drawing a breath.

She went on to explain in a shaky voice that Cato had confronted George because of the trouble George had caused him with Doak Posey. He said that George was lying about him, making trouble for him every way he could. He wanted it stopped. He wanted George to shut his mouth, or he'd shut it for him.

George didn't back down from Cato. He said he hadn't lied about anything. He said that Cato got what he had coming on account of him killing little Satchel and stealing Roscoe Hammer's hound dog, and all the other things he'd done. He told Cato he wanted Satchel's collar back, the collar with his name tag on it. It wasn't in the gunny sack with Satchel that day.

Cato told George to meet him in Harmony Park the next evening, just before dark. He wanted to meet near Donut Bay, by the low-water dam. He told George he'd bring the collar and they could settle everything between them.

"Later on," Harriet said, "I tried to talk George out of it. I told him he had no business meeting up with Cato alone. There would be trouble, I was sure, and I didn't want him hurt."

But George wasn't afraid of Cato and he was eager to get Satchel's collar and to get all the trouble finished. To his way of thinking, there was nothing to be afraid of; he'd dealt with worse than Bobby Cato many times. He'd have nothing of backing down. His mind was made up.

"So when that evening came," she said, "after George left on foot, I took the keys to Gertie's Ford sedan and drove to the park by a different route. I took the pistol with me and I parked the car over by the ballpark on the other side of the tracks. Then I went and hid behind some big cedar bushes near the dam. I hid there and shook and wept from fear. I had trouble breathing and was afraid my heaving was loud enough to be noticed. I waited."

Soon enough, Cato arrived. He wheeled around in his blue sedan with big fins and made a quick cloud of dust. He got out and lit a cigarette and paced. At times he walked so close to the cedars where Harriet hid, she could smell the smoke from his cigarette. Then George came walking around from the other side of Donut Bay.

The two of them, George and Bobby Cato faced off and began talking in low voices that Harriet couldn't make out. Then one of them said something that sparked and Bobby Cato pushed George. Then George pushed back and before you know it they were all tangled up, each trying to throw the other to the ground. In the middle of all that, Bobby Cato threw a wild punch that caught George in the right temple and sent him to the ground in a heap. While George tried to gather himself and get to his feet, Cato found an old tree branch just the right size and took after George with it. He whaled on George again, and again, and again. George put his arms up, and even his feet too, trying to protect himself, but the branch was the size of a baseball bat and Bobby Cato just kept on whaling. Finally George's strength gave out, his arms dropped and he lay in a bloody puddle, unable to fend off anything more.

"Cato pulled back for one more blow," Harriet went on, "and I knew that one more might just be the end and I came from behind the cedars with that pistol dangling and I screamed at the top of my voice. Stop, I screamed, again and again. And I raised the pistol, though it was too heavy for me and made my arm tremble. Stop, I said, or I will kill you, by God I swear."

Cato heard Harriet and looked up. He could see the pistol was too heavy for her trembling arm. He saw her trying to hold it with two hands, and still it was too heavy. And he laughed a great, heinous laugh.

"Leave my George alone, Bobby Cato, or I swear by God I will kill you right here!" Harriet exclaimed.

"With a gun you can't even hold, you old bat," Bobby said, laughing and coming at her.

"I told him to stop, again and again. And I tried to pull the trigger to fire a warning shot, but I could not make my hand do even that. And he came closer and closer and I tried to hold the pistol steady towards him, but my arm was weak and I couldn't do it. Stop! Stop! But he kept coming."

"I should go," Roscoe said, jumping to his feet. "This is making me really afraid, Miss Harriet. I really should go home."

She turned to him. "Please, young Roscoe, don't. I need to tell someone and there is nobody to tell. You already know more than anyone else. Please, I need to tell it all."

Roscoe sat back down and suddenly Harriet became more calm. As she told the rest of the story, she seemed peaceful. Her words weren't rushed as before. Her breath was even, and she was able to face Roscoe normally. It was as if she was releasing a small fish.

"He reached toward me, laughing, and with a hateful look in his eyes. He reached for the gun, which was bobbing uncontrollably in my hand. I tried to pull the trigger, but I couldn't do it...something kept me from it. And then he reached out and grabbed at the pistol and his hand wrapped around mine and he tried to pull it away, the pistol. He pulled hard and his hand was against my fingers and the pistol went off. The sound it made was deafening. It hit him in the neck and blood spewed on me. It startled and angered him, but still he pressed forward against me and the pistol. His eyes rolled as if he might stumble and fall, but in one last surge he grabbed again for the pistol. And again his hands wrapped mine and the thing went off a second time. That shot hit him in the forehead and pitched him backward over the edge and to the creek bottom below the dam. I heard his back crack on the rocks. Then I saw a pickup truck coming fast down the road from the other end of the park. It was Benny Ybarra and a fishing buddy of his. I guess they heard the gunshots. I hid behind the cedars again and watched them load George into the pickup. They sped away to the hospital. It all happened in an instant it seemed."

Roscoe sat silent, white-faced, afraid. What had he heard? His mind raced, the place was spinning. His stomach rolled and he wanted to stand and run, but his legs felt week. He was eight years old and had heard a women confess to killing a man with a pistol. He would never be the same, and even at his age, he somehow knew it.

"Miss Harriet," Roscoe said softly, "I really have to go. I need to go home to my family. I don't know how to make all of this better. I need to go home."

"Roscoe," Harriet said calmly, "hear one more thing, please. What I have told you here today, should you be asked about it, you must tell the truth. I could not live with myself were you to do otherwise. What I've done is done. I am ready to answer for my actions and to be judged. But I cannot have you telling lies for me. That I could not suffer. Promise me, the truth, Roscoe, the truth."

"Good bye, Miss Harriet," Roscoe said. And then he left her.

When Roscoe walked into the house his father was reading the paper. He looked over the top and spoke. "Are you all right, Roscoe? Where have you been?"

"I was at Gertie's. I'm fine," Roscoe answered, trying to gather himself. "When am I supposed to meet with Officer Odom?"

"Oh, I told him we'd see him on Saturday. I wanted to be with you and I really can't take any more time off right now. He was fine with that."

"So Saturday?" Rosoce asked.

"Right."

It was Wednesday. He had two days to make the most important decision of his life.

CHAPTER 21

H e didn't need both days. After a patchy night's sleep and a school day at Masonhall during which he was so preoccupied that Mrs. Sweeney scolded him for daydreaming, Roscoe made his way straight to Gertie's.

"Is Miss Harriet here?" Roscoe asked Gertie. He had a knot in his stomach the size of a regulation baseball.

"She is indeed, Roscoe. She's in the kitchen taking cookies out of the oven. Play your cards right and I think she'll give you one with some cold milk."

Roscoe found Harriet in the kitchen. She smiled when he came in.

"Hello Roscoe," she said cheerfully. "Do you know what I've been doing today?"

"No ma'am, what is that?"

"I've been baking cookies and listening to Ziggy Elman records. Do you know who he is?" she asked.

"No, I don't."

"He was a famous jazz trumpeter who played with big band leaders like Benny Goodman and Tommy Dorsey. He had some great hit songs like *Zaggin' with Zig*, and *Let's Fall in Love*. Fabulous musician, truly. Would you like a warm cookie?" she asked, sounding strangely upbeat.

"No thank you, Miss Harriet. I can't stay long today, I just came to…"

"Yes, Roscoe, I know. You came here today to tell me that when you meet with Officer Buster Odom, you will tell him the truth about the things I shared with you. I know you are worried that something bad will come of this for me, but you needn't be. As I said, I am ready to answer for my actions. If I am to be judged, then I believe I will be judged fairly," she said, smiling.

"I would judge you as innocent, ma'am, I swear I would," he said, his young eyes drooping at the corners.

"Well, dear boy, I am not innocent. I took actions. I did certain things and could have done different things instead. A man is dead and that is not an unimportant fact. And I had a hand in it. I have been over it in my mind again and again. I could not let him kill George, and surely he would have. Sometimes there is not a good answer."

"Yes, ma'am," he replied, standing to leave. "But I am sorry. I know I have to tell the truth, but I can't see any good coming from it."

Then Harriet did something she had never ever done. She moved toward Roscoe and gently hugged him. She smelled of choco-late-chip cookies.

"Don't be sorry, Roscoe. You truly are the innocent one in all of this. I am proud that you feel compelled to tell the truth, as we both know you should."

Then she looked in his eyes. "I had to tell someone my story. I couldn't tell George, because he would blame himself. He will any-way when it all comes out, but that will be later and he will be healed and stronger by then. I told you and I wish I had not. But you did me a great service by listening without judgement and I am grateful to you. You are wise and strong beyond your years."

"Thank you Miss Harriet," he said. "I better be going now."

"Oh, Roscoe," she said, smiling again, "I forgot to tell you how I came to be a fan of Ziggy Elman."

"Yes?"

"His mother was my only friend at Madeline's School for Girls. I kept track of her through the years. She once invited me to the Casa Loma ballroom in St. Louis to hear her son, Ziggy, perform with his orchestra. You never know where or when you might meet someone nice, someone to be your friend. You never know how things will turn out."

"That's right," he said, thinking to himself about George Mabry. He hurried home against a sharp wind. His load felt lighter, and he was hungry for dinner.

Saturday morning, Roscoe woke up early, took his bath and dressed before going downstairs. He wore the clothes he had laid out the night before, his very best, the outfit his mother had bought him for class pictures. Brown corduroy trousers with cuffs. A grown-up undershirt and a long-sleeved plaid shirt in heavy cotton with a wide and pointed collar that opened a third of the way down his chest. And of course, his leather shoes. What he did not wear, which he had worn for class pictures was the dickey, a make-believe turtleneck contraption that went under the shirt — too much, he thought. He brushed his teeth and combed his hair with a crisp tight part, held in place with just a little wax. His dad had always told him that when you have a difficult job to do, try and look your best, it will make you more confident. He went downstairs with all the confidence one boy could wear on his back. His was ready for Buster Odom.

In the kitchen he found Laura humming a pleasant melody, washing dishes. Hannah was in the living room, on the floor playing with her toys. Andy and Frank were nowhere in sight.

When he spoke, it startled his mother. "Where's dad? He and I are supposed to go see Officer Odom."

"Oh," Laura said, "I didn't hear you come downstairs. You snatched me out of a nice daydream." She folded the towel and examined her oldest child, smiling. "You look so nice, Roscoe. That's the outfit we got for your pictures. So handsome you are!"

"I thought I'd better try and look my best for the meeting."

"For your appointment with Buster Odom? Didn't dad tell you?"

"Tell me what?"

"The meeting with the officer has been cancelled. He and your dad talked yesterday and decided he didn't really need to interview you after all. Nice surprise, huh?"

"I'll say," Roscoe answered, blood moving back into his face. "What did dad say to him?"

"I'm not sure, but I think he just told the officer that this whole situation had been pretty intense for everyone and unless there was something specific that he hoped to learn by involving you further, that he'd appreciate him leaving you out of it. Buster is a good man and when he thought about it, I think he just decided to call off the meeting."

"Wow! That is so great. I wasn't looking forward to it; I mean, I was actually dreading it. I've never even been in the police station. Wow." Roscoe slumped into one of the kitchen chairs and looked aimlessly toward the window. He couldn't believe the news. Perhaps the most feared event of his young life had evaporated before his eyes. How had it happened?

"Your dad took Andy down to the recreation center to sign him up for baseball in the spring; he will be back pretty soon," she said as she ran her hand softly across his precisely combed hair. "Since you look soooo sharp, I've got an idea."

"What's that?" he asked.

"After lunch, dad can look after Hannah and Andy, and you and I can go to the movies. How does that sound? There's a new one out that I thought you might like, *Abbott and Costello Meet Frankenstein*. Just you and me, what do you say?"

Roscoe's day had taken an unimaginable turn for the better. He'd gone from spilling his guts about Harriet's confession, and watching all the misery that was sure to follow, to a day at the movies. Abbott and Costello, no less. And, at the invitation of his mother, whose recent inattentiveness had nearly broken him.

"I'm going to be a shortstop!" Andy proclaimed, bounding through the door. "Watch out Phil Rizzuto, Andy Hammer is in the line-up."

"Lots of confidence, this one," Frank said, laughing.

"Hey dad, no meeting today. Mom told me." Roscoe said, ignoring his little brother.

"Right," Frank answered. "Buster was real understanding. You're glad, I guess?"

"You're not kidding," Roscoe answered enthusiastically. "And you know what else?"

"What?" Frank asked, glancing in Laura's direction.

"Me and mom are going to the movies. We're going to see *Abbott and Costello Meet Frankenstein!*"

Frank smiled at Laura. His wife was trying to claw her way back.

"No way!" Andy protested. "What about me? I want to go to the movies too."

"Just me and mom," Roscoe answered, feeling important for the first time in a long time. The universe was twisting in his direction. It was about time.

CHAPTER 22

Roscoe believed it was the approaching Christmas holiday that muted the town's interest in the mystery of Bobby Cato's death. After all, Mitchell, like so many hundred other little towns across the country, was still tender from the ache of empty wartime Christmases and her citizens would not be robbed of another Yuletide by the unexplained demise of a scoundrel like Cato. Snow was on the ground and goodwill was in the air; as for Bobby, well, a violent man met his violent end — just how and at whose hand were questions that would have to wait, maybe forever.

Fatty's theory about the conspicuous disinterest in Bobby's death had little to do with the holiday. People didn't like Cato he reasoned, they didn't care about him and they felt safer with him gone. Had George Mabry died that day along with him, most peoples' concern — with Roscoe, Fatty and Harriet as noted exceptions — would have withered just as quickly and for largely the same reasons.

All of this was of some but insufficient comfort to Roscoe. Every day, as he passed by Gertie's and the old potting shed, his eyes and mind were drawn back, back to the place where he alone had learned how it happened, how a man who may have had some future act of goodness in him died. The story would not leave him; it would never leave him he feared.

Haunted as he was, Roscoe was still only eight years old, and Christmas was coming and it made for a good diversion. Trees, and lights, and music. Snow and happy shoppers. And of course, the bounty, the glorious bounty. What Roscoe was about to learn is something that most youngsters learn at about his age: When it comes to the loot, all Christmases are not created equal.

He could have seen it coming. It started with a dramatic increase in his father's gushing about the Motorola.

There were about a million televisions in the entire country at that time, which meant that there were about a dozen in Mitchell, Missouri. Actually, there was no "about" about it; there were folks who kept track and there were exactly twelve televisions in Mitchell, and eleven were in the homes of the town's elite. The one that was not, the Hammer family Motorola, was the result of an enormous raffle sponsored by the American Legion. Tickets were sold throughout the entire county, and Frank Hammer, an otherwise practical man, found the prospect of exchanging two dollars for the chance at a life-changing event utterly intoxicating. Moreover, the beneficiary of this particular raffle was the family of a returning WWII vet who lost a leg in France. Frank bought three tickets, one in honor of each of his three children whose lives would be forever charmed when he won, as surely he would.

A farmer from sixteen miles west of Mitchell won first place, a new Cadillac worth three thousand dollars. It turns out he already had a Caddie and decided to sell this one so he could buy a new bailer. Farmers.

Second place went to an eighteen-year-old kid who won an all-expenses-paid weekend in St. Louis, where he and his guest would enjoy VIP seats at a Cardinals baseball game and lunch with Number 6, Stan the Man Musial. Competition to occupy the position of "guest" was vicious.

Third prize went to Frank Hammer. It was, without exaggeration, the only time in his entire life that he had won *anything*. It was a ten-inch Motorola television monitor mounted in a mammoth console that also incorporated an LP turntable and stereophonic speakers. From the day it arrived, he referred to it simply as "the sweet Motorola". It was his first, and as things would turn out, his only walk on the moneyed side of the street. His children would see and hear things that most of the children in Mitchell, Missouri would not. They would have what he never had, an advantage.

Frank waxed lyrical about the television from the first moment the delivery men switched it on and for a month he couldn't stop. That was October. Then, through the next two months, the family and even Frank began to take the thing for granted. Roscoe's classmates were permitted an afternoon off to watch the televised World Series in the Hammer living room. More routinely, there was the evening news, the morning weather report, a kiddie clown show originating from St. Louis, the Arthur Godfrey Talent Scouts, and the never-to-be-missed Jack Benny Show. In just a matter of weeks, it all became rather old hat for the privileged Hammers.

Until just before Christmas, that is. That's when Frank started up again. The Motorola was a technological miracle. It was a beautiful piece of furniture. It was the future of everything. At one point he even said, "It's like Christmas came early to the Hammer house." And that's when a bell went off; Roscoe knew something was up. The family — more particularly he — was headed toward what would be referred to years later as the "lean Christmas".

He had entered the season with a comprehensive, some might have said piggish, list of longings. He had even gone to the trouble of arranging his desires by category. First athletics: a new baseball glove, hockey skates, a football helmet. Next weaponry: a bow and arrow set ("a real one please"), a BB gun, a new pocket knife. Finally, the obligatory academic category: a chemistry set. He scribbled a note promising to add more to the academic category as things came to mind. And, in his letter to Santa cataloguing the coveted bounty, he offered a special thank-you for the family's Motorola. It was a shameless attempt to head his father off at the pass.

It did not work. The "lean Christmas" came with conviction equal to the winter that brought it. In summary — because there is no point in dawdling with the details — Roscoe Hammer got the following for the Christmas of his eighth year: a pair of colorful pajamas, a colossal chemistry set from Santa which Andy joked was like a "cooking set for girls", a very nice parka, for which he was dutifully appreciative, but which he knew he needed whether it was Christmas or not, and, of all things, a Philco transistor radio — yes, a transistor radio.

In addition to the foregoing, Roscoe got a nice package from his Great-uncle Benny. Benny was a dental specialist who lived in Arizona where he earned a fairly handsome living manufacturing false teeth. He had a swimming pool and a Thunderbird convertible, and lived alone as far as anyone knew. He had sent Roscoe a Christmas present every year since his birth. He had, for reasons unknown, summarily ignored the birth of Andy and Hannah, which caused a once-a-year glare from Laura.

"Does your uncle *not know* we have other children, or does he just *not care?*" she would ask Frank with a look.

Of course Frank had no idea because Uncle Benny was odd and Frank made sure he had no occasion to talk to him. The fact that Benny continued to send Roscoe something each Christmas was just one of those peculiar things that almost all families learned to take in passing.

This particular year, Great-uncle Benny's package was extraordinary. Roscoe had learned, even at his tender age, that Uncle Benny was quirky. And so he opened the box — larger than normal — carefully, as though it might contain a bomb or some spoiled food or a live animal. What it contained was none of these. Inside the cardboard box, Roscoe found a Smith-Corona portable typewriter, a copy of Mark Twain's memoir, *Life on the Mississippi,* and a ten-dollar bill.

There was also a note.

Young Roscoe. This year's bounty is more, well, more eclectic that usual. I have for most of my life planned on writing great sweeping novels about romance and adventure and grave danger. Well, it turns out I have been too busy for such undertakings, what with the demand for perfectly white and straight teeth. And so, alas, I think I shall not be needing my trusty typewriter. I am, after all, at an age where a good strong fart could drop me dead like a bag of rusted bolts. It strikes me that you may be the Hammer with big stories in you. If that is true, then you now have something to write them with. The 'f' key flies a little, but I think your dad could straighten it with some needle-nose pliers. The book by Twain should be of interest to you as time passes. You will want, and I hope will have, your own adventures. And for the ten bucks, well it is an insurance policy of sorts. If the typewriter and book don't have Christmas morning sizzle, as I suspect they do not, then go and buy yourself something fun with the tenner. Make sure it is something non-lethal. I'll be in touch, and until then, warmest Yuletide regards, Uncle Benny.

"The man's a lunatic," Laura said after finishing the note.

"And so your side of the family is so perfect?" Frank responded, laughing. "Focus on the ten-spot. And, who knows, maybe Roscoe will be a great writer."

"Yes," she said, "and maybe he'll grow up haunted by the memory of weird relatives, relatives from your side of the family."

As the day wound to a gentle close, Roscoe came down from his bedroom and took a seat at the kitchen table where he could watch his mother finish drying the day's dishes. From where he sat he could also see Hannah playing with her new toys on the living room floor. Their eyes met.

"Hi, Roscoe," she signed. "Where are your toys?"

"I put them away in my room," he tried to say. But it came out, "I put them up in the air." She looked up as though she might be able to see them floating above her.

Roscoe took a spoon from the drain rack on the counter, moistened it with his breath, and then let it hang magically from the tip of his nose. Hannah giggled with delight.

"You are funny," her tiny fingers said.

"You are pretty," his answered perfectly. She smiled broadly.

Laura, who had watched the exchange out of the corner of her eye, folded her dish towel and turned to Roscoe.

"I forgot to show you my favorite gift, Roscoe," she said warmly.

"What do you mean, what gift?"

"Come back to our bedroom and I'll show you."

Roscoe followed his mother down the short hallway to her bedroom and stood back while she opened the door. He stepped into the doorway and saw it, resting majestically on an elegant carved plant stand, right in front of the room's largest window.

"The Christmas cactus," he said wistfully, as if to no one in particular. "I'd forgotten it."

"I hadn't," Laura answered. "It has started blooming. Isn't it beautiful? I wanted it right there by the window where it would get lots of light and where I'd see it each morning."

"When did you bring it up from the basement?" he asked.

"Just a few days ago. I didn't want you to see it until today. It's my favorite Christmas gift. A special gift from you, Roscoe. I love it."

"From me and Mr. Mabry," he added with a smile.

"That's right, you and Mr. Mabry. The next time I see him I'll have to thank him."

"Sure mom, like you're going to see Mr. Mabry. I doubt it."

"You never know, Roscoe, you never know."

Laura Hammer stood behind her son and draped her arms lovingly around his neck. Then, she almost whispered. "The radio was your father's idea. Don't be disappointed. I know it's hard to imagine but I think you'll grow to really like it. It will make your world bigger. And you can use Uncle Benny's money to buy a football helmet if you want."

"Thanks, mamma," he said. "I think you are right about the radio. Dad tries hard on presents, doesn't he?"

"On presents and almost everything else, son, yes he does." She paused for a moment and then went on. "I have some news, Roscoe. I'm going to be working at Gertie's after the first of the year. I'll be helping her out."

"At Gertie's?" Roscoe asked, turning toward Laura.

"Yes, that's right. Will it bother you to see me there when you come in with your friends?"

"No, huh-uh. At least I don't think so. Why are you doing it?" he asked.

"Well, actually it's perfect for me, for us. I can take Hannah with me and I can keep an eye on her. Gertie needs the help because Harriet is able to do less and less as time goes on. And, we can use the extra money."

And there it was, the answer he expected, the money. It was an answer that would linger sadly for the rest of his childhood. Roscoe's parents tried so hard, harder than anyone he knew, but there was never quite enough money. It caused him to believe that money could keep you safe. Of course he was wrong.

That night, after Andy had fallen asleep, with the volume turned low, Roscoe carefully tuned the Philco to what would become one of his most favorite radio programs of all time, *The Whistler*. He fell asleep to the sounds of its famous opening narration, which could not have been more appropriate.

I am the Whistler, and I know many things, for I walk by night. I know many strange tales, hidden in the hearts of men and women who have stepped into the shadows. Yes… I know the nameless terrors of which they dare not speak.

The bedroom door was slightly ajar and Frank stood silently with his ear near the crack. He heard the radio and smiled. He had gotten his boy a good gift. He felt lucky.

CHAPTER 23

On January 20th, Roscoe's entire class, along with Mrs. Sweeney and Fatty's mother, Margaret Gilchrist who served as the third-grade room-mother, all crowded into the Hammer living room to watch the first presidential inauguration ever televised. They huddled before the "sweet Motorola" and stared at it with their mouths gaping, as if the thing was magic, or maybe had come from outer space.

There were children on the floor, in the easy chairs and on the couch, where Penny Barksdale had Fatty trapped tightly against the end. When Harry Truman put his hand on the bible to take the oath of President of the United States, Penny put her hand gently on top of Fatty's and whispered in his ear.

"You could be President one day. I really think you could," she said, leaving her hand on his. Her touch flushed his cheeks bright red. His face, his ears, his whole head felt hot, and something like a slight tremor ran down his leg. Fortunately, all the eyes in the room were on the Motorola. All except for his mother's. She was standing at the back of the room and witnessed the short and tender episode. Penny was a pretty girl and came from a good family, a family held in very high regard across all of Mitchell. Margaret's heart pounded with a dizzying combination of pride and joy and sadness. For her, it was one of those moments when a parent knows that they will never be as happy as they are when their children are still children. The best of times might be slipping away, she thought.

"Margaret," Laura whispered from behind, "could you come into the kitchen and help me with the cookies and punch?"

"Oh, yes, sure," Margaret said, wiping an inconspicuous tear from the corner of her eye.

In the kitchen the two women worked together preparing the treats as though they had done it a million times before, the way two men might mow a lawn together, with a kind of native, unrehearsed choreography.

"Randall tells me that you've begun working at Gertie's. Are you enjoying it?" Margaret asked.

"I am,very much, yes. It's perfect for us. I take Hannah with me and Gertie and Harriet are both wonderful. And I see so many people there, customers I mean. I'm always home when Roscoe and Andy come in from school. I think it has been good for me. And of course, the extra money comes in handy, no matter what Mr. Truman says about our vibrant economy," she added, laughing.

"Speaking of little Hannah," Margaret started carefully, "I have wanted to find a way to tell you how sorry were all were when she got sick. We just felt awful. Randall blamed himself. I couldn't reason with him. He has always been so fond of Roscoe and all of you."

Laura stopped what she was doing and made sure she had Margaret's eyes before she spoke. "We are equally fond of your little boy, you must know that. I will tell you the truth, for a time I was willing to blame anyone I could for Hannah's illness. But I was wrong and I regret those feelings more than I can tell you. If Randall sensed blame from me then I am ashamed, thoroughly ashamed. Please assure him that what happened was nobody's fault, not his, not anyone's. And please make sure he knows he is always, always welcome in this house."

"I will, Laura, I promise," Margaret said smiling. "You know, I've been thinking about taking in some ironing as a way to make a little extra money myself. It wouldn't be much but it would help out. And, I could do it right at home and be there when the children come in from school. Like you said, I think that's important."

"Good for you," Laura replied smiling. "I think you have a very good plan."

Margaret looked in the direction of the living room. "You are so lucky to have a television! What a wonderful thing."

"We sure are," she said. "You know Frank won it in that American Legion raffle? He can't get over it."

"I know...what a great thing!"

Laura thought for a moment and then spoke. "Margaret, in March of each year, we cheat just a little before spring, and we have a picnic. We think it makes spring come sooner. Anyway, we always invite some folks, and this year, if you can, I wish that you and your family would come and join us. It's nothing fancy, just a nice picnic. I wish you would come."

Margaret smiled a very slow, natural smile. "We'd be pleased," she said. "You'll let me know what I can bring?"

That day the United States of America got a new President, Fatty Gilchrist got his first girlfriend, and his mother got a new friend, which she would need more than she could know.

CHAPTER 24

I n Mitchell, Missouri, February was the calendar's cruelest month. The sky held to grey and the cold was dense and unrelenting. This was the month when winter harvested her victims — old trees, wounded birds, stray cats. When Basil Cobb came through the door at Gertie's, he held his arms tightly around himself and waited for the warmth of her old furnace to reach him and for the sound of the counter bell to bring Gertie out from back of the store where she was busy stocking shelves.

Basil was a slender, frail-looking man with cropped white hair and thick eyeglasses that magnified his deep shadowy eye sockets. The founder and sole owner of Cobb's dairy was well-liked and respected by his friends and neighbors in Mitchell, and by all of his customers statewide. He was an industrious man, successful in business by way of hard work and wits, and charitable with his treasure. He gave to the church, to the Rotary Club, to the Masons, and to the hospital. Gertie was surprised to see Basil that day but welcomed him warmly. Regrettably, he had come with bad news.

The small-town dairy business, like so many other small businesses in towns like Mitchell, had come under the pressure of larger, well-capitalized, city-based competitors. Cobb's, Basil explained, had seen profits decline to the point that the dairy's very existence was threatened. Changes had to be made, and Basil thought it his responsibility to visit with each of his customers and explain why.

The large diaries who were cutting into Cobb's revenues and profits, operated without traveling sales people, people like Henry Gilchrist. These big outfits had production facilities and workers, surly clerks who took customer orders over the telephone and delivery truck drivers. They didn't have salesman like Henry, who made friends of all his customers and in return earned twice as much in wages and sales commissions as any order clerk or truck driver made. All in all, his competitors' costs were lower and so were their prices; such was the arithmetic of misery for Basil Cobb.

Henry Gilchrist, as beloved as he was by his customers and Basil himself, was no longer affordable, at least not in his current role. He would be offered the position of a delivery truck driver and would be permitted to solicit customer orders while making deliveries. His wages would be reduced considerably, but a job for him would be protected, no matter how intense the competition became. Basil explained all of this to Gertie slowly, methodically, as if he had gone through it in his mind a thousand times, not for her benefit but for that of his own conscience. He would visit every one of Henry's customers, more than fifty of them, each time with the same anguished explanation.

One ominous footnote which Basil shared with Gertie because she knew Henry well and was especially fond of him, was that the delivery job was "physically demanding" as he put it, and not particularly well-suited to man of Henry's size and condition. He, Basil, could only hope for the best. Time would tell.

Gertie, charitable as always, thanked Basil for the personal visit and the explanation. She said she would pray about it; maybe she could help somehow. When he was gone, she went into the empty screened porch on the south side of the house. Closed off since the time of her husband's death, it was dark and dusty-smelling. There, in the cold, she began to make a plan. She wasn't waiting for God's purpose to be revealed — she had her own purpose in mind.

CHAPTER 25

Roscoe and Fatty walked together, in light jackets, at an uninspired pace. To his right, across the street, Roscoe caught the first glimpse of forsythia. Against a still-dull landscape, it gave just a hint of brilliant yellow, and with it the promise of spring. For Roscoe it was a quick, vibrant reminder that things change. Things always change. It's funny he thought, when things are good, we think they will never change. And when things are bad, we think they will never change. But change comes…it just does, it always does.

"Do you think it matters who shot Bobby Cato?" Roscoe asked Fatty without looking at him.

"I don't know," Fatty answered. "That's one of those think-about-it questions you like to ask. You should know by now that thinking about things is not my strength."

"You think about things as much as anybody else. Why do you act dumb?"

"It's not an act."

"What do you think?"

"I think that if you ask George Mabry, he'll tell you that it seems like it was either him or Bobby Cato who was going to die. He'd say he's glad it wasn't him."

"I'm asking you, not George."

"I'd agree with George."

"That's it?"

"I told you I'm not a thinker."

"Do you like Penny?" Roscoe asked, changing the subject.

"You know your dog, Ranger? Well, if God-forbid Ranger should die and lay in some alley or somewhere for say a week, and get all smelly and rotten....well, if I was starving I would rather eat Ranger's dead flesh than be Penny's boyfriend."

"Jeez," Roscoe replied, "I think she's pretty. And smart, too."

"Then you be her boyfriend. You're smart. You're not pretty, but you are smart."

"Maybe I will."

"I doubt it. She wouldn't like you."

"Why not?"

"Weird hair. You got weird hair. She likes my hair. She told me so."

"Don't ever mention Ranger dying again. You can talk about my hair, but don't talk about Ranger dying."

"I said, 'God-forbid'".

When Roscoe and Fatty found George Mabry lying on Eudora Whitely's side yard he looked dead. He was on his back with his arms outstretched. His good eye was shut tight and his bad one was covered with the patch Roscoe had first seen in the hospital.

"You think he's all right?" Fatty whispered.

"I think he's asleep. Does he look like he's asleep to you?" Roscoe asked, craning around to get a closer look at George. Finally he gathered the courage to tap the toe of his boot. "Mr. Mabry, are you all right?"

George squirmed, snorted and then brought himself off the ground and up onto his elbows. Looking straight into the bright sun, he squinted and strained to get a fix on his visitors.

"Hello Roscoe boy. I couldn't make you out at first. And your pal is with you I see."

"Hi Mr. Mabry," Fatty and Roscoe answered together.

"You caught me snoozing. I ain't got as much go-power as before the hospital and all. I run down a little quicker. We got us a nice warm snap and the sun hits Eudora's side yard just perfect. The grass is warm. It put me out like an old cat," George said laughing. "What are you two knuckleheads doing?"

"We've been to Cobb's for a soda," Roscoe answered. "You look a lot better than when I visited you in the hospital. A lot better for sure."

"That's a fact Roscoe boy, I am a whole lot better. Except for being down to one eyeball," George said, pointing to the eye patch. "I'm worried I'm going to get all the bushes in town crooked, what with my impaired vision and all."

"Does it hurt?" Fatty ventured carefully. "The one that's gone I mean."

"Na, hell no," George replied laughing hard. "There ain't nothing there but a sewed-up hole. You wanna see?" he asked, moving his hand to the patch.

Fatty was so alarmed and afraid, he threw his arms up as though he was trying to block gamma rays. "No, no! Holy Jesus, don't do it!" he screamed, flailing and stumbling backward.

"No way!" Roscoe chimed in, turning his head away and shielding his eyes from what was about to be the most horrible thing he'd ever seen, a deep black hole in a man's head.

Well, all this hysteria put old George into such a laugh that he fell backwards into the same position where the boys had found him, flat on his back. He was laughing so hard he let go a tiny squeak of a fart, which he didn't notice but Roscoe and Fatty did. They looked at each other and giggled like two girls. George Mabry, Mitchell's monster, had made a joke and passed a little gas laughing at it. He was being something no one in town, including Roscoe and Fatty, had ever seen him be, he was being playful. A near fatal beating at the hands of Bobby Cato had changed him.

George worked his way back up and rested with his elbows on the ground. "Sit down here for a couple of minutes, boys. It's been a while. How was your Christmas?"

"Great," Fatty offered first. He and Roscoe both sat down on the warm grass with their legs crossed Indian-style.

"Mine too," Roscoe said. "I got a radio, a Philco."

"Did you now?" George said. "You'll have a good time with that, you will. I had a radio once. How about you young Gilchrist?"

"Football gear. Helmet, shoulder pads, pants," Fatty answered, beaming.

"That's great."

"What about you Mr. Mabry?" Fatty asked. "How was your Christmas? Did you get anything?"

"Look right over yonder," George answered, pointing toward the walk leading to Eudora's front door. Parked there on its kick-stand was a used bicycle with a basket on the front handlebars and some fake saddlebags draped over the back fender. The frame was faded blue, but the tires looked brand new, with gleaming white sidewalls and shiny chrome spokes. "She's a cruiser. I bought her for myself from Billy Dill. It was my Christmas present to me. Never had a bike before, ever. She's beauty don't you think?"

"Ya, she is a real beauty," Roscoe offered cautiously.

"She's a she. It's a girl's bike," Fatty blurted out.

"Well, yeah, you're right it is. But that was the only used one Billy had and he said it might be a good precaution anyhow in that I hadn't ever rode one. He was saying it might help me not get my nuts racked while I was learning. Plus, ain't nobody going to confuse me with a girl, that's for sure."

"How are you doing, learning to ride it, I mean?" Roscoe asked.

"Not too bad. By the middle of spring I should be real steady on the thing."

"You can put some of your smaller trimming tools in those saddlebags," Fatty said, wishing he hadn't made such a thing out of the bicycle's gender.

"And books," George added.

"Books?" Roscoe asked. "What books?"

"Library books. I got me a library card, my first one of them too. Making some changes, I am," George said proudly. "No more grumpy, dumb George Mabry stumpin' all over Mitchell acting mad as hell all the time. It's a new George boys. Upgraded transportation, new learning, a lighter heart."

Roscoe and Fatty looked at each other wondering what to make of this bike-riding, library-card-carrying George Mabry, his attitude, his antics. How had this happened, they wondered? For a few moments neither of them nor George spoke. It was an awkward pause for the boys, but George seemed very much at ease. Finally, as though coming out of a short trance, George spoke.

"A radio, you say?"

"Yep, that's right. A Philco," Roscoe answered, happy to see the conversation reignite.

The thought of the radio nudged George into a smokey reminiscence, a recollection that once shared would be remembered by Roscoe and Fatty forever.

When he was in his late thirties, early forties maybe, he owned a very nice console radio with excellent reception. He was encouraged by a cohort to tune into a broadcast emanating from Milford, Kansas, of all places, featuring the medical pontifications of a Dr. John R. Brinkley. Brinkley was ultimately exposed as a colossal fraud, a man with sketchy professional credentials, boundless avarice and phenomenal salesmanship, all seasoned with a vague, midwestern religiosity. And, oh yes, he also had a radio station of his own.

The good doctor Brinkley conceived — based on who knows what — a suspicious but attention-getting theory that by surgically replacing certain male organs with ones taken from goats, that the patient's youthful vitality could be restored. Using his radio transmitter to promote his preposterous fountain-of-youth scheme, Brinkley actually found men willing to undergo the procedure *and* pay handsomely for the privilege. He performed several of these gland transplants and then spent a good part of the rest of his life explaining away the more-or-less disastrous results. He was ultimately sued into oblivion.

"What glands?" Roscoe asked breathlessly.

"Gonads," George answered flatly, looking down at his lap for emphasis.

Fatty had a growing interest in biology and had done enough research to know what to call things. "Testicles?" he asked, "Is that what you're saying, testicles?"

"Yep, gonads," George answered.

Roscoe and Fatty looked at each other, speechless. How could such a horrific hoax work, they wondered?

"No damn way," Fatty exclaimed. "Huh-uh."

"Who would do that?" Roscoe asked. "Who would pay someone to do that to them?"

"Who the hell would *perform* the operation?" Fatty added. "That's about the sickest thing I've ever heard. I think I might puke!"

"Are you making this up, Mr. Mabry?" Roscoe asked, hoping beyond hope.

"Yeah," Fatty added, displaying his growing command of mild profanity, "is this a lot of bullshit, Mr. Mabry?"

"Nope, it's true. That doctor made a bundle, too. Tells me a couple of things," George answered.

"What?" both boys asked in unison, wanting George to somehow make sense out of this nightmarish report.

"There's some fellas out there who are way smarter than me, but there's some out there who are way, way, way dumber than me. And, young Roscoe, it tells me that you should watch out where you tune that radio. There's something about it, radio and quacks seem to go together."

All three sat there on Eudora's side lawn without speaking for quite a little bit. The boys were stunned by George's story and he seemed tired from its telling. Finally, it was Fatty who decided to change the subject.

"Mr. Mabry," he asked, "do you think it matters who shot Bobby Cato? Roscoe asked me. What do you think?"

The question caused Roscoe to stiffen. If Harriet had told George all that she had told him — and it had always seemed to Roscoe she would when the time was right — then George might assume that Fatty already knew who had killed Bobby Cato, that he had learned it from Roscoe. He might think the boys were baiting him. It seemed like Fatty's question could lead to trouble. To make things more tense, George was very slow to answer.

"Somebody saved me," George finally said. "That's what matters to me. Who it was, well, I guess I'd like to know. But I'm glad they saved me." Then after another pause, he added "I've got some ideas of my own, but I'd never guess at it. Guessing might get somebody in trouble. But just between the three of us here, I think it might have been some of the Mexicans who fish below the dam. I've always treated them right, decent, more decent than they are by most folks in town. They like me. They bring me tomatoes in the summer. I think they would try to save me from Cato, and I don't know, but I think they might have a gun. But I'd never guess about it cause they don't deserve to get in trouble, even if they did it."

Roscoe was silently stunned. He could tell that George didn't know what had happened that day in the park. *Harriet hadn't told him.* For all he knew, Roscoe was still the only living person, other that Harriet herself, who could explain what had happened to Bobby Cato. As it always had, the story made him feel alone, alone and a little afraid.

"Gonads," Fatty said to himself, drifting back to the story of Dr. Brinkley. "Who would do that? How could that happen?"

Buster Odom's police cruiser had a horn, just like every other car in Mitchell. But Buster preferred to use a quick burst on the siren to get attention. And on that day, the siren got plenty of attention from George, Fatty, and Roscoe, all still sitting in the sun on Eudora Whitely's side lawn.

Buster rolled down his window and said, "Hey George, Eudora called into the station. Said she saw you laid out on the lawn and thought you might have had a heart attack or something. Looks like you recovered."

"I had dozed off before the boys here came along. Everything is okay. Never felt better."

"Roscoe, and you, Gilchrist, you fellas going to be here a while?" Buster asked.

"No sir, we were just getting ready to go," Roscoe answered nervously.

"Either of you ever ridden in a police car?"

"No, never," Fatty answered quickly, with a certain eagerness that made Roscoe wince.

"Come on then," Buster said, "get in and I'll give you both a ride home. I need to talk to both of you about something."

Roscoe stiffened again. What could Buster want with both of them? Was this the interview he had dodged before? Buster seemed proper and official, but then he always seemed proper and official.

The boys slid into the back seat of the cruiser. "Roscoe, you come sit up front with me," the officer said. Once Roscoe was in, Buster pulled away and gave the siren one more short shot for good measure. Roscoe hoped to see Officer Odom smile, but he didn't. Whatever he had on his mind, he considered it serious.

CHAPTER 26

Frank Hammer, a man more than a little bit skeptical of organized religion, was fond of saying that Mitchell was full of loosey-goosey Catholics, reasonably flexible Episcopalians, and hickory-stick Baptists who had never gotten over the repeal of prohibition. And so, when it came to the planning of the Hammer family spring picnic, he would admonish Laura, who was in full charge, to please cull the guest list for known Baptists. The affair always fell during Lent and it would afford any good Christian a number of opportunities to violate Lenten resolutions; Catholics and Episcopalians, skilled at self-forgiveness, could deal with it, but not the Baptists.

"Wouldn't a loving God look the other way when it comes to lemonade pie?" he would ask. "Or, for that matter, a tiny nip of good whiskey after such a miserable winter? Our little event is popular enough, we don't need to suffer those do-gooders."

Laura too believed that it was time for fun, time to smile and look ahead. And she made plans and built a guest list accordingly. The attendees, she thought to herself proudly, would surprise everyone, especially Roscoe. There would be no Baptists, but there would be surprises and fun.

And the afternoon they were rewarded with could not have been more beautiful, sunnier, more peaceful than had it been plucked from mid-April or early May. Soft white clouds floated high against a sky of mostly pale blue, and there was a constant, easy breeze from the West. Frank moved two picnic tables together, end to end, and at the edge of the back lawn he built a magnificent barbecue pit, an altar of sorts, where all the sacrificial meats — brats, dogs, and pork steaks —

would be prepared. And when the pit was ablaze, when the two tables had been trimmed, the guests began to arrive. And from there on, the afternoon and evening only became more interesting.

First came Gertie Paulson, with two pans of fried chicken and a lazy spray of fresh vegetables. She promised that Harriet would be along soon, with an apple cake and a guest of her own. Then came the Gilchrist family, the whole crew, Fatty, his sister, Henry and Margaret, hauling hot rolls, fruit salad and a giant bowl of green beens. Roscoe was stunned to see them and went immediately to greet his friend.

"I didn't know you were coming," Roscoe whispered.

"Neither did I," Fatty replied, smiling. "Your mom asked us."

Then — dangerously enough it seemed to Frank — the Reverend Gleason and his tragically unsatisfied wife Nancy appeared. The rector scanned the gathering as if looking for prison escapees, quickly abandoned Nancy to the other ladies in the group and found himself a comfortable spot by the barbecue pit, where he could sip Pabst Blue Ribbon beer and make small talk with Frank and Henry.

"Cut me off when I begin to slur," the Reverend said with a nervous laugh. Frank and Henry just looked at each other and smiled.

Soon Althea Woodson came along, with two beautiful lemonade pies and a bowl of sweet potatoes. Nobody's winter had been harder than hers and she was ready for sunshine and laughter.

Right behind Althea came the O'Sullivan family, eight strong, lugging folding lawn chairs and gallon jugs of fruit punch and iced tea. The O'Sullivan clan came from the loosey-goosey Catholic category and had proven in years past that they could be counted on for a good time. Their crew of children guaranteed that all the kids would have a playmate or two.

And then, across the early green lawn, came Harriet Merchant and George Mabry, arm in arm, looking as bright and shiny as movie stars. They moved gracefully, and looked proud and happy. Harriet wore a long white summer dress and her hair was pulled back in a tight, proper bun, and in her left arm she carried a colossal white apple cake. Her smile was wide and unrelenting. George too looked marvelous, in stiffly starched light brown trousers and a soft floral-print shirt with a broad collar. His hair, a few lonely grey strands, was combed against a perfectly straight part, and his shaved face glowed pink and shined with Aqua Velva. He was, without a doubt, as clean as he had ever been in his life. No one, except perhaps Laura, knew what to make of them, but what everyone knew that day was George Mabry and Harriet Merchant were very close friends, very close indeed. Roscoe, like Fatty at his side, was — in the words of the book his father had given him so long ago — *bewildered*. Whatever was occurring that day in his own backyard was unusual and important. He could tell.

Introductions and polite exchanges. People sat. Food — *so very much* food — moved willy-nilly around the table. Folks were happy and… accepting. The afternoon chit-chat was warm and nice, a kindly diversion for anyone nursing old winter wounds, as so many at the table were.

All the children, with Roscoe and Fatty as leaders, gobbled their food and then left the table for the lawn where they played and laughed and took turns swinging. After a while, some clouds which had not been predicted began to gather in the late afternoon sky. People looked cautiously upward and some took the threat of rain as a cue to address the crowd.

Gertie Paulson stood and almost immediately had everyone's attention. She spoke slowly, with enough precision to make it clear that she had given what she was about to say a good deal of thought. She started by thanking Laura and Frank for such a lovely afternoon. As a historical marker of sorts, she proclaimed that this had been her twelfth Hammer family picnic and she enjoyed every one of them immensely. But this one, she explained, coming off such a difficult winter, meant more to her than all the others before.

"This last winter reminded me that spring comes just when it seems you cannot live another day without it," she said. "And friends show up just when it seems you cannot make it through another day on your own. Today I am thankful for the coming of spring and for all of you, my friends."

A short pause and then she went on. "Winter also reminded me that I am not getting any younger. As you know, Laura Hammer has been helping out at the store, and I think it has been good for both of us. But the truth is, I think I must cut back my own activities even more in this new year and so I have asked Margaret Gilchrist and Althea Woodson to join Laura in managing almost all of the day-to-day affairs of the store. I discussed this with Harriet, with Laura, Margaret and Althea and all have agreed enthusiastically to this new setup. As Laura can attest, the pay at Gertie's is modest, but the work is honest and the customers make for a very nice day, at least most days. So that this new plan might be as financially beneficial as possible to those involved, we will be opening a pie and coffee cafe of sorts in the old screened porch on the south side of the house. Mr. Frank Hammer is handy with tools and has promised to help me get the porch into proper shape. If the pie shop does well, then we may add carry-out barbecue to our menu later. Althea, as you all know, is something of an artist when it comes to barbecue."

"What about you, Gertie?" Reverend Gleason asked, by now with just enough Pabst beer in him to make him look woozy. "What are your plans?"

"Well, other than my dear sister, my only relation is small collection of cousins who live in California. I've decided that if I am to see them before I die, which I believe I should, then I need to travel there while I can still find my way around a train station. I'll be taking a long time, maybe more than a month, as it will likely be my last visit. I thought this might be a good time to make you all aware of these plans, as so many of your families will be effected by the changes. It's been my privilege to serve you all as good loyal customers, and I will miss doing that more than I can tell you. But time passes, and people like Laura and Margaret and Althea will be good for Gertie's." With that, Gertie smiled, nodded her head politely and then took her seat.

"Thank you, Gertie," Laura said. "I think I speak for my new co-workers when I say that we are excited about this new arrangement, and will do our very best, though we no doubt cannot match the standard you've set all these years. Would now be a good time for some lemonade pie?" she asked, scanning her guests.

"Excuse me, please, but before that could I say something?" Harriet said softly from near the end of the table where she was sitting beside George.

"Of course, Harriet, what is it?"

"I don't think many people here knew it, at least not until today, but George Mabry and I have been good friends, affectionate friends I would say, for quite a long time. And, for reasons that are no longer clear to me, we kept our friendship a secret. Today is a happy occasion for me because it marks an end to that secrecy. George lives, or I should say sleeps, in the potting shed behind the house and has been careful to remain unnoticed there for so very long. A couple of the more curious youngsters here today have gotten to know George and have figured out his living arrangements I think. We want you all, our friends, to know what they know: George has been back there in that shed and will continue to be for a long, long time I hope. From now on, instead of feeling he must sneak around, he will be free to smile and wave as he comes and goes which is his true nature. I nearly lost my good friend this past winter and it taught me that there is no time in our short lives for hiding away in the shadows."

"Here, here!" proclaimed Joseph Gleason, raising high a can of Pabst. "Might I say that St. Agnes has also had what you would call a private relationship with George for many years, private at his request, let me hasten to add. Because St. Agnes is his parish, he has been tending our shrubbery for free for as long as I can recall. He considered this his contribution to the church, and what a fine contribution it has been. Our grounds are the envy of the Catholic parish," he said, and then added, looking toward Mr. O'Sullivan, "no offense intended."

"None taken, Father."

"And so," the Reverend continued, struggling to realign his now foggy thinking, "as our parishioners here today know, we maintain a fund that is reserved for special occasions of need, special situations. The vestry has approved my request to tap this fund so that we might buy George a glass eye. Praise the Lord."

"A glass eye?" Henry Gilchrist whispered to Frank. "How much does one of those boogers cost?"

"We are told it will be painted a perfect match," Reverend Gleason continued. "It will, of course, not move — swivel, you might say — in harmony with the good eye, that's understood. And so, when watching activities in motion, a ping-pong match, or something akin to that, George will need to move his head back and forth following the action so that his good eye and the artificial one don't appear completely out of whack."

"I think they get the idea, Joseph," Nancy said nervously. The Reverend sipped his beer.

"I think that is marvelous," Althea said. "We can't do what God can do, but there's no harm in coming as close as possible. We women know that."

"And I can get rid of this Captain Hook business," George said, pointing to his patch.

"Pie anyone?" Laura asked hoping for takers.

The discussion about the glass eye had caught Roscoe's and Fatty's attention. They stood waiting, not far from the table, wondering if any more might be said.

"Roscoe boy tells me he got a radio for Christmas," George said to Frank, who replied with a smile and nod. "I told him I had a fine radio once."

"Oh shit," Fatty exclaimed. "He's going to tell them about the gonad doctor! My mom's sitting right there. Holy cow!"

"Mr. Mabry," Roscoe jumped in awkwardly, hoping to redirect the conversation, "did you ride your new bicycle here?" It worked.

"I did indeed, Roscoe," he answered. "I rode alongside Miss Harriet and carried the white cake in my front basked. I parked it out front, near the porch."

"Did you say *bicycle*?" Reverend Gleason asked, stretching out the word. "Out front you say?" he added, trying clumsily to extract himself from the picnic table bench. "Do you mind if I take a spin, George?"

"Help yourself, Padre," George replied enthusiastically.

"Joseph! For goodness sake!" Nancy said, with the look of terror coming across her face.

"Hold this for me," Gleason said, handing her his can of beer.

"Oh my God!"

"They say you never forget how to do it, Nancy," he proclaimed, heading around the house.

While the other guests whispered to each other, Roscoe and Fatty made their way around the house, expecting to witness something funny or calamitous. They would not be disappointed.

Nancy Gleason put the beer on the table and tried to catch up with her husband before he could mount Mabry's bicycle. Several of the other adults, all but George and Harriet, followed behind her with the idea of helping or being entertained. And the kids, all except Hannah who was alone on the swing, came in a covey behind them. They were all too late. By the time the crowd got around the house, the Reverend Joseph Gleason was weaving his way down Sand Plum on old George's bike. He used the entire street, lazily looping from curb to curb, howling with laughter.

"It's true, Nancy," he shouted, "you never forget how!"

The look of panic had no sooner left Nancy Gleason than around the corner in his rattle-trap delivery truck came old man Hattan, with fresh eggs and live chickens in the back. He headed south down Sand Plum, straight toward a half-drunk Episcopalian priest on a bicycle. He saw Gleason first and began to honk. Joseph looked up, saw Hattan headed right toward him and began to lose control — of the bicycle and his emotions. He swerved one way, Hattan, guessing wrong, swerved the same direction. Then they both tried to dodge the other, in the opposite direction. They seemed destined to collide.

"Sweet Jesus!" Nancy Gleason screamed. "Watch out, Joseph. Jump off!"

"Eject, Padre!" George shouted from the backyard, laughing.

As the Reverend and Hattan got closer and closer together in what looked like a horrible, unintended game of dare, Nancy Gleason, the first lady of St. Agnes, fainted right at the feet of Laura, Althea and Margaret. With her in heap, looking momentarily dead as a mackerel, her husband bounced over the curb and into widow McKenzie's lawn. Hattan miraculously pulled his delivery van to a screeching stop in the street, but at least two or three dozen fresh eggs fell off the truck and splattered. Adding to the bedlam, three live chickens somehow popped out of their crate and ran wildly all over the place.

Once Nancy had been fanned back into consciousness, once Reverend Gleason was on his feet, and once Frank Hammer was able to calm old man Hattan, then the chaos became funny. While Roscoe held Ranger at bay, the other children used apple bushel baskets to capture two of the three escaped chickens. The last one got under JL Woodson's pickup truck, parked at the curb where it had been all winter, and hunkered down. The only kid small enough to get under the truck and game enough to accept the assignment was Roscoe's brother Andy. He disappeared beneath the truck, and the next thing anyone saw was a fat hen, its legs held together in a small hand coming out from under. Hattan grabbed the bird, put it back in its crate and went on his way. The crowd, exhausted by now, began to move slowly toward the backyard, where Harriet sat beside George, who was enjoying a big piece of lemonade pie.

While everyone walked off, Andy crawled out from under the truck, brushed himself off, and hollered to Roscoe.

"What is it?" Roscoe asked, turning around.

The two brothers were alone. "Look what I found stuck up under Mr. Woodson's truck." He had a dirty, tattered strap of some sort to Roscoe, and asked, "What do you think it is?"

In an instant, Roscoe knew the answer. There was a piece of metal attached, a tag. He rubbed it. He almost choked. He knew what it was. "It's nothing, just some junk," he told Andy. "Go on, hurry up, momma's serving pie." Andy shrugged and ran ahead, leaving Roscoe alone.

At that moment, Roscoe felt something he'd never felt before. The air was thin, and he couldn't catch his breath. The sky seemed to spin and he thought he heard ringing in his ears. His hands shook as he held the thing and rubbed the tag. He didn't need to clean it to know what it said: *Satchel*. And in an instant, the conversation came back to him, the one between his dad and JL, it came back like a loud ringing bell.

Hit a possum or raccoon the other mornin' in the middle of that downpour; never even saw the thing. Knocked the muffler loose I think.

Once again, he alone had the truth — Bobby Cato had not killed Satchel, it was JL Woodson, and it was an accident — and again, all alone, he would have to decide what to do with it. It wouldn't take him long. He walked calmly to the back alley, made sure nobody was looking his way, lifted the lid off a fifty-five-gallon garbage can and threw the collar and tag inside. There was nothing to be gained by purifying history. Cato didn't kill Satchel, but he was still a victim of his own violence, that hadn't changed.

Roscoe rejoined the group, trying not to look like he'd seen a ghost, which of course, in a way, he had. He didn't know it but this day, more unusual than any other he had ever known, was about to become indelible. What Roscoe experienced next would prove without a doubt, to even the most skeptical, that God does exist.

First, what he sensed was that the sounds around him, the idle conversations between people on either side, were muted; he could hear them, but only barely. And the same thing happened, in a way, with his field of vision. He could see children playing, adults talking, people laughing, all on his right and his left, but everything was smokey, grey, hazy. All he could see clearly was his baby sister, Hannah, swinging by herself. She was beautiful. She was smiling.

Then — and he only knew it because of the vague sense he had of others around him — a clap of thunder came. And then Andy threw a rubber ball for Ranger to fetch, and the ball went under the bushes near the swing. Then there was another clap of thunder and hazy people looked toward the sky. But not Roscoe. He still could only focus on Hannah. Ranger barked at the ball because he could not retrieve it. And another clap of thunder sent ladies, almost silently in Roscoe's periphery, busy to the task of clearing the tables. And then Ranger barked again at precisely the same time another loud blast came from the sky. *And that time, Roscoe saw it.*

He saw Hannah's head turn first toward Ranger, and then to the sky. And before Roscoe could convince himself that it meant anything, the sky boomed again, and his baby sister's head turned skyward once more. This time Roscoe saw it and so did George Mabry. Roscoe glanced his way and saw that with his one good eye, George had seen the same thing he had. Only George and Roscoe saw it. *Hannah could hear.*

Roscoe stood like a statue while people went scurrying indoors. Hannah never stopped swinging. The sky went quiet and a gentle rain began. When Roscoe saw his mother on her way to fetch his sister, he hollered.

"Momma, wait," he said. "Watch."

Laura stopped and Roscoe whistled as loud as he could. There was no response from Hannah.

"What's wrong with you Roscoe?" Laura asked, perplexed.

Then George Mabry put two fingers in his mouth and made a whistle as loud as had ever been heard in Mitchell, Missouri. It sounded like a Burlington Northern train whistle. And Hannah turned her head. And Laura saw it.

"Again, George!" Laura screamed.

And old George put forth and even louder whistle. And again, Hannah turned toward the sound. George looked at Roscoe and smiled peacefully. Maybe the wand had worked.

The last image Roscoe had of that evening was one of his mother holding her baby daughter in her harms, alone in the rain. Hannah laughed at the rain and Laura was sobbing.

That night, after everyone was gone, after Andy and Hannah had been tucked into bed and the rain had stopped, Roscoe went alone into the back yard, sat at the picnic table and looked at the sky. Soon, his father found him there.

"Big day," Frank said, putting his arm around Roscoe.

"Dad," Roscoe asked, "do you ever cry?"

"Sure I do," Frank answered. "What made you think of that?"

"Mom was crying with Hannah in the rain," he answered.

"She was happy. She was crying because she was happy."

"Do you ever cry because you're happy?"

"I cried when you were born," Frank said. "It was one of the happiest three days of my life."

"What was the fourth?" Roscoe asked, predictably.

"Well, the day I married your mother has to be up there pretty high on the list." Then, after a pause, he added, "But today would be pretty high too. Today was a great day."

"Do you think Hannah will get her hearing all the way back?"

"I don't know, but I think we have reason to be hopeful. I have a good feeling about it."

Roscoe sat silently for a while, just looking at the sky. It was hard for him to comprehend all that had occurred that day. He remembered something important he needed to tell his dad.

"Me and Fatty are going to be on a baseball team together this spring. The Mitchell Police Department is sponsoring a new team and Officer Odom asked us to be on the squad."

"That's terrific. Good for you and Fatty. You'll have fun. What's the name of the team?"

"He let us choose the name. The Bandits!" Roscoe announced proudly. "We thought that was a perfect name for the police department team."

"Good choice," Frank said, laughing. "Great choice."

After a quiet moment or two, Frank spoke. "Today, when I was watching Reverend Gleason on that bicycle, all I could remember was JL's funeral," he said. "I kept recalling how Pastor Robert Earl Woodson told me he liked your name. It sounded like someone who knows what he's doing, he said. I couldn't stop remembering that."

"Do you believe in magic?" Roscoe said.

"I do." Then, after another moment, Frank waxed softly into the dark night, "Ladies and gentlemen, your pilot for this transatlantic flight will be Captain Roscoe Hammer. The starting pitcher for this afternoon's New York Yankee game is rookie Roscoe Hammer. Tonight's guest conductor for the St. Louis Philharmonic Orchestra is Maestro Roscoe Hammer. We are proud to have with us this evening, Congressman Roscoe Hammer, from Missouri."

"I believe in magic too," Roscoe said. "I think you are right about Hannah." And then, happy to have his dad at his side, he let one of the best nights of his life fade away.

CHAPTER 27

St. Louis, Missouri – 46 Years Later

The prosecuting attorney for Saint Louis County sat alone in his office nursing a small hangover, the product of his victory celebration the night before. After six consecutive campaigns, six victories and six parties, he found himself wondering why he'd chosen the life of an elected official. He felt like every four years he had to go looking for steady work. He could have joined a firm, where by now he might have been a partner with several years under his belt and a good-looking bank account. Instead, he had chosen the life of a mutant — part lawyer, part politician. Oh well, nobody made him drink last night's champagne, he told himself. And it had been his career choice to serve the people, nobody twisted his arm. Stop complaining, he thought to himself.

What was really bothering him was that at last night's victory party, for the first time ever, none of his children could be there. His two boys and his daughter were all three off somewhere in various stages of building their own lives. They were having babies, buying houses, over-working at under-paying jobs, putting new tires on old cars, being ambitious, being hopeful, being happy. They had always been at his victory parties, which seemed secretly right to him because *they were his victories*. But, then, as he remembered thinking when he was a young boy, time passes and things change. His family, like Pastor Robert Earl Woodson's, had gotten "strung from hell to Christmas".

He looked at the file on his desk and rubbed his temples. He had been through it once quickly and could tell that it would not be a simple prosecution. The case looked simple, but experience had taught him that old lesson, a lesson to which, in the words of a book his dad had given him years earlier, we are strangely resistant: Reality is always more than we can see and the truth is always more than we can know. He was leaning toward a grand jury and could already hear his critics.

"The others are here, sir. They are waiting in the conference room," his secretary said with just her head through the door. After more than fifteen years, she knew him well enough to know when it was best not to be all the way in his office.

"Thank you Maxine," he replied. "Tell them I'm on my way. Is there some coffee in there?"

"Yes, sir, a fresh pot. By the way," she continued, now easing all the way in, "Judge McElroy called and wants to take you to lunch at his club. A congratulatory gesture, I think."

"Ugh. Can you put it out a couple of weeks? I talked to my dad this morning and I think I need to go see him in the next day or two."

"Is everything all right?" she asked.

"Oh he's fine, I'm pretty sure. But the lady who cares for him, Adella is her name, I talked to her too and she says he's not eating well. I just think it's time for me to look in on him, that's all."

"I'll handle Judge McElroy. Do you need me to make any arrangements for you down there?"

"No thanks. I'll stay in the old house with dad. Maybe I'll sleep in my old bed," he answered laughing.

He picked up the file on his desk and headed reluctantly off to his meeting. In the conference room he found County Police Chief Ray Hoskins, Detective Mike Mulligan, the lead investigating officer in the case, and Assistant Prosecuting Attorney Janet Preston.

"Congratulations, Roscoe," Hoskins said cheerily. "Sorry I missed the festivities last night. Your sixth term, that's impressive."

"Thank you, Chief," he answered politely. "But it's not hard to win when you're running unopposed. Me some, Opposition none, a landslide."

"Becoming unopposed, that's the hard part, huh?" the Chief replied. "This is Mike Mulligan. He's our lead on this case. I think you guys have met, right?"

"Sure," Roscoe answered, shaking hands with Mulligan. "Good to see you Mike."

"Thank you sir," Mulligan replied in a stiff but respectful way. "Look forward to working with you."

"Let me introduce you to your primary coordinate from our office, Janet Preston. Janet has been an assistant prosecutor for six years. Very experienced. SLU Law grad."

"Somebody's favorite law school," Hoskins joked, referring to Roscoe's alma mater. Janet smiled and shook hands with both men.

"You got it," he agreed. "Anybody else want coffee?" he asked, pouring himself a cup.

"I'll take some, sure," Chief Hoskins said. "Should we have Mike take us through the case?"

"Yes, let's have a rundown. Go ahead Mike."

The second of seven kids born to a good Catholic south-side family, Mike Mulligan was as cop as they come. His father and his grandfather were cops. Two of his younger brothers were cops. A sister worked in the coroner's office. At family dinners they talked Cardinal's baseball, Republican politics and heinous crimes.

In a way that made everyone feel slightly awkward — even his own Chief — Mulligan stood up to conduct his heavily rehearsed briefing. It was crisp, efficient and seemed organized in such a way as to suggest that the police department had done everything it could to make the prosecutor's job easy. He spoke to Roscoe and Hoskins but never made eye contact with Janet Preston. His "primary coordinate" like hell.

The victim: Michael Scarbo, a thirty-three-year-old part-time auto mechanic, never married. Moved to St. Louis from Philadelphia as a kid. Met the accused four years ago and moved in with her after a year. Fired from his most recent job for stealing tools. Bragged to co-workers about "keeping his girl in line the old fashioned way". He was a big — correction — *very big* drinker.

The accused: Mary Lewellen, thirty-two year-old single mother of two girls, ages ten and five. Her husband, their father, killed one week after the birth of the five year-old in an industrial accident, an explosion. A registered nurse at St. Vincent's, Lewellen grew up in St. Louis,

attended Rosati Kain. Her parents are deceased, but she has a grandfather living in a special home for late-stage dementia patients. It's
across the river in Washington Park. On her days off, like the day of
the murder, she takes the old guy home with her, sits him on the front
porch and lets him wave to people who walk by. She puts a baby-gate
contraption across the stoop so he can't wander off. According to official records at the nursing home, he hasn't spoken a single word to
anyone in two years. In other words, as far as this investigation goes,
he is no help at all.

The motive: So far, no eye-witnesses, but it's pretty clear that this
guy liked to abuse her. The investigative team has documented three
trips to the ER in the last year with suspicious injuries. Cracked ribs.
Broken collar bone. Bruised kidney's with blood in her urine. In
every instance, she had some unconvincing explanation. We interviewed his co-workers and hers. His said he bragged about it, in
detail, especially when he was drunk. Hers said they were suspicious
but she wouldn't talk about it. When she was arrested, the medical
team took photos of neck bruising and scarring on her back. She told
the arresting officer that this guy Scarbo had been beating her for
three years and he always threatened to kill her little girls and her if
she spoke to the authorities or tried to leave him. As abusive situations go, pretty standard stuff.

The day of the murder: So it's Lewellen's day off. She has her
grandfather out on the porch. Scarbo, according to Lewellen and tox-
icology, had been drinking since about ten in the morning. Lewellen
saw a train wreck coming so she sent her two daughters three blocks
down the street to play with the daughter of one of her co-workers, a
friend, another nurse at St. Vincent's. This friend, Ann Lewis, says the
girls got there around noon. Scarbo got wound up about something
and started choking Lewellen. The neck bruises confirm this. She
broke away. He stalked her around the room for a few minutes and
then decided he needed a shot of vodka. He took one and, boom,
went down like a bag of bricks, passed out cold. She got her grandpa
up and took him to the home in Washington Park; it's about a twenty-
five minute drive. She checked him in, confirmed by their logs, and
then left. She went back to the house and found Scarbo still passed

out on the floor. She went to the garage and got the knife, a long filleting knife. Back inside, she straddled him, and plunged the thing
straight into his heart. One stab wound, bingo. The medical examiner says the trajectory of the knife wound suggests a right-handed
assailant, which she is. According to Lewellen, he rolled slightly to
one side, moaned, and then died. His blood pooled in a manner consistent with her story. She then drove to the bar, ordered a beer and
told the bartender to call us.

The arrest: Our guys picked her up. They took her beer glass as
possible evidence and questioned the barkeep. According to him, she
had blood on her arm, her right arm, and a slight smear on her cheek.
But he said her hands were clean. And our examination of the beer
glass would confirm this. It was clean, except for prints, his and hers,
but no blood. By the time the arresting officers arrived, she had
washed the blood off her arm and cheek. She was clean as a whistle.
They took her to the precinct where she gave a detailed statement, a
full and complete confession.

"And so, to summarize," Mulligan said, taking his seat, "Scarbo
was a low-life loser and his girl friend is a murderer. Pretty straight-
forward."

"Questions?" Janet Preston asked.

"Fire away," Mulligan replied.

"The knife, anything on it but his blood?"

"His blood type on the part of the blade that penetrated. Nothing on the handle excepts some smears. No prints. No blood. Pretty
clean actually. Forensics found a chemical contained in women's
hand cream. That lines up logically. In the hospital, they use that
sanitizer stuff about a hundred times a day. Hand cream figures. On
the upper part of the knife blade they found some dried blood but the
type didn't match him or her."

"Probably catfish," Hoskins said, laughing.

"What type?" Janet asked.

"B negative."

"Rare?" Roscoe asked.

"Very," Janet answered before Mulligan. "What about the girls,
her girls, did they witness any of the abusive episodes?"

"You mean the fights?" he replied, mocking her a little.

"You know what I mean."

"No, they never witnessed any of the 'episodes'. When he got wound up, if they were home, he'd lock them in their room. They could hear but not see their mother getting beat up. There were entries in the oldest one's diary about it. 'Mommy is screaming, Michael is shouting, mommy is crying,' that kind of thing. Anything else?" he asked.

"The knife was a fishing knife, right?"

"Yeah, one of those filleting knifes."

"Was Scarbo a fisherman? Any poles or reels or tackle boxes or whatever in the garage?"

She had him. Mulligan didn't know and knew he should.

"We need to check that out," he said sheepishly. "I'm not sure, but the team may know. I'll get back to you."

"That would be great, detective. And the murder wound, one single stab wound you said, right?"

"Correct."

"Lucky shot I guess," Janet replied.

"She's a nurse," Mulligan answered with a smug grin, "I think they teach them where all the vital organs are located." Janet glared.

"Why would her hands be clean?" Roscoe asked, breaking the tension between Preston and Mulligan.

"No good answer for that one, sir," Mulligan answered. "Lewellen has no explanation. Says she can't remember."

"Did you find any blood on her beer glass?"

"None."

"In her car? The steering wheel?"

"None."

"Doesn't add up, does it? She stabs this guy, gets blood on her arm and, according to the bartender, on her cheek, but her hands are clean?"

"Missing piece, I agree," Mulligan answered, feeling a little defensive.

"What about this grandfather? Does he know anything? Did we question him?" Roscoe asked.

"It's like questioning the wall, sir. He doesn't even know his own name. He hasn't spoken a word in two years. There's nothing there. Or if there is something there, it would take Sigmund Freud to get it." Then, after a momentary pause, Mulligan went back on the offensive. "So, sir, I'm not sure what the problem is. We have a confessed murderer, murderess if you like, a dead body, a murder weapon, a truckload of motive. What else can we do for you?"

Before Roscoe could answer, Janet spoke. "You *do not* have a confessed murderer, which, by the way, is the word I prefer. You have a woman who stipulates to the fact that she killed her boyfriend with a knife. There's a big difference."

"I'm leaning toward a grand jury on this one," Roscoe said.

"Roscoe, really, a grand jury?" Hoskins asked.

"What the hell are you guys talking about, a grand jury?" Mulligan asked, losing what little composure he had left. "You have a confession! Most of the time you're bitching because we can't bring you a suspect. Now you have a confession! What are you worried about?"

"I'm worried about a jury's reaction to the evidence we have, the evidence that you, Detective Mulligan, have provided. I'm worried about what they call the battered woman's defense. I'm worried that we might not really know who killed this guy. I'm worried that my dad isn't eating right. I'm worried about the economy. I have a lot of worries, detective."

"You're talking about self defense, right? Well, from what I've read, the threat of harm has to be imminent. Without that, the self-defense argument doesn't hold up. Well, this guy, asshole that he was, he was *asleep* for god sakes! He was unarmed! Did I mention he was passed out! How the hell was he an imminent threat to anyone?"

"Imminent," Janet said calmly, "is a non-specific reference when it comes to time, suggesting only 'very soon'. Your imminent might be in the next five minutes. Mine might be in the next five days. The key is the certainty of the event, the timeframe for its occurrence is subjective."

"Is that so?" Mulligan replied, looking a little stupid. "You learned that in lawyer school, did you?"

"No, I learned it in grammar school."

"Okay, okay," Roscoe said, trying to restore order. "Unless we've got a witness that will testify that Scarbo was uncontrollably contrite and had ordered roses for Ms. Lewellen with a hand-written note of apology, then I'm going with a grand jury. We're going to test-drive this one."

"Respectfully, sir," Mulligan began, "this is crap! You have a reputation for prosecuting criminals. Lewellen is a criminal. She was living with an animal who beat her up, but that doesn't give her the right to kill him. You need some polling data from a grand jury? And, oh by the way, her lawyer, PD Martin Gray, he's still on training wheels. I don't know how we could lose this one."

"Detective Mulligan," Roscoe began calmly, "may I address your concerns? First of all, as Janet pointed out, we do not have a confessed murderer, we have a woman who says she stabbed a man, there's a big difference. I am just guessing, but I'll bet that she and her lawyer will come up with some reasons why she did it. And if we get to trial, emphasis on *if*, that training-wheels guy you mentioned, Martin Gray — who by the way is a damned good lawyer — he won't be her lawyer. By then, a special interest group will have lined up her legal team. They will come swooping in here from New York or LA or Chicago wearing $1500 suits and looking like lawyers in the movies. They will put someone like you, Detective Mulligan, on the stand. Because they have vast research resources, they will know that you are married and have two daughters. Then they will put a picture, this one from your investigative file, in front of the jury. They will ask you what the welts on Mary Lewellen's back, the scars on her back, what they look like. And you will answer that the scars are in the shape of a belt buckle. Members of the jury will gasp, as properly they should. Then this out-of-town lawyer who looks and sounds like Gregory Peck will ask you this: 'If someone did this to your wife with a belt, and if that same person said they would kill your wife and your daughters, what, Detective Mulligan, would you do? Would you take action to defend the people you love, or would you parse the meaning of imminent"? And, because the law is an imperfect thing, it will not matter one whit what your answer is because every man and woman on the jury will have answered the question for you in their own minds.

And then your lawyer — regrettably that would be me or Janet — one of us would then spend the next several days trying to instruct that jury as to the finer points of the law and we'd be lucky if they didn't fall asleep. That, Mike, is how this will go. And so, if you don't mind, we're going to test-drive this one with a grand jury."

"Yes sir, got it," Mulligan answered.

"Janet, I've got to be gone a few days. How much longer do we have with the current panel?"

"About five weeks," she answered. "They only have a couple of cases before them and one should be settled next week."

"Let's get the ball rolling with this panel, and try not to extend their term. You know the routine."

Mulligan couldn't stop himself. "She'll be running the case with the grand jury?"

Roscoe smiled at Hoskins and then turned to answer Mike Mulligan. "Janet is more than capable. I know she and you will make a great team."

With that, the meeting broke up. Hoskins and Roscoe shook hands. As everyone was on their way out of the conference room, Roscoe tapped Mulligan on the shoulder. "A minute in private, Mike?"

"Sure," Mulligan answered.

"I like you and I think you have a promising future. But the next time you come up here for a meeting, find a way to participate without insulting one of my assistant prosecutors. Unless, of course, you have a personal future in mind that involves shopping mall security. Are we together?"

"Yes sir, we are."

When everyone was gone, Roscoe walked back to his office. "Maxine," he said, "have you called Judge McElroy's office yet?"

"No sir, I will right away."

"No, no, I've changed my mind. If he can do it tomorrow, let's go ahead. I'll leave town right after lunch. Let's see if that will work."

"Will do."

CHAPTER 28

The drive from St. Louis to Mitchell takes two hours or so, depending on weather and traffic. In a helicopter — which is how he had made the trip three years earlier — you can get there in forty minutes. On this day, the roadway was empty and the sky was clear and the memory of that flight flooded back.

Maxine gave him the first sketchy, frightening report. His mother had been walking across a parking lot when a child someone had left alone in the car blasted the horn. Startled, she stumbled backward and tripped over a parking curb. The next person who pulled into the lot found her unconscious, her head resting in a small pool of blood.

She was rushed to the hospital by ambulance. The outlook was not good.

The police pilot told Roscoe that the Mitchell Police had informed him there was room to land the helicopter on the hospital lawn. There wasn't an actual pad, but the ground was flat and dry. "Only steps to the door," he said.

"Thank you for this, I appreciate it very much. And pass along my thanks to your Chief, I didn't get a chance to."

"Don't mention it, sir."

Suddenly it seemed, they were there. And minutes later he was in her room. His dad, looking more afraid than Roscoe had ever seen him, threw his arms around his son. "I'm so glad you're here," he said.

"What are they saying, dad?" Roscoe asked.

"It's not good, son. She's been in and out a little, but there is swelling. They can't do much about it except wait and hope. If it gets worse they may have to cut a hole in her skull — his voice caught on the words — to relieve the pressure. But for now they say to wait and hope. That's what I've been doing."

And that is what they did together for the next two hours. Roscoe took only two very short breaks to call his brother Andy in New York and his sister Hannah in Colorado. "Should I come right away?" they took turns asking.

"I can't tell yet. I'll let you know. Just sit tight. Pray."

Somewhere toward the end of the second hour his mother drew a very loud breath, loud enough to be noticed, exhaled slowly and then died. Somehow he and his dad both knew right away that she was gone. It was as if they could feel her leave. His father's face was drawn, grey, vacant. He began to cry. There were tears but no sound.

"It's time to come," he told his brother and sister. "She's gone."

The evening following visitation, Roscoe, Andy, Hannah and her husband Kevin sat around the old kitchen table eating pizza and drinking chianti. The wine, which they found in the back corner of the pantry, was cheap and old, and why not with bad pizza on a black day. Symmetry.

"Where'd you get the pizza?" Andy asked his brother.

"Pete 'Shaky' Bondero's Pizza Parlor," he answered. "A Mitchell mainstay for a long time."

"What's with the 'Shaky' thing?" Hannah asked.

"Sound's like a gangster's name to me," Andy said.

"Actually, I think the guy, he's dead now, had some kind of neurological disorder. That's what they did back then, they'd take someone's disability or infirmity and turn it into a nickname. 'Fish-eye' Gomez. 'Booger' Stanley. Do you remember that poor kid? Allergies. Nose running all the time. Even grownups called him that. Very politically incorrect by today's standards."

"Cruel," Hannah said, grinning. "I'm going to go check on dad."

"Let me do it," Kevin said.

"Thanks, honey," she said.

"So here we are," Andy said. "I can't remember the last time we were all here at the same time."

"My two big-shot brothers," Hannah proclaimed, smiling. "A big-city lawyer and a New York banker! Who'd have thought?"

"I read an article last week about the top ten professions toward which common people feel hostility. Guess what two were at the top of the list?" Roscoe asked.

"I saw the same article," Andy replied. "Let's think of ourselves as exceptions."

"Exceptional exceptions," Roscoe promptly replied.

"Did you two see how mom and dad have copies of both of your diplomas hanging in the living room? Those degrees were their crowning achievements. My little liberal arts BA didn't make it onto the wall of fame. The fate of an only girl, I guess," Hannah, said.

"Poor kid," Roscoe said with a chuckle. Then, after a short pause, he became serious. "You know mom must have talked about all the sacrifices they had to make for our education a hundred times. I never remember dad mentioning it even once." Then he turned to Hannah and took a lighter tone. "So if you and Kev have to make sacrifices to educate those boys of yours, and you think they should know it, make Kevin do the dirty work. They'll remember you in a better light."

"Sacrifices won't cover it, not with four boys," she laughed. "Armed robbery maybe. Anyway, Kevin has already started telling them how expensive it is going to be every chance he gets. He calls it 'guilt on layaway'. My seven-year-old will be so guilt-ridden by the time his turn comes, he'll probably run off and join the circus."

"An honorable profession," Kevin said, coming back into the room. "Your dad is still asleep. I think he may be out until morning."

Roscoe took a last sip of chianti. "I'm going to go back to the funeral parlor for one last look. The casket will be closed tomorrow, right? Would anybody care to join me?"

"I'll go with you I guess," Hannah said.

"I'll pass," Andy said. "I don't want dad to wake up with all three of us gone."

"I'll stay, too," Kevin said. "Andy needs somebody to drink with."

"Always thinking of others," Hannah joked and then kissed her husband on the cheek. "We won't be long."

On the short ride to the funeral home, Hannah and Roscoe talked about Andy. Earlier that day, Andy had confided in Hannah that he and his wife Alexis, or "the Countess" as Hannah referred to her, were having problems. Apparently Andy had tired of the investment banking grind and all the tech company deals. In the latter case, he saw grey clouds collecting on the horizon and didn't want to wake up one morning as part of a burst bubble. But mainly, he was after some normalcy. He was weary of the Hamptons, where all his neighbors were "aging rock and roll stars and boozed-up, third-tier novelists". Oddly, he longed for suburbia. He wanted a lawn mower, a mailbox at the curb, a big mall. But, the Countess wasn't interested.

"Why do you call her that?" Roscoe asked.

"One time she told me with unexplainable pride that some obscure branch on her Tennessee-rooted family tree was occupied by a splinter faction of Spanish royalty."

"Is she Spanish?"

"No. But she was runner-up in the Miss Tennessee Pageant once."

And so, the truth was, Alexis the Countess was back in New York weighing her options, not in the hospital recovering from gallbladder surgery as Andy had told his father. And he, Andy, had enlisted a head-hunter in an effort to find him a normal job in a normal city with sprawling, well-groomed suburbs.

"Does Andy have enough money to get free of her?" Roscoe asked.

"Truckloads, I think," Hannah answered.

"Good for him, my brother. Then I say, get on with it. Life's short."

Inside, they made their way slowly to the side of their mother's casket. Neither spoke for a few minutes. They gazed at her corpse as if they were looking at an old picture album.

"Did you want to come back here for one more argument with her?" Hannah asked, smiling. "If you did, you're too late. She's already dead."

Roscoe grinned. "Once again, she gets the last word."

"She worried about her relationship with you. Did you know that?" Hannah asked, now more serious. "She talked to me about it."

"I would call our relationship a slow dance of forgiveness," he said, never taking his eyes off his dead mother. "I know you probably don't remember things this far back, but when you were sick, everything was pretty rocky. But by the time you were ready to start school, your hearing was almost completely restored, all the trips to St. Louis had ended and life had gotten back to normal. Mom had been working at Gertie's for three or four years and times were pretty good. The things that had gotten her and me off track never really resurfaced, but then again they never completely went away either. It was like having one of those lifetime viruses in you that goes dormant but never moves out. From then on it was a little bit easier for her to make me mad and vice-versa. It was like there was always a good argument lurking just below the surface and we both had to work at keeping it there. But all in all, I think I feel the way you should feel when your mother dies. Memory is benevolent; the good stays and the bad slowly slips away. I'll miss her."

"Me too," Hannah offered. "One time she told me that being a parent was the most important thing you will ever do and, ironically, you can't practice it ahead of time. You become a parent and you learn on the fly. And when you make mistakes, the most precious thing in your life, your child, is on the receiving end."

"Her way of saying she did her best, huh?" His voice had an edge on it.

"I suppose so," Hannah answered. "Don't get all judgmental. Our mistakes might be different ones, but we've made them, haven't we?"

"I guess we have at that," he answered, smiling at having been mildly upbraided by his baby sister. "The only way to avoid them is to be in a childless pagan marriage like Andy." They both laughed.

"I always thought dad would go first, didn't you?" Hannah asked.

"An actuary would tell you that was the correct bet. You think he'll be all right with her gone?" Roscoe asked.

"I don't know, but I think so. Kevin and I have talked a little, and if dad wants to come to Colorado and get a place nearby, we'd like being able to look in on him. We'll have to see what he wants to do. I don't think we should even pose the question for a few months."

"Right."

"Amy will be here tomorrow? Isn't that what you said earlier?"

"Yes," he answered. "Kit is getting married in a couple of months, nice boy from Chicago. She and her mom were there yesterday for a bridal shower thrown by Kit's future mother-in-law. They flew back to St. Louis today and will drive down in the morning. Timing on these things is always a mess."

As Roscoe drove them slowly down Mitchell's darkened streets toward their first home, neither he nor his sister spoke. He angled his dad's big, awkward Mercury into the gravel driveway using the doorknob-like affair Frank had attached to the steering wheel, a throwback to the days before power steering. His dad's fondness of simple technology made him smile.

"I kept the wand, you know? I still have it," Hannah said, looking at her brother.

"Huh?"

"Your magic wand, you left it in my bedroom the night you came home to see me and Kevin walk into senior prom. I've kept it all these years. I think it's worked. Me and Kevin, our kids, we've been lucky. Maybe I should pass it along to Kit. We will be getting an invitation I presume," she said grinning.

"Invitations trigger wedding gifts, right? You're liable to get two." He paused for a second and then added, "I'm glad you've felt lucky. Nobody deserves it more than you, Hannah."

The ringer on the cellphone attached to the dashboard of his car was turned all the way up and it jolted him back into the present. He blinked and found the off-hook button.

"Hello."

"Roscoe, it's Janet. How's the road to Mitchell?"

"Janet. Hello. The road is empty, quiet. What's going on there? It hasn't even been two days, is there a problem?"

"No, no problem, just a quick update on a couple of things you left me notes about."

"Go ahead."

"Well, first," she started, "there wasn't a single piece of fishing gear or tackle in the garage. They interviewed a couple of Scarbo's coworkers again and they said he had never ever mentioned fishing.

And there's nothing you do with that kind of knife except clean fish, so I'm told. I've got Mulligan checking with Missouri Wildlife to see if either Lewellen or Scarbo had a fishing license. He doesn't strike me as the licensed type, but who knows? The blood on the knife that wasn't Scarbo's type, there's still no good explanation. Mulligan keeps mumbling about his theory that her hand slid down the handle and she cut herself on top part of the blade. When I present him with the blood-type analysis, he argues that the medical examiner's lab team isn't one hundred percent committed to the B-negative finding. They are 'reasonably certain' but not positive."

"Why not?" Roscoe asked.

"Supposedly the sample size was small and may have been partially wiped, they can't tell for sure. If it was, whatever was used may have corrupted the analysis, blah, blah, blah. I say it's B-negative. And anyway, we went back and looked at all the photos taken at the time of the arrest, and there were absolutely no open wounds on her hands, none, not even a hangnail. That blood can't be hers and that means there is an unexplained gap in the story we're constructing for the grand jury."

"When will you be ready for the grand jury?" he asked.

"Day after tomorrow."

"That's fast. Good job."

"The last thing, her clean hands. We still have no good explanation for this one. The bartender is rock-solid that there was blood on her arm and her cheek, but her hands were clean. Analysis of the beer glass, the five dollar bill she paid him with, the steering wheel and door handle on her car, all clean. She left the crime scene with clean hands. We don't know why, and if she knows, she isn't saying."

"What does she say?"

"That she can't remember."

"Was the blood on her arm and cheek Scarbo's?"

"She says it was, but she washed up in the bathroom at the bar before the arresting officers got there so there's no way to confirm it."

"What was the bar?"

"Ah, … the Tarpon Bar and Grill, I think. Yeah, that's right. Just off Delmar."

"Why there? Any idea?" Roscoe asked.

"She says she overheard someone at work talking about it or something. She's not really sure. How do you pick a place for a drink after you've stabbed someone to death, right?"

"She has a little memory problem, doesn't she?"

"Yeah, she does."

"Okay. Keep the ball rolling, you're doing a good job. By the way, I had lunch with Judge McElroy before I left town today. I need to tell you about our conversation when I get back."

"Intriguing. Drive carefully. I'll track you down if I need to."

His focus returned to the road in time to spot a distance marker: *Mitchell - 40 miles.* About forty minutes to find out why Frank Hammer wasn't eating right. He came around a bend in the two-lane and down a gentle slope to find a Missouri Department of Transportation worker straddling a tractor, mowing weeds on the shoulder. His posture suggested a lack of job satisfaction. The sight reminded him of his old friend Fatty Gilchrist.

All through school, the two of them had remained best of friends. But somewhere during the high school years, their interests began to diverge along pretty clear lines. Fatty, who had grown taller and more muscular than almost anyone in their grade, no longer answered to the nickname, except of course when Roscoe used it. To everyone else, he was Randy. He was a gifted, graceful athlete, a standout in almost every sport, but football was his first love and he was fabulous at it. He was very popular.

Roscoe was more academic, a lover of books, and science, and space exploration and even art, and his grades were stellar. He admired Fatty, along with all of Mitchell's other athletes, and he cheered them on wildly, but from the stands. The differences in their interests never really separated them, but instead seemed to connect them more closely. It was as if each saw the other as his natural second half. Separate, they were all right, but together, they were extraordinary, as they had been from the age of seven or eight.

By the time the boys graduated high school, Roscoe's academic achievements had earned him a partial scholarship to Saint Louis University, a grand Jesuit institution. Fatty's grades, on the other hand, had slumped to the point that he found himself academically ineligible to attend any of the larger schools that would have given him a full scholarship, a no-show job, a car, and God knows what else to come and play football for them. He did what other similarly situated knuckleheads did, he went off to an obscure two-year college, Cimmeron County Junior College, in Cimmeron, New Mexico. According to plan, he would play football there for two years and meanwhile a posse of tutors, along with a lenient teaching staff and administration, would rehabilitate his grade point average and then he would move on to Ole Miss, or LSU, or in the worst case, the University of Missouri. According to plan.

Roscoe's first term away was tumultuous. He studied hard, found a part-time job, and his grades were excellent. Between his junior and senior year in high school, Gertie Paulson had passed away. Just a year or so later, during his first semester at SLU, Harriet and George died, her first, with him following in a month and a half. Both of them died peacefully and of natural causes. People who knew them were pretty sure that their last years had been their very best. Sad news, Roscoe found, hits hard when you are away from home for the first time. He was lonely and too much of his childhood was finding its way to the graveyard. Those first difficult few months ended with an unexpected call from Fatty. Things had not gone according to plan.

"Where are you?" Roscoe asked over the phone.

"Home, Mitchell," Fatty answered. "Halfway to anywhere."

"What happened?"

"They gave me the boot, Roscoe. A slap on the ass and a train ticket home. Adios."

"Why? What went wrong?"

"Just about everything went wrong, pal. Me and the coaching staff didn't see eye-to-eye. My teammates were a bunch of gap-toothed idiots from Oklahoma and Texas. I never thought of Mitchell being, well, sophisticated, but I'm telling you, these guys were almost prehistoric. And their personal hygiene was for shit, they stunk. And, in keeping with my recent past, my grades were not so hot. Let me put it another way, I was flunking out. After only one semester!"

"You were flunking out of junior college? I didn't even know that was possible," Roscoe exclaimed.

"You know me, always pursuing higher and higher levels of underachievement," Fatty answered laughing.

"So now what?" Roscoe asked.

"I've been offered a position at Doak Posey's station. After a short apprenticeship there should be lots of opportunity for advancement," he announced with mock enthusiasm. "I plan to climb the corporate ladder."

"Doak's station?" Roscoe asked. "That's pitiful."

"Oh, it's only temporary," Fatty answered. "I've got my application in at NASA. They just don't have any astronaut openings right now." He laughed at his own joke. It was the last time Roscoe would ever hear that sound.

CHAPTER 29

H e pulled into Mitchell and thought to himself how shabby the town had become. The global economy everyone liked to talk about had not been kind to places like Mitchell. Everything seemed to be splintered, and blistered, and sagging. Lawns and gardens had gone too long untended. People had even pulled mobile homes into their backyards and angry dogs kept on thick chains killed the grass where they paced and made mud. It dawned on him that maybe his hometown needed to start completely over.

But things were brighter on Sand Plum Street. He passed Gertie's and found it looking largely unchanged, still all white and tidy and with green grass and perfectly shaped bushes, once the pride of old George Mabry. In the back, still enshrouded in wild honeysuckle, and with moss caked on its roof, the old potting shed still stood, looking like a three-dimensional postcard of his youth. *Wish you were here!* And his boyhood home just down the street, it was immaculate with its crew-cut lawn and towering oak trees and porch painted grey to match the shutters and roof. Frank Hammer believed in keeping things neat and trim. If he couldn't do it himself, which by now was generally the case, then he'd spend his last dollar to have it done. Letting things slide was not an option.

Adella met Roscoe at the door, hugged him, and whispered that Frank was in the living room watching television.

"He's just not himself," she said, rolling her eyes. "I don't know."

In the living room, with the television blaring, Frank sat in his chair and sipped red wine. At the sight of his son, he worked his way to his feet and gave Roscoe a big hug.

"My boy, what brings you here?"

"Wine, dad, at four in the afternoon?"

"This is the wine time, son. I usually watch *O-frah*. Have a little wine, maybe some cheese, maybe a little chocolate. You want some wine? Why are you here?"

"Dad, it's *O-prah*. No, no wine, thanks."

"That's what I usually watch," Frank said. "But today, no, because we got the tennis players at Wimbledon in her place today. Very pretentious sport if you ask me. Those Brits, calling it 'the gentleman's finals' and all that sort of horseshit. In America we don't call anything 'the gentleman's this or that' do we? Who'd believe us if we did?"

"Dad, Adella says you're not eating right. What's wrong?"

Frank Hammer looked toward the kitchen to make sure she wasn't looking in, then put his hand up as if to shield the answer. "Her cooking, it's slipping."

"Dad, I don't believe you, Adella is a fabulous cook."

"Stick around son, have a meal or two, then let me know what you think," he whispered.

Roscoe decided, and Adella quickly agreed, that he should take his father out to dinner and Adella should have a richly deserved night off.

"Thank you, Jesus!" she said.

"Where shall we eat tonight, dad? I'm buying," Roscoe asked.

"If you're buying, then I say Angelo's Steak House."

"Sounds good to me," Roscoe answered. "You have a taste for steak?"

"I have a taste for steak and a thirst for whiskey," Frank answered enthusiastically.

Frank fell asleep in his chair for about thirty minutes, a normal part of any afternoon, according to Adella. Roscoe used the time to get his things into the house and splash some water on his face. Then he phoned Amy.

"I can't tell how he is," he said, frustrated. "He's thin, but then he's never been heavy. And he's shaky, I guess, but sometimes I feel shaky and I'm thirty years younger. He says Adella's cooking is slipping, which, by the way, has her more than a little annoyed. The atmosphere is unsettled, what can I say?"

"Take him to dinner, Roscoe. Be calm."

When they came through the door at Angelo's, Frank waived at the waiters and bartender as if he knew them. They responded in kind, which Roscoe noticed with a combination of pride and worry. The hostess seated them at a nice out-of-the-way table and took their first drink order.

"Beefeaters and tonic, please," Roscoe said, thinking of a drink that might last a while.

"Jack Daniels, on the rocks, snifter please," Frank said, thinking quite the opposite.

"What's with you and the whiskey, Dad?" Roscoe asked. "You never drank it at home."

"Rarely, you're right, though once in a while I guess. Made your mother nervous. I guess nervous is the right word. Her dad was a drunk, you know? I guess that's where it came from. Or maybe she was just afraid of too much of a good thing, I don't know. Some people, too much. Some people, not enough. Anyway, to answer your question, I like a drink now and then. I asked Adella to get a bottle for the house, but she refused. Church of Christ, she is. No booze, no dancing, no nothing. Dreadful tribe, a very negative bunch. So, it's me and Angelo's, once in a while. After all these years, that's what it's come to, me and a decent bartender, every now and then."

They ordered steaks, cooked rare, and baked potatoes with all the fixings, and enjoyed manly small talk for almost two hours. Then Frank, who had been more in charge than it appeared, got to the important matters.

"Your wife and kids, everyone all right?" he asked.

"They are all great, dad," Roscoe answered. "Kit's going to have a baby soon. You're going to be a great-grandfather."

"Where? I want to be there!"

"Well, as you know, they live in Chicago. But the first time they bring the baby down, I'll come and get you and we'll drive up together to see him."

"*Him*, you said. So you're expecting a boy?" Frank said, laughing.

"I'm hoping for ten toes and ten fingers....that's all."

"I want to bring a gift. You need to let me know ahead of time."

"I will, dad."

"We Hammers are gift givers, you know. You keep me posted."

"I will, dad," Roscoe answered again. Then, after a pause, he asked, "Why are you so thin, dad. Why so thin?"

"I'm drinking more wine. And I eat chocolate sometimes. It's the way of the French. Keeps you thin."

"Dad, come on, please. What's going on?"

Frank paused, sipped the last drop from his glass, rattled the ice cubes and then answered. "Roscoe, I've got a little situation, a problem, a medical problem. Normal for my age. Nothing much to do about it. I've been to the doctor and anything extreme that might change the situation, well, I'm not doing it. The clock ticks, time passes. It's natural son."

"Dad, what are you talking about. What doctor? That Dr. Brayton? I've heard he is a cocaine addict who got his medical degree in South America somewhere. He's been married three times and has practiced medicine in four different states. You're basing your plans on a prognosis from him?"

"Nobody's perfect, Roscoe," Frank answered. "Could I get another whiskey please?" he asked in the direction of the bar. The drink came and they both drew a long breath. Owing to the fact that alcohol does have some positive effects, the conversation between them became calmer, softer.

"So, your family, your kids, they're all good?" Frank asked.

"Yes, dad, they're fine. They have been the center of everything for me. Not that you and mom haven't been important, but they are my world. I hope you've understood."

"I am proud of you for that, son. Always remember."

"This medical condition of yours, anything more you want to say about that?" Roscoe asked gingerly.

"No sir, nothing more to say."

And with that, Frank drank his drink, slowly, savoring the thought that his oldest boy had been more in love with this family than anything else on earth. And Roscoe sipped his gin, wondering what his dad was dying from.

Over coffee, Frank moved to what he considered some important details. It seemed that when Gertie Paulson died and her sister Harriet soon thereafter, their wills stipulated that Laura Hammer, Margaret Gilchrist and Althea Woodson could sell the store and the real property at their discretion. Half of the proceeds was to go to a fund for the beautification of Harmony Park, and the other half was to be split equally between Laura, Margaret, and Althea. It turned out that Laura's one-third of one-half equalled a rather amazing ten thousand dollars. She and Frank placed this money in an interest-bearing account, and now, thanks in part to the soaring interest rates during President Jimmy Carter's administration, it had become eighteen thousand dollars. What, he wondered, should he do with it?

"I don't need anything that costs eighteen thousand dollars," Frank said flatly.

"Give it to Hannah," Roscoe offered. "She has four boys to get through college."

"What about you? What about Andy?" Frank asked.

"I'm fine, and Andy, well, Andy is loaded, dad. He made a lot of money."

"Did he? Good for Andy. I'm not surprised, he's smart."

"I'll take care of getting the money to Hannah if you want me to," Roscoe offered.

"That would be good. I'd like you to do that for me."

In the dark car on the way home Roscoe asked his father a question that had been on his mind for longer than he could remember.

"Have you been happy, Dad? In your life I mean, have you been content?"

"Of course I have," Frank answered flatly. Roscoe was suddenly glad that he couldn't see his father's expression and neither of them spoke for what seemed like a long time.

"I didn't mean anything by the question, Dad. I didn't mean to upset you."

"I'm not upset son. I'm a little, well I guess a little surprised. You don't think about your kids wondering things like that about you. At least I never did. I hope I didn't come across as unhappy."

"No, no, you didn't, not at all. You just never know for sure what's going on in the life of another person, even if that other person is your father. I just wanted to ask you while…" His voice trailed off.

"While I was still around?" Frank said, rescuing his son with a gentle laugh.

"Yes, I guess so," Roscoe answered with a chuckle.

"Maybe, the question you really meant to ask me is whether or not I was happy with your mother. Could that be the question?"

Roscoe had trouble bringing himself to respond and once again, Frank threw him a rope. "If that was the question, the answer is still yes. I loved your mother very much. We were neither one happy with the other every moment of every day. But most days were good and yes we were in love."

"I'm sorry that things were not always perfect between me and mom," Roscoe offered, struggling to give the awkward conversation a new direction. "I'm not sure why that was."

"Laura was a little too concerned with mistakes she felt she had made. She was convinced she'd made more than anyone else. I told her that was a fool's calculation. We know all our own missteps and we know so few of every one else's. You can't help but come out on the short end of that arithmetic. I didn't have much luck talking her out of it. It worried her and made it hard for her to be happy with herself sometimes. When people feel that they've failed, it squirts out in all kind of ways, and there can be collateral damage. She loved you a lot and she knew you loved her too. You shouldn't worry about that."

Roscoe pulled the car into the driveway. "We're home."

"Do you still think of it that way, as 'home'?" Frank asked.

"Yes, I do, dad. I guess I always will."

"That makes me feel good. A home is what we all try to make, isn't it?"

"You did a good job of that, dad. You *and* mom."

"There was another thing I used to tell your mom about mistakes."

"What's that?"

"Our mistakes always seem bigger at night. 'Wait until morning,' I'd tell her."

"I vote we go in, watch the news, and then go to bed."

"Agreed," Frank chimed back. "You might have noticed that it's a Japanese-made TV. No more Motorola. Damn shame."

"Tomorrow I'm going to buy you your own bottle of bourbon. We'll hide it from Adella."

"Now you're talking!"

On the nightstand in the bedroom he had shared all those years with his little brother, Roscoe found the Philco radio. His feet hung over the end of the bed but he slept soundly without moving.

CHAPTER 30

The next morning the air was light and cool and Roscoe went for a walk. He had been informed by Adella that Frank was unaccustomed to rising any time before eight or eight-thirty and so it was her habit to get to the house at about seven-thirty, early enough to have coffee ready. She offered to come earlier if Roscoe needed her but he insisted she keep to their normal routine; he could find coffee somewhere around town if he wanted it badly enough.

As he walked, the sun came all the way up and splashed light on a town that was as uninspiring by foot as it had been the day before by automobile. He passed dingy houses, one after another, where people on their porches — some reading the newspaper, some just drinking coffee — stared at him as though he had come to town to foreclose on mortgages or to sell narcotic drugs or to burn the churches. He wasn't from around there, their eyes seemed to say. He wanted somehow to tell them just how much he really was. Then again, who cares, he thought to himself, the time was near when he'd have no more connection to Mitchell. Maybe that was for the best — the place disappointed him beyond measure.

Back at the house he found Adella busy in the kitchen. The aroma of the coffee was overshadowed by the smell of something even better in the oven, cinnamon rolls she made from scratch the night before while he and Frank were at dinner.

"Umm, those smell so good, Adella!" Roscoe said, peeking through the oven door. "You made them last night? You were supposed to be taking the night off."

"It was no bother, really."

"I don't know if dad will gain any weight, but I'm pretty sure I will."

"What do you think?" Adella asked. "How is your daddy? He doesn't talk to me about his health and all that kind of thing."

"I'm not sure, Adella. He didn't tell me very much. But he's getting up there and I think, well, I think he's not great. But his spirit is good. I credit that to the care and company you give him. I'm very grateful. He is too, even when he doesn't act like it."

"I'm grateful to you and your family. You all have been very good to me. Your daddy is a good man. I wish I could do more for him."

"Is he up?" Roscoe asked looking toward the bedrooms.

"He's in the shower. He came out and got a cup of coffee earlier. I don't know how long he's been awake. When he came out, he had a list he'd already made this morning. Things he wants to do while you're here. It is over there on the counter," she said, pointing.

Roscoe took the list into the living room, sat at his father's tiny, cluttered desk and read it. What he saw, scribbled in fitful cursive, were the last few requests of a man who was not in the habit of making many.

Fishing with Roscoe
Light bulbs in garage
Lawn mower blade
Money to Hannah — Soon — Before
Gift for baby
Bourbon

"I hope you don't mind," Frank said, his voice coming from behind Roscoe. "It's just a few things I'd like to get done while Adella's cooking and I have you captive. Might take us a couple of days. Have you got the time?"

"I've got as many days as we need," Roscoe answered. "Let's have a cinnamon roll and then get started. You look great this morning. Showered, shaved, all shiny."

"I slept good. The whiskey might have helped."

The two of them then set about cramming a day and a half's worth of activities into the next four. The pace left plenty of time for impromptu naps, Frank's of course, and occasional telephone updates from Janet Preston. And there was time for walks together, for afternoon wine with Oprah, and long, meandering conversations. He reported to Amy that his dad looked better, was eating better, seemed more engaged…but, and this he did not report, he knew in the back of his mind that his father's every glance, every slow smile, every touch was a farewell. The end was coming.

"I've decided about the baby's gift," Frank announced, waking from one of his short naps with a sudden snort. "He or she won't be able to use it right away, but not too far down the road they will get a lot of fun out of it."

"What is it?" Roscoe asked, smiling.

"A Radio Flyer wagon. They have them at the hardware store. I've seen them! We can get it while you're here and you can take it back with you. That way, when the baby comes, boom, you've got the gift right there. What do you think?"

"Perfect, just perfect. It's a great plan."

"And Roscoe, you saw the list. The thing about the money for Hannah, you understand, right?"

"Yes, I do," Roscoe answered. "I'll take care of it as soon as I get back to St. Louis. Don't worry."

"Speaking of that, when do you plan to go back?" Frank asked, trying not to sound plaintive.

"Maybe day after tomorrow," Roscoe said. "We'll have to see. You and I still have some things to do. Light bulbs in the garage. Fishing."

"And the lawnmower blade, we've got to get that off so I can have Bill Sanborn sharpen it for me."

"That's right."

The job of changing the light bulbs in the garage took Roscoe somewhere he had not been in twenty-five or more years. He and Frank went there together — clearly, these were meant to be joint activities — and his dad quickly found a comfortable place to relax, sitting on the edge of an old spare tire that leaned against the wall. From there, he reckoned, he could visit with and supervise his son without over-exerting. Roscoe took a step ladder off a pair of wall-hooks and positioned it beneath the first light in a row of three. Before climbing up, Roscoe turned slowly around, taking in all the artifacts of his childhood. There were old worn gardening tools shipped here presumably on the Mayflower, a hopelessly snarled string of Christmas lights, an unimaginable cache of landscape sprays and chemicals, all undoubtedly carcinogenic and all in containers old enough to be seeping at their seams, plastic packages of mouse and rat traps at the ready, a strangely shaped brush that Frank used to get bugs off the bumper of his Mercury, a wad of cotton gardening gloves and a half dozen brushes dried stiff with old paint. Many men from Frank Hammer's era were not tidy anywhere except in the garage; quite the opposite, Frank Hammer was tidy everywhere except in his garage.

"I once knew a guy who fell off a ladder while changing light bulbs in the garage and killed himself. His head cracked on the concrete floor like a melon," Roscoe said as he made his way upward.

"Be careful then," Frank answered flatly.

"Hand me the bulb, dad."

"Get the old one out first. One step at a time. You're always in such a damned hurry."

Amidst such banter, the team of Frank and Roscoe Hammer worked their way through the installation of three new, bright light bulbs for the Hammer garage. Before he came down the ladder for the last time, Roscoe turned and asked his father a question.

"Dad, why don't you ever ask me about my job?"

Frank thought for a moment and then answered, "I don't know why. Is there something you want to tell me about your job?"

"Oh, no," Roscoe replied, laughing. "I was just wondering, that's all. For the record, the job is fine."

"It's interesting that you bring that up," Frank offered, after another thoughtful pause. "Not too long ago, I got hungry for some pancakes. Adella makes glorious pancakes, but, as you know, she's been in a kind of *healthy* cooking phase. Yogurt, fruit, bagels, that sort of thing. So, anyhow, I made up some kind of excuse and snuck down to the diner, sat down at the counter and ordered a short stack from the young lady I see there anytime I go in. She pours coffee, tell's me 'good morning' and takes my order. She probably does that about fifty times every day, who knows, maybe a hundred. Well, the guy three stools down from me orders pancakes too. Mine come and they are delicious, perfect. The guy down the way gets his, takes one bite and starts complaining. He says his have lumps in them. He starts raising Cain and the young lady, she's a nice person, she says she'll take the pancakes off his bill. Well, he says he doesn't give a damn about the bill, he just wants some pancakes without lumps. Well, finally the cook has to come out — and by the way, he's the owner of the place — he comes out and tells this guy to take a hike. The guy gets up, takes a nickel out of his pocket and slams it down on the counter. 'There's your tip, you bimbo' he says to her as if she made the lousy pancakes. And then he stomps out."

"What an asshole?" Roscoe interjected.

"No kidding," Frank replied. "So the young waitress, she's pretty upset, teary-eyed and all, and I overhear her talking to another waitress. I'm not listening in you understand, but I can hardly help hearing. Anyway, she says she has a kid whose having a birthday and he wants a new bicycle. She emphasizes the word 'new'. But she can't afford a new bicycle and she's wondering if he'd be all right with a used one. And she says she's working two jobs and she never gets much time with her kid, and that her life is pretty much crap. She might not have said crap, but that was her meaning."

"And so you left an extra big tip?" Roscoes jumped ahead, smiling.

"It might have been a little more than normal."

"How much?"

"Son, come on down from that ladder before you crack your skull," Frank instructed. "The amount of my tip is not the point of my story. The point of my story is that every kid in the world wants a new bike, at least once in his or her life. And every kid deserves to have a mom and a dad who can spend time with him or her, teach them things, help them through rough spots. Every kid has that coming. But a lot, and I mean a lot of people have jobs like this young lady, shit jobs, if you'll excuse my language, where these simple dreams are just that, dreams. But none of my three kids ever had to suffer with that kind of job. My kids could buy bicycles and spend time with their children because they had good jobs. So maybe I don't ask you about your job much, but let me tell you, I'm grateful for your job. I'm grateful."

Roscoe stared at his dad and his dad stared back.

"Fifty bucks," Frank said without flinching. "The pancakes were damned good. No lumps."

That night, they finished Roscoe's visit as it had begun, with a steak dinner at Angelo's. And there was, of course, whiskey. And with the drink there came tall tales of earlier lives and of paths not taken, of dreams full of promise and, to Roscoe's surprise, of exotic women who Frank had brushed up against, but only that. His father was freer than he had ever seen him.

When they were back home, and when Roscoe had his father in bed, Frank looked up through tired eyes and said something his son could not have expected.

"When I was a kid, I looked forward to bedtime," Frank said to his son. "I did because sometimes, when I slept, I would have a dream. And the dream would not be a happy dream or a sad dream, it would just be a good story. Not scary, and not fantastical, it would be just a good story. And so, he said with the whiskey stretching his words and thoughts, when I said my prayers, as I always did before bed, I would pray for a dream. I would pray for a good story. Sometimes it came, sometimes not. But I always prayed for it." He paused and his eyes batted. "Do you have a good story you can tell me, Roscoe? Not sad, not happy, just a good story to help me sleep?"

Roscoe thought for more than a moment, waiting to see if his father might just drift on into sleep. But Frank's eyes kept batting and finally Roscoe answered. "I have a hell of a story to tell you," he said.

And then, Roscoe Hammer did what he had been waiting almost half a century to do. He told his father the story of his life. He told him about Harriet and George and Satchel, about Bobby Cato and the crazy mixup with JL Woodson. He told him about the accident the night of that awful rain and about how afraid he had been when he was supposed to meet with Buster Odom. He told him about the magic wand.

And while Roscoe told the story, Frank blinked in and out of sleep. It was as if Roscoe was giving him what he most wanted, a dream.

So Roscoe went on, telling the whole story, all the secret parts, and along the way he told how his friend Fatty figured in. And the telling of the story somehow made him feel calm, peaceful, content, as if he was turning a caught fish safely back into the water. And then his father was fully asleep.

Roscoe took the bottle of Jack Daniels and a plain glass and went to the living room where he had learned to walk. He sat in his father's chair, poured a short drink and opened an old picture album. He found the article about Fatty, read it, and in the dark he sobbed. He put his hands on his face to try and make it stop.

CHAPTER 31

1965 was a big year for the Hammer family and characteristically, Frank decided to mark the time with new technology. He invested far too great a percentage of the family's wealth in a new camera being marketed by an inventor with the rather dull name of Land. The camera, called Polaroid for some unknown reason, was a breakthrough. In lay terms, it promised that you could take and develop photographs, all in one fell swoop. No photo lab, no waiting; memories in moments at your finger tips, so the marketing went.

What wasn't known about the Polaroid, which by the way came not in a customary camera case, but rather in what could only be described as a small piece of fine luggage, is that it took something like a Patton tank crew to shoot and process photographs at a live event, a live event like the night Hannah and her date Kevin walked into the Senior Prom.

People were lined on both sides of the walkway leading into the Mitchell High School gymnasium. As it was in towns all across the country, the layout was like Oscar night when movie stars floated like angels into the Dorothy Chandler Pavilion in Los Angeles, California. Young girls in long, ostentatious gowns, and scrubbed and eager boys in rented tuxedos made their way happily into the biggest social event of their lives. Roscoe was home for the occasion and also to celebrate early his own graduation from law school. And Andy came home too, as he was on the cusp of graduating from Princeton and entering a period of his life that result in great personal wealth and marital agony. They, Roscoe and Andy, were Frank's camera crew. And when the time came, when beautiful, glamorous, joyful Hannah made her way down the walk, Frank stretched out the accordion-like Polaroid and began to flash like a madman. He called for more film packs, more flash bulbs. Photos, like magic, came grinding out of the end of the Polaroid and had to be swabbed with developing slime and preservative slime. "Don't touch them with your fingers," he shouted. "We don't need photos of your fingerprints."

At one point, when Hannah was just about to enter the gym, Frank steadied himself like a UPI photojournalist for a final shot. Sadly though, Beverly Deffenbaugh, an innocent bystander, stepped into the line of fire, and when the Polaroid went off, it flashed in her eyes from no more than eighteen inches. She stumbled backward as if she had been shot with a deer rifle. Frank panicked, dropped the Polaroid, and went to her aid. Andy recovered the camera which continued making sounds like you might hear in the dentist's office. Finally a memorable snapshot of Beverly's cavernous mouth and flaring nostrils developed. It was, in a word, horrifying.

"That's a keeper," Andy said, dryly.

And as they were gathering up and preparing to go, that's when Roscoe glanced across the walkway and saw standing at the very back, hidden it seemed, his best childhood friend, Fatty Gilchrist. He was thin, gaunt maybe, but peaceful looking. His eyes met Roscoe's and then jumped away, as if to give him, Roscoe, an out. But Roscoe stayed on him and finally they shared a smile. And when the crowd cleared, Roscoe went to him and they shook hands like proper young adults should do.

"How the hell are you?" Roscoe asked.

"I'm fine, yeah, I'm good. And you?"

"I'm okay too, I guess. About to finish up law school. Then, who knows what."

"I've kept track of you, through our moms, you know, and I'm proud of how things have gone for you, how you've done, I mean. Your future's bright I think."

"Hey, you want to go to Pud's and have a beer? We can really catch up," Roscoe said.

"I came here to see Hannah tonight. I've always thought of her as my other sister. She looked fabulous, didn't she? When I think how things could have gone. So, anyway, Pud's, sure, great, I'll see you there in a few minutes."

At Pud's, Roscoe ordered a draft beer and Fatty asked for a coffee, black.

"Coffee?" Roscoe asked.

"I've learned that I like beer a little too much," Fatty offered flatly.

"And so, what's going on with you?" Roscoe asked after a moment.

"Well, the astronaut job never came through," Fatty answered with a small, slow smile. "And I topped out at Doak's, and so then I went to work for the highway department, and that has been pretty much spectacular. Two weeks off every year, healthcare insurance that's pretty good if you never get sick, and, did I mention, a chance to get one hell of a suntan every year. It's glamorous."

"So what's next?" Roscoe asked, trying to sound upbeat.

"Vietnam."

"What?"

"I enlisted, Marines. At my age, with good appraisals from MHD, they say an officer position is possible. No guarantees, I mean going in I'd just be a grunt, but there are possibilities."

"Wow. There are a lot of people with questions about this war, Fatty. Are you sure about this?"

"It's Randy," he answered, and a shock wave went through Roscoe. "That's what I go by now, Randy."

After an awkward silence, Roscoe tried what seemed right. "Are you okay? If you are and this is really what you want to do, then great. But if you aren't, then..."

"Then what?" Fatty responded. "Look Roscoe, I don't know if I'm okay or not. But I do know some things. I know that I haven't done much with what I was given. I could have done better. You've done something with yourself. Most of the guys I know have too. This is a chance for me to do something important. I need that. I need to make myself proud."

"But you could stay here with the highway department, you could progress, move up. And you won't get shot. A lot of things could be worse."

And then Fatty said to Roscoe something he'd never forget, a thought he would take to his grave. "There is not much worse than feeling like you've let yourself down, is there?"

Though by local lore Mitchell was halfway to Vietnam, Randy Gilchrist never made it there. He was mowing grass on a steep shoulder on Highway 49 when a cloudburst came. The rain made the grass slick and his tractor slid and caught on a random boulder, flipped over, and pinned him underneath. He drowned in six inches of rain water. Four days later, on the very day they buried the best friend Roscoe would ever have, Tommy Corcoran's wife gave birth to triplets. The Oklahoma Tire and Supply Company gave them a brand new washer and dryer, the idea being there would be a lot of diapers to clean.

CHAPTER 32

When Roscoe come in from his morning walk, he found Adella, alone in the living room, looking at the album he had left opened on the footstool the night before. She was sitting the same chair where he had sat and was reading the clipping about Fatty.

"Can I get you a cup of coffee, Adella?" Roscoe asked gently, trying not to startle her.

"Oh, Roscoe, I didn't hear you come in. No, let me get you a cup. I was just reading this newspaper story. I didn't mean to be snooping or anything, truly I didn't," she said, closing the album.

"Don't be silly. Sit back down there and let me bring you a cup of coffee. And nothing in this house if off limits to you. You are part of this family."

Roscoe brought two cups in the from kitchen and handed one to Adella.

"Cream and sugar, right?"

"Yes, sir, that's right. And thank you very much."

"The boy you were reading about, the young man, rather, he was my best friend," Roscoe said, his eyes dropping. "We grew up here together."

"That's very sad," she replied. "So sad."

"It was a long, long time ago. I was just looking at that last night and remembering what it was like when we were kids. I miss him. I miss that time of my life."

"I bet you do," she replied.

"Today, we fish!" Frank announced coming into the room. "What are you two doing anyway, making lazy, slacking? Adella, may we have some of your fine scrambled eggs this morning? I feel I'm needing extra protein today. And maybe a biscuit? I'm partial to those simple canned ones from the fridge. Sonny boy, are you ready for a big morning of catch and release?"

"No keepers?" Roscoe replied.

"Oh, hell no. Fish scales and guts everywhere, not to mention you've got to murder the poor things first. Nope, it's only sport with me. Adella feeds me fine without me dragging home a bunch of bottom feeders. The more I think about it, I hope we don't even catch anything."

"Breakfast will be ready shortly gentlemen," Adella said brightly. "And I have a can of corn you can use for bait if you like."

"Superb," Frank said. "The poles are already in the trunk of the Merc. We are set." Frank gobbled an ample breakfast at a school boy's pace and then they were gone.

When they were there in the park, on the bench at the edge of Donut Bay, Frank held his pole in one hand and rubbed his belly with the other.

"That woman can cook, can't she?" he said with a smile.

"Dad, when I got here, you said Adella's cooking was slipping. Now you've got nothing but praise. What changed?"

"A few days with my son, that's what. A few days with your boy can change everything. I've had it real good, and you remind me of that."

"We all have," Roscoe replied smiling.

Frank squirmed on the bench, dug into his pocket and pulled something out. He held it tightly in the palm of his hand for a few seconds and then, without looking, he handed it to Roscoe.

"What's this?" Roscoe asked, even though he could tell perfectly well what it was. "Where'd it come from?"

"It's a bullet. It's the last bullet from George Mabry's pistol."

Roscoe was stunned. He tried to speak but the words had too little air behind them. "How did you get it? What's going on, dad?"

"I took it out of George Mabry's pistol myself, more than fifty years ago. I've hung on to it ever since. Not sure why, maybe I knew somehow that this day would come."

"I still don't know what you're talking about, dad," Roscoe replied.

"In the story you told me last night, the part where you were going to meet with Officer Buster Odom but then the meeting got canceled? Remember?"

"Yes, dad, I remember. It was one hell of a relief. I remember it well."

"Well," Frank said slowly, cautiously, "here's the whole story. After Harriet told you what she did, about the encounter with Bobby Cato, about the shooting and all, she knew she had burdened you with too much. She went to Officer Buster Odom and told him the same story she told you. She said she would leave it in his hands, but that she didn't want you to be caught up in the middle of it."

"She told him everything?"

"Yes, everything. And then he came to me and said he wouldn't be needing to talk with you after all because new information had been made available to him. I thanked him but I didn't ask him about this new information. I figured let well enough alone. But I could tell he wanted me to ask him about it, he wanted to tell me the story. And then, because I think he couldn't stand not to, he just blurted it out, the whole sad business."

"What did you say?" Roscoe asked, increasingly caught up in his father's telling of the story.

"Damn," Frank replied. "At first that was all I could think to say, just *damn*. But then Buster looked away from me and talked as though he was thinking out loud, if you know what I mean. He said that Harriet had told him where she hid the pistol, but that until he had the weapon in hand, all he really had to go on was the wild remembrance of a cooky old lady — not much of a case really, not enough to go on. Then he turned and looked at me in a way I'll never forget. And then he spoke. He said that he wouldn't be able to get out to the park to look for the pistol for a couple of days on account of him being pretty busy and all. Now Buster Odom was a good man and a fine police officer but he was never over-worked, never what you would call real busy. Then he just looked at me and didn't say anymore for what seemed like quite a while. Finally he just said, 'who knows if it will be there when I can get to it'. And then I knew what he was getting at."

"Oh no," Roscoe said, with a sense of where the story was headed.

"Your mother and I talked it over. We talked it over good. It wasn't anymore her idea than mine, we agreed. We agreed between us that it would be best for everyone concerned, best for the whole town, best especially for our family if that miserable episode would just fade into the past. We agreed that if Officer Odom found the pistol and was then obliged to carry on with some kind of investigation or to press charges against Harriet, that no good would come to anybody from it. Bobby Cato had been bullying good people, hurting good people, scaring them, all the time he was alive, and now it looked like he could do even more harm from the afterlife. And so we decided what to do. We came out here together, we looked in the tall weeds right over there and we found it. Then we came together and sat on this very bench, side by side, without talking for quite a while. I took the last bullet out of the cylinder and put it in my pocket and then your mother held out her hand. I gave her the pistol and she laid it in her lap. She was wearing a plaid flannel skirt and I remember what the thing looked like laying there against the fabric. She smiled at me and without saying a single word, she pointed to the middle of Donut Bay. The pistol was too heavy for her to throw. And so I did it, I threw the thing as far out there as I could. We vowed that day to never speak of the matter again. And we never did."

"Jesus Christ, dad!" Roscoe exclaimed. "I don't know what to say. I'm dumbfounded. Christ, why didn't you ever say anything about this?"

"Like I said, we just felt that to say anything more about it would just keep breathing life into the tragedy."

"But you could have at least told me. Why not me?"

"The truth? We told ourselves that we wanted you to be able to forget all of it, to let it drift away, and that talking about it would work against that. But the truth was, we didn't say anything to you because we were never certain that we'd done the right thing, plain and simple. We didn't know for sure then and I don't know for sure now.

Your mother and I, we weren't raised to hide things, to conceal and deceive. But in this case, that's what we did, right or wrong, that's what we did. I won't speak for your mother, but I didn't want to sit my little boy down and tell him I had done something that seemed right but might not have been. I've worried that I did the wrong thing for a long time. Right or wrong is a tough question when you have to decide it for yourself, not from some rule book or some ancient code."

"Don't you see, I've had the same worry, dad? Just because Buster Odom decided not to talk with me, I still could have come forward, and I didn't. And I've never known if I was right not to."

"You were a child, Roscoe, we were grown people, there's a big difference. Anyway, if it would have helped you for me to tell you about it, for that matter, if it would have helped me, then I wish I had. When you told me the story last night, I could see that you and me, we've been toting the same bucket of water, me for more than half my life and you for most of yours. I say we put that bucket down."

Roscoe stood up and went behind Frank and put his left hand on his dad's shoulder. With his right hand he threw the bullet as far as he could into the silver-plated surface of Donut Bay.

"About right there?" he asked Frank pointing to the tiny splash.

"Yep, just about right there."

Roscoe moved back around, sat on the bench beside Frank and steadied himself by putting his hands on his knees. Looking straight ahead, he asked his father a question.

"Are you afraid, dad?"

"Afraid of dying?"

"Yes."

"A little bit I guess. It's actually kind of hard to concentrate on your own death, even if it's just around the corner. It's a slippery idea. You focus on it, you put your mind against it and your mind, it won't stay put; pretty soon it slides off one direction or the other. Before you know it you're wondering how to keep the neighbor's cat out of your flower beds, or maybe what's the best price on new tires for the Merc. Maybe we're not meant to ponder it. But it is discernible, and yes a little frightening, if I'm down right honest about it."

"I guess it is a natural part of living, isn't it?" Roscoe offered.

"They say that it is, yes, and I suppose from a comfortable distance it seems so. But I have to tell you that up close it doesn't seem real natural. Enjoying the company of your children is natural. Walking on a beach with your wife is natural. Putting a caught fish back into the water because you know down deep that the life running through it is the same life that runs through us, that's natural. Picking a ripe tomato is natural. The prospect, rather the *certainty* that all of that will end, at least as far as we know, that seems *unnatural*."

"Anything I can do?" Roscoe asked.

"Only what you have done so well these few days. I've had a great time having you around here," Frank answered. "I can't wait for your next visit," he added with a quick wink.

"Good. I say we take Adella to dinner with us tonight. I think she'd like that. What do you think?"

"I think you are right. She'd like that very much," Frank answered. "Maybe somewhere kind of nice so she can dress up a little."

"Why not let her choose?"

"Perfect. Let's get out of here before we catch something. Help me up, I've been on this bench too long."

When Roscoe gripped his dad's hand to help him stand, his skin felt like paper.

CHAPTER 33

J anet had been close. The name of the joint was The Tarpon Tavern, not the Tarpon Bar and Grill, though, as Roscoe would learn, they served food and booze and so either name would have done. The original owner no doubt favored alliteration. The place was a small-ish, red-brick, flat-front building with large windows full of neon beer signs splashing the promise of good times out into the street. The front door was solid steel, the kind you might expect to see on a strip bar or an illegal betting establishment. A long black awning shaded the front windows and above the awning there hung a giant fake-looking fish, a tarpon he supposed, though he was no expert on gamefish species.

Inside Roscoe found a stereotypical St. Louis saloon, with dark wood tacky to the touch from years of cigarette smoke, and a long shiny bar that ran from near the front door straight to the back of the place where a partition wall hid a tiny grill kitchen on one side and the restrooms on the other. In the middle of the room there were a dozen or so wooden tables with oak chairs. All over the walls there were fish, some looking real and some not quite. Some were mounted in what seemed expert fashion, while others, which appeared to have been var-nished, were just kind of slung whimsically here and there. One large bass had a laminated news photo of Bill Bidwell, the owner of the St. Louis Cardinals football team who had taken his team and abandoned the city for sunny Arizona, sticking out of its mouth. The fish was either eating Bidwell or spitting him out, it was hard to tell.

There were no patrons in the bar when Roscoe came in, which favored his purpose for the visit. The bartender behind the far end of the bar was, he hoped, the one who was working the day Mary Lewellen stopped in for a confession. He was a short, tight-skinned man, maybe in his mid-forties. He looked up when Roscoe entered and smiled broadly.

"What can I get you, pal?" he asked.

"You have Bud?"

"I do, in bottles, not on draught."

"A bottle will be fine," Roscoe said, still scanning the place. "So this is The Tarpon Tavern, huh?"

"You might should say, it *was* The Tarpon Tavern," the bartender replied. "Things are changing."

"How so?"

"The new owner, my boss, he plans to turn the place into an internet cafe. Kids with laptops ordering lattes and mochas. I can hardly wait."

"He doesn't go for the fishing motif, huh?"

"No sir, he does not. Got big ideas this one. Can you imagine what tips are like in an internet cafe. I think I am coming to a fork in my career path."

"Let me ask you a question," Roscoe started, taking a sip of beer. "Where you working when Mary Lewellen came in? You know who I mean?"

"Yeah, I know who you mean," he replied, looking suspicious. "I was here, who wants to know?"

"I should have introduced myself. I'm Roscoe Hammer, the St. Louis County Prosecutor. My team is handling the Lewellen case."

"Oh, yeah, I think I've seen your picture in the paper before. What can I tell you? I covered every last bit of what I could remember with the police two or three times. Something new come up?"

"No, the case is before the grand jury, so I can't really discuss it, but I was just curious and wanted to come by and see this place in person."

"Swanky, huh?" the bartender said, laughing.

"Had you ever seen Ms. Lewellen in here before?"

"Nope. Not me, and the police talked to the owner and all the other barkeeps and nobody ever remembered seeing her in here before."

"And she just ordered a beer, washed up in the bathroom and then told you to call the police, is that right?"

"Yeah, in a nutshell, that was it. I mean she drank some of her beer. She stood up and went over there and stared at the wall of shame for a few minutes while she sipped. Nothing else I can remember."

"Wall of shame?" Roscoe asked. "What's that?"

"Over there," he replied, pointing to a collection of photographs in cheap individual frames hanging on the far wall. "You know how some joints give you a personal mug when you're a regular, well the previous owner, my original boss was into all this fishing crap and so if you were a regular, you could put a picture of yourself over there on the wall." Roscoe stood up and walked over to the wall and studied the photos. "They are supposed to be in some kind of fishing pose, I guess. Most of those old timers haven't been in here in years. Most of them go way back, according to my old boss. The new guy, the internet cafe king, he's going to trash all this old fishing shit and paint the place grey and white."

One photo, near the center of the collection, caught Roscoe's eye.

"Do you recognize this one, the one of the young woman standing in the surf holding a fly rod?"

"No. I know which one you mean. There's a shadow covering her face, the rest of her, in the bikini and all, if anybody that shape had been in here I think I'd remember. Who knows?"

"But you said Lewellen stood over here and stared at the photos that day while she was drinking her beer, is that right?"

"Yeah, she did. It was just kind of like she was daydreaming a little, you know what I mean?"

"Did she say anything?" Roscoe asked.

"She asked me if I'd ever been bonefishing in the Bahamas. I told her I wouldn't know a bonefish if one jumped in my lap. And the Bahamas, don't I wish? That was it."

Roscoe took the photograph of the young girl off the wall and slid the backing out of the frame. On the back of the picture he found in simple handwriting: *M.A.L. Freeport.* He walked back over to the bar and handed the photo to the bartender.

"You sure you don't recognize this one?"

"Nope. Like I said. That kind of figure doesn't show up in a place like this."

"What about Lewellen?" Roscoe asked. "She's young, slender."

"Well, she had on a baggy t-shirt when she was in here that day, so I'm not so sure about her figure. But she has dark hair and this girl looks like a blonde to me."

"Hair color can be changed."

"Yeah, I guess it can."

"Do me a favor," Roscoe said, "show this to the other bartenders, maybe even some of the older regulars and ask if anyone knows anything about her. I'll come back in a day or two and see if you've got anything. Will you do that? And ask your new boss if I can borrow the photo when I come back."

"I can guarantee you he won't care. He's already told me to trash all the old stuff. He wants to get the painters in here. I'll check around with the other guys."

Just then Roscoe's cellphone rang and the turned away from the bartender to answer it.

"Hello, this is Roscoe Hammer," he said.

"Sir, it's Maxine."

"Oh, yes, Maxine, what is it?"

"Ms. Preston called and would like to schedule a briefing with you before her case goes into final deliberations. She was hoping to meet with you tomorrow and I thought I should check with you before scheduling it."

"No, of course, Maxine, that's fine," he answered, slightly bewildered. Such a meeting was the kind of thing Maxine would routinely schedule on her own. "Maybe you could order in some sandwiches and we could meet in my office over lunch?" He waited a moment for Maxine to answer. When she didn't, he thought maybe they had been disconnected. "Are you there, Maxine? Sandwiches?"

"Ms. Preston has been working very hard, sir, if you don't mind me saying so. I thought, just perhaps we could do better than sandwiches in the office....sir."

"Lunch at the Carlton Club, maybe? You think that would be better?"

"I could make a reservation for you, sir. A table by the windows? I think she would find that very, well, very motivating. A nice reward. People on your staff work so very hard, sir."

"None harder than you, Maxine."

"Thank you sir."

Roscoe folded his phone shut and took one last mouthful of beer. About that time a young, well-dressed young man came through the swinging doors that separated the bar from the grill.

"Hey boss, meet the County Prosecutor," the bartender said.

"Roscoe Hammer," Roscoe said, extending his hand.

"Oh, yeah, I've heard the name. Nice to meet you." They shook hands and then the young man continued. "What brings you in? We've had quite a few official visits since that Lewellen thing. All the attention isn't exactly great for business, you know what I mean? But, we want to be helpful, right Dave?" he said, looking at his bartender.

"Mr. Hammer was wondering about this young lady," Dave said, handing him the photograph. "I told him I'd never seen her, but maybe you have."

"Nope, not me. Call Ronnie, his number is over there on the Rolodex. Ask him about her." Then, to Roscoe he added, "Ronnie's my night manager and bartender. If anybody knows anything about her, it would be him."

While Dave telephoned Ronnie, Roscoe asked the bar owner if he could borrow the photograph for a few days.

"You can have it. We're taking all these stuffed fish down. I guess that's what you call them, right, stuffed? Mounted, whatever, they're coming down. Gotta keep up with the changing times, you know what I mean? In another week or two all those photos will be in the dumpster out back. Hey, I gotta run. Nice meeting you. Dave will fill you in if he gets any info from Ronnie."

"Thanks, nice meeting you too. I appreciate the help."

Dave's phone conversation with Ronnie was short. He hung up and turned back to Roscoe.

"Ronnie knows her, not by name, but he remembers her. Said she used to come in regular with her old man five or six years ago. They split up and the guy moved somewhere out of state. She came in another couple of times, but then just stopped. That was it. There was nothing special about her, according to Ronnie. The previous owner begged her to put her picture on the wall because he wanted men to think women like her came in here regularly, which of course they don't. But anyhow, that's all he knew."

"No name? Not even a first name?"

"Sorry, no. You might as well take the photo with you. I overheard him tell you he didn't care. Nobody around here is going to know anymore than Ronnie. He's kind of the official Tarpon historian."

"Thanks for your help."

"No problem. Come back for a latte some time."

CHAPTER 34

T
wo very different perquisites adorned the St. Louis County Prosecutor's job. The first, with which Roscoe Hammer was
immensely comfortable, was a low-slung, under-featured Chevrolet
Impala in a color very close to dull army green. The second, a mem-
bership to the Carlton Luncheon Club, a lofty perch on the 37th floor
of the Laclede Gas building in downtown St. Louis, made him feel
like one more public sector sponger in an ill-fitting suit. He didn't
like it there one bit, but he went now and then when duty called — as
it seemed, at least in Maxine's eyes, it did today. He sat alone, in the
warm glow of the city's gentry, waiting for Janet Preston to arrive, and
tugged at his suit jacket, trying to make a rowdy lapel lay smooth.

Before Janet arrived, Peter Davenport bounced through the door
with three short, well-scrubbed men wearing three-piece suits in tow.
He saw Roscoe out of the corner of his eye and motioned for the three
musketeers to go on to his table across the room while he stopped to
have a word with the county's top lawyer.

"Roscoe," he said energetically, "good to see you out mingling
with your electorate."

"Peter, how are you?" Roscoe replied, extending his hand. "Who
are your menservants over there?"

"Them? Oh, bankers," he answered with mock disgust. "It takes
a peculiar type to be a banker, you know it? I don't need to borrow
any money, and I will make deplorable banker jokes through all of
lunch. I will pretend to forget their names. I will sip martini's while
they drink iced tea. And in the end they'll pick up the tab. They have
beautiful offices, fabulous suits, enormous personality deficits and at

the end of the day they have nothing to show for their efforts, no buildings built, no criminals incarcerated, nothing. Odd, don't you agree, rather like moles? So, what brings you down into the dark center of the city today?"

"I have a luncheon briefing with one of my assistant prosecutors, Janet Preston. I think Judge McElroy has talked to you about her."

"Preston, yes, yes he did. Your nominee, I take it?"

"My recommendation, yes, she is."

"Well," Davenport said, scratching the back of his head, "she sounds good, but she's a little more unknown than we'd like, to be honest with you."

"We can take care of that over the next two or three years...the right cases, the exposure."

"The right results," Davenport added with a sly wink.

"You don't need to worry about that, Peter."

"Well, we'll see. Anyway, I'm having a little meeting with the Judge after lunch, over on the quiet reading side of the club. Maybe you could join us? We could talk about her a little more."

"If the timing works out, I'll come find the two of you. Don't be too hard on the bankers."

Janet Preston came into the room and the maitre d' directed her to Roscoe's table. Before she had taken five steps every idle eye in the room had gone to her. A Buddhist would describe her aura as perfectly balanced. She was pretty but not glamorous, intelligent looking, professionally dressed in a simple but not dull dark blue suit. She moved with confidence but not pride, and without seeming flirty or overly familiar, she offered everyone she passed a broad, engaging, genuinely friendly smile. In many ways, she reminded Roscoe of his daughter Kit who had only recently left a job with one of the major television networks and was on the verge of making him a grandfather for the first time. Like her siblings, Kit always worked hard and had taken nothing for granted. The very same could be said of Janet.

"What a beautiful place!" she exclaimed.

"Your first time here, I take it?" Roscoe asked.

"Yes. What a treat."

"Maxine felt you deserved a nice lunch. She has a very high opinion of you."

"What a sweetheart? You're a good boss, but she makes you an even better one. An assistant can make so much difference. I hope I have one like her someday."

"I'd say there is a good chance you will," he replied, looking peacefully out the window. "When I come here, which is not often, she always requests a table by the window. I like seeing all the people down on the street, on the sidewalks, eating hamburgers and big folded slices of pizza while they windowshop. They are more like me than the people in this room. As I get older, I grow more and more certain of that."

"Well, anyway," she replied, "it's very nice. Thank you and thanks to Maxine."

"So, where are we on the Lewellen case? They go into final deliberations tomorrow, is that right?"

Janet drew a breath and began to answer when a server stepped to the table.

"Let's order, and then you can fill me in," Roscoe said. "Everything here is very good. I like the swordfish, but anything you like, fire away."

They ordered, the waiter disappeared and Janet started.

"Yes, final deliberations tomorrow. I don't expect it to take long. We've shown them everything we have and I sense that they feel they've gotten what they need. We laid it all out in a fairly traditional way. The police findings, the medical examiner's report, the timeline, which by the way works pretty well, a couple of expert witnesses on the psychological dimension of domestic violence, and of course, Lewellen's own testimony. We didn't bury them with a lot of extraneous stuff. My assessment is that her testimony overshadowed everything else."

"Convincing?" Roscoe asked flatly.

"Very."

"To you?" he probed further.

Janet paused for a moment, took a drink of water and then got, as far as he was concerned, to the heart of the matter. "Yes and no," she answered. "And before you call me indecisive, let me explain."

"Take your time," he said with a kind smile, "no hurry."

"The grand jury believes, I believe, the court reporter believes, the janitor with his ear to the wall believes one thing: Scarbo would have killed her and her daughters. Who knows when, or how, or what would have triggered it, but it has been clear to everyone in the courtroom that this guy was going to do it. When she tells her story, the story of her life with this guy, it is utterly believable. When she speaks, you can tell that she is more at peace now than she has been in five years, even though she could be headed to jail. In jail she won't be bull-whipped with the buckle end of a belt. In foster care her girls won't be poisoned with prescription pain killers, one of Scarbo's favorite threats. She doesn't come across as proud or defiant or indifferent. She just seems....peaceful, I guess. It's as if she did what she felt she had to do, and now, whatever happens, she'll be okay. If you believe her, and all the evidence supports her claims, then you are left where you always are in these cases: Was there any other reasonable course of action? Why not just leave him? Couldn't she have gone to the police? Why didn't she?"

"How did she handle those questions?" Roscoe asked.

"Interestingly, with simple facts and very little emotion. She has a job, and she's the sole support for two young girls. She has $480 in the bank. She owns the house, but it carries a $300,000 mortgage. Her car has 85,000 miles on it and needs tires. Her only blood relative is an aunt in California who lives on Social Security. Just leave? And go where? Leave the house behind, leave the job behind? She did a great job of stepping through the impracticalities of the why-not-just-leave-him scenario. And in the background, the jury is reminded again and again, that if the plan doesn't work, if things don't go just right, Scarbo will kill all three of them. To top off that part of her testimony, she related to the jury an episode that left them speechless. One night Scarbo started spinning out of control, punched her around pretty good and then decided to walk down to the mini-mart for a pack of cigarettes. She took the girls and went to a shelter on south Grand. The next day, she went to pick them up after school and learned they had already been released to Scarbo. She found both of them at home, at the kitchen table with Scarbo, each eating a bowl of cereal. On the table there was a vial of Vicodin. When Lewellen walked in, he picked up the vial, shook it, laughed and whispered 'next time'. You know what Vicodin would do to a five year old?"

"What about protection, the police?" Roscoe asked, already knowing — as any good lawyer does — what the answer would be.

"Mulligan testified, and honestly boss, he did his best and a pretty good job. The grand jury must have submitted a half dozen specific questions to him — how much protection, during what hours, for how long, what about the girls at school, etcetera, etcetera. As I said, he did his best, but to his credit, in the end he told them the truth, that the police could not watch Scarbo, Lewellen and her girls twenty-four hours a day, indefinitely. If he was determined, Scarbo would get an opening, a chance to do what he said over and over he would do if she involved the police."

"You said yes and no. What's the 'no' part?"

"It's not what she's telling us, it's what she may be leaving out. It's as if there is part of the truth she's decided is too risky to tell. But that doesn't make sense to me. She went into this risking a prison sentence, foster care for her kids. How could the whole truth make it a riskier proposition? But, my instinct is that something's missing. Unfortunately maybe, I don't think the grand jury shares my instinct. I think they believe they are dealing with the whole truth."

"Nobody gets the whole truth, not us, not the police, not the jury. There's always something missing. What you have to hope is that whatever it is, it wouldn't redefine a just outcome. This isn't a perfect business we're in."

"We're not going to get an indictment. I'm sorry. I feel like I've let you down," Janet said, looking away.

"Come on, Janet, you should know you're not letting me down. This is what we do. We assemble facts, we ask questions, we present what we have to the grand jury, we advocate for the people. The grand jury makes a determination. If we disagree strongly enough, if we feel we have a case, then the statute provides that we can proceed to trial anyway."

"Have you ever done that?"

"No. I've never been willing to substitute my opinion for the collective opinion of jury of average citizens. When I was young enough to do that, prideful enough to do that, thank God I wasn't the prosecuting attorney. Overtime you learn to trust your neighbors."

"So this one is over?" she asked.

"Yes, it's over."

Roscoe wanted to tell her about his trip to the bar, about the picture on the wall. But to what end? She was trained to gather and present evidence, to arrange that evidence so that it would serve as proof of something. The photo wasn't evidence, it didn't prove anything, it only gave rise to curious calculations, to speculation. It meant something, he was sure of that, but at the same time it meant nothing. It wouldn't help her, just as it had not helped him.

"You'll handle the press conference. Lay it out for them plain and simple. The grand jury did not indict, period. The substance of the case, the evidence, the testimony, it's all sealed. When they ask about the grand jury's reasoning, you can give them only one answer. The grand jury's job is to decide if there is probable cause to believe that a crime has been committed, and if there is probable cause to believe it was committed by the accused. Since the accused in this case stipulated to the act of killing Scarbo, you can only conclude that the jury decided that it was not a criminal act, that is was a justifiable because of the demonstrated threat that Scarbo posed to Lewellen and her daughters. That's as much as you can give them. You'll be all right, yes?"

"I can handle it. Will you be there?"

"No, I won't, which leads me to the next thing I wanted to talk to you about," Roscoe answered, looking across the room to the quiet reading side of the club where a half dozen newspapers hung on special racks and big leather sofas and chairs were arranged to encourage leisurely reading or friendly discussion.

On the far side of that part of the club, near floor-to-ceiling windows that looked out over the Mississippi River, he could see Judge Lawrence McElroy and Peter Davenport locked in conversation. McElroy was the circuit judge in charge of the St. Louis County grand jury. The oldest and most tenured sitting judge in the history of the county, he was solely responsible for selecting jurors for each of three, four-month panels for the year, for appointing a foreman for each panel, and for helping prosecutors organize case material that was put before the grand jury. Lastly, jurors were permitted to submit questions pertaining the law to the judge, even though he did not preside over the process the way a judge would in a normal trial. He was the most widely respected judge in all of eastern Missouri, and was well-known and admired throughout the region. Because of his role in managing the grand jury, he was very familiar with all of the county's assistant prosecutors. Janet Preston was his favorite.

"You see Judge McElroy over there?"

"Yes, who's he with? I don't recognize him?"

"That is Peter Davenport. He's a prominent, very successful, and very old commercial real estate developer, not just here, nationwide. He's a Republican with lots of influence in state and regional politics."

"Have your paths crossed?" Janet asked, cautiously.

"Early on he was helpful to me....well, at least not hurtful. We've always kept a respectful distance, each of us knowing sort of intuitively that the other is not our cup of tea. I'm a Republican because way back when, I had to be one thing or the other. He's a Republican because God hates Democrats."

"He looks ancient," Janet said.

"Eighty-five, eighty-six, something like that. Older than Judge McElroy who is turning eighty-three this weekend."

"Wow, and still all that influence?"

"Yes, regrettably, because he's still going. He's never stopped, in business or in politics. Once you stop, it's like taking your hand out of a bucket of water. It's as if you were never there. But as long as you keep going, the influence continues. People like Davenport know that."

"What are they talking about? It looks serious. Do you know?"

"They are talking about the end of my career and the beginning of yours."

CHAPTER 35

F rank Hammer was sitting at his kitchen table with a drab, grey bathrobe pulled tightly around himself. On the table there was a tablet, a yellow legal tablet, and a ballpoint pen.

"Adella," he hollered, "I need your help."

And she came to him quickly, dutifully, as she had for so many years.

"What is it? How can I help?"

"My handwriting is no good anymore, I've tried, believe me, it's damn near illegible, looks like hieroglyphics. I need for you to write some things down for me, some personal things. Your penmanship is still perfect. Will you help me?"

"Of course I will, Mr. Frank. But is it important? I really think you should be in your bed trying to rest."

"What it is, Adella, is much more important than my rest. Are you ready?"

Adella took up the pen and looked at him with resolve. Whatever it was, she was ready.

"This goes to Roscoe, my son."

Roscoe, you are my oldest child and so these final details fall to you. When you read this, I will be gone, on my way to whatever is next. It occurs to me that I may have no way of knowing if you comply with my requests, but then again, you have no way of knowing that I won't. So, just do, please.

The allocation of my remaining assets is of course spelled out in my will. These assets are not vast, and the arithmetic of my distribution is simple: I have loved the three of you equally and so the three of you shall receive

*an equal share. In no case will the amount change your lives, and in no case
will it measure up to the joy you have given me.*

*I wish to be cremated and placed beside your mother. Jeffery Jessup,
the boy who took over the funeral home from his old man, he knows all of
this. Now the tricky part. There shall be no ceremony. I cannot take to the
great beyond a final image of my three, wonderful children in a sad circle at
the graveyard. No ceremony. I fear Hannah, my baby, may object to this.
Of the three of you, she was the most churchy. But you and Andy, I'm confident, can persuade her. If you wish, at some later date, when it is convenient to be together, have a little drink and remember all the great
times...there were so many. That will be ceremony enough.*

*The only thing not spelled out anywhere is the disposition of the old Mer-
cury. I hope, Roscoe, that you being the oldest will take it for yourself. Drive
it back home and take it through St. Louis's best neighborhoods on warm summer days. Drive slow and tune the radio to a station that plays Sinatra — roll
the windows down. I am sure that Hannah and Andy will not object to this
one, slight imbalance. I like to think of you enjoying the last little shred of me.*

*Always — and this is the most important thing — always remember
that the three of you have been the center of my life. You have made me
proud and grateful and happy. Remind Hannah and Andy of this every
chance you get.*

*And, oh yes, young Jessup has already been paid, remember that. He
is trustworthy I suppose, but who knows?*

"I guess that's all," he said, smiling at Adella. "Do you think it
sounds okay, not too maudlin? I don't want it to sound all pitiful."

"I've got it all down, Mr. Frank, every word," she answered, trying not to cry. " I think it is beautiful, not maudlin, not pitiful."

"Well, I think it is important to have some things, some specific
things, down in writing. That way people don't have to be wondering.
You know what I mean?"

"I do, sir, yes I do. And the way you have put all this is very good,
very, very good. Now you should go and rest, and not worry about
these details."

"That's what a man does, Adella," he said softly. "A man must
worry about the details."

"Well, you've done enough, I think."

"You know, Adella, I roam around this old house, and I look at the pictures, the souvenirs, the knickknacks, and what I see, all I see, is my life, my beautiful life. And I don't want it to end. But I will not go out a complainer. God hates a complainer and all too soon, his opinion of me will matter greatly. I was given everything I needed, Adella. There was a time when I thought I wanted a million bucks in the bank, an amount that would make my family safe. But it turned out that I didn't need that, they didn't need that. What we all needed was what we got, and more. I'm tired. I don't want to go to the hospital, I want to stay here."

"I know, Mr. Frank," she said, almost whispering. "The doctor said that there's nothing they can do for you there that we can't do here with your medicine and all."

"Good."

"And I know about the bottle of Jack Daniels. I know where it is. And so, if you need your medicine, you tell me. And if you need your Jack Daniels, you can tell me that too. I brought my nightclothes, and my toothbrush and my face cream. And so I'll be staying here for a few nights, just until you are better."

"Thank you, Adella," he said slowly, "I'll have just a touch of whiskey if you are sure you don't mind."

CHAPTER 36

"The fact that I ran unopposed in this last election was not an accident," Roscoe said to Janet.

"What do you mean?"

"I mean it was *arranged*. It was part of a deal, a deal brokered by Davenport and some of his cohorts, a deal with the Democrats."

"What kind of deal?" she asked, alarmed.

"The Democrats had a young guy, an impressive young guy they thought about running against me. He's about to become a partner at Snow and Gladden. West Point graduate, Army Ranger, Notre Dame Law — like I said, impressive. Well, Davenport and team went to their peers on the other side and offered them a deal. You keep the Army Ranger out of this one, and we will persuade Roscoe Hammer to make this his last term."

"Why? What were they after? Were you party to this deal?"

"No, I was not. To answer your first question, what they were after is an orderly transition to a younger Republican St. Louis County prosecuting attorney, someone whose career is more in front of them than behind. They were after an organized transfer of this job from one Republican to another, a controlled succession. They want to hold this seat, my seat, and they know they can't do it with me very much longer. So, from Davenport's perspective, it's a smart move. I get to go out on top, as they say, and the Party gets four years to prepare my successor."

"And the Democrats, what do they get? Why take such a deal?" Janet asked with her eyes wide.

"They avoid the worst thing in all of politics, running against an incumbent," he answered. "Two years ago, in United States Senate and House races, more than eighty percent were won by incumbents. And this is a Congress with approval ratings below twenty percent. Of all the factors you can imagine — education, gender, wealth, good looks, height, weight, ethnicity, hair color, shoe size — in a political contest, absolutely nothing is more predictive of the outcome than incumbency. It trumps all the others....*combined.* An incumbent can cheat on his spouse, steal from charities, burn churches and drive drunk and still get re-elected."

"Why aren't you furious? Can they just run you out of the job like that?"

"I was at first, and so was Judge McElroy. And, so was Rusty Solich," he said, referring the St. Louis County executive whose career as the county's top politician had largely coincided with his own. The two had been good personal friends and staunch political allies for twenty-five years or more.

"But finally, we all, including me, concluded that the plan made sense. It's time for me to move on, to try something else while I still have time for a second act. And the Party needs new young, strong people in big jobs. Pretty soon, Rusty will face the same thing, and he knows it. And so, even though I could bow my neck, run again four years from now and take my chances, I'm not going to. It's not what's best for me or my family or the job."

"What *are* you going to do?" Janet asked slowly, cautiously.

"In the short term, I'm going to convince people that you should be my successor. Longer term, I'm not sure."

"You're kidding. You can't be serious!"

"I'm serious, yes. And so is Judge McElroy. And so is Rusty Solich. You have a pretty good base of support. And the Judge is over there right now trying to broaden it with Peter Davenport. Yes, Janet, I'm serious. We all are."

"Oh, I don't know boss," Janet said slowly, placing a worried hand over her mouth. "I don't know if I can be the person you're after. The last thing I want to do is let you down, conclude your run by losing the job to the Democrats."

"Come on Janet, what are you talking about? You've got to want this job. An attorney of your caliber would be paid three times what you're making with us if you went to a firm. Why would you stay unless you aspired to higher office, which, by the way is nothing to be ashamed of? This young Democrat, I may have made him sound too good. He's beatable. You are a better lawyer. And you will have had ten years experience as an assistant prosecutor. We have four years to get you ready, trust me, we can do it."

"Of course I would love the job, the truth is I've dreamt of it," she admitted, trying to keep her voice low. "But do you really think I'm ready?"

Before Roscoe could answer, he saw Judge McElroy approaching them from over her shoulder. "Hold on, the Judge is coming over," he whispered. "You are going to be invited to his birthday party. Very big deal. Act surprised."

"Roscoe, Janet, how are you?" McElroy asked, pulling out a chair and planting himself at the table. "What luck running into you, Janet? They — whoever they are — are throwing me a very big birthday party this Saturday night at the St. Louis Club. I would love it if you would come. Lots of people will be there, from the ruff-n-tumble Irish, my folks, to the creme de la creme, my wife's crowd. Roscoe and his lovely wife Amy will be there, and I do hope you will join us. Not that it is of any particular interest to you, but of great significance to me and Roscoe, I'm told there will be free booze. We'll seat you and your date at my table. Please say yes."

"Why of course, Judge, I'd love to be at your party. You can count on it. Maybe I'll buy a new outfit. It sounds like quite a bash."

"One condition, Janet, you must save a dance for me. There will be an orchestra and dancing, and if I do say so myself, I'm pretty smooth on the dance floor. You and I will make the crowd take notice. Agreed?"

"I'll try to keep up. Sounds wonderful."

Then turning to Roscoe, the Judge's look became more serious. "Could we have a quick word in the lounge area?" he asked.

"Don't bother moving," Janet inserted alertly. "I need to use the restroom."

"Thank you Janet," McElroy said. "Truly, all we need is just a minute or two. If I'm gone when you get back, I'll look forward to seeing you Saturday night."

As soon as she was out of earshot, Judge McElroy gave Roscoe a quick report on his discussion with Davenport. "The asshole may be a problem," he said flatly. "She's not enough this, too much that. She's a she. She's too unknown," he grumbled, avoiding the word Roscoe knew was hiding between the lines. "You know his line of ancient bullshit as well as I do. I just wanted you to know that he will have to be dealt with. I'm still in her corner, so is Rusty. And we'll have a couple of mystery guests at the party whose ears we can bend. We can get this done, Roscoe, but we've got some tough sledding ahead. Oh well, we Irish love a good brawl," he concluded with a laugh.

"I'll miss you, Judge," Roscoe said.

"You mean when you're not in the job anymore, or when I'm dead?"

"Either."

Leaving the dining room, McElroy passed Janet on her way back to the table. He made a silent Fred Astaire move and gave her a happy wave. And then, turning back to Roscoe, he signaled a "thumbs up".

"You look preoccupied," she said to Roscoe who was gazing out the window, looking again at all the people on the street below. "Is something wrong?"

"No, no, not at all," he answered wistfully. "I was just thinking how, you and me and all our colleagues in the office, we're the lawyers for all those common people down on the sidewalk. We're their lawyers. When they get swindled, or when they get mugged, or when their kids get shot at by gang-bangers, it falls to us to advocate for them, to help them find justice. It's a great job, Janet, and you'll be fabulous at it. I'm positive."

"Thank you Roscoe, I owe you a lot. I'm going to try and make you proud."

"Remember, at the Lewellen news conference, keep it short and simple. Don't let them bait you, right?"

"Got it boss."

Judge McElroy's report played on Roscoe's mind that night and all the next day. He knew that the Judge had understated the trouble he saw ahead with Davenport and his cronies. *Tough sledding?* He knew better. It would be what his father called a "snot-slinging, eye-ball gaugin', ear-bitin' free for all". Don't bring a knife to a gun fight, he reminded himself. He had a plan.

"Sir," Maxine said, bringing him back into the moment. "Ms. Lewellen is here whenever you are ready."

"Thank you, Maxine," he answered, looking over his shoulder to make sure the photo was still there. "Bring her in, please."

Mary Lewellen's expression was a cautious, curious combination of relief and fear. She looked pretty in a simple way, with her hair pulled back into a ponytail, and little or no make-up. Her blue eyes avoided his as she carefully extended her hand.

"How do you do, Ms. Lewellen. Please have a seat. My name is Roscoe Hammer and I am the St. Louis County prosecuting attorney. I promise you that this won't take long."

"Yes, I know who your are," she answered evenly.

"First, I am required to remind you that you are entitled to have your attorney here with you for this meeting if you wish. It's your right."

"My attorney said I didn't need him, that all the questions were over, that the case was over."

"He's right. This case has ended. We are left with only a few formalities," he answered, moving slightly in an effort to catch her elusive eyes. "The grand jury has decided not to indict you in the death of Michael Scarbo, your former boyfriend and housemate. Do you have any questions or about their decision?"

"No."

"As I believe your lawyer has explained to you, all the evidence presented to the grand jury in your case, all the testimony, the forensic findings, everything displayed or discussed will remain secret. Any of your personal documents or belongings will be returned to you. Do you have any questions about this?"

"No."

"There are some legal papers in this envelope that spell out in a formal way what I have just told you. I suggest you keep these documents where you keep other important papers," he said, pushing the packet toward her. "They are your record that the grand jury found no probable cause to believe you had committed a crime." Just then he saw a tiny smile come across her face. "Did I say something amusing?"

"No, no, it's just that people like you imagine that people like me have important papers, that's all, I didn't mean anything by it." Then, taking the envelope, she asked, "Can I go now?"

"Just one more thing," Roscoe said, standing up. "I need a glass of water. Would you like one?" She shook her head as he walked to the console on the wall to his right. "Janet Preston, the assistant prosecuting attorney responsible for your case is holding a press conference right now to convey the grand jury's decision. We hope this will spare you any unwanted encounters with the news media. This is important because you too are bound by the rule of secrecy."

When he turned to walk back to his desk, he saw what he had expected and feared. Her eyes were glued to the photograph he had placed alongside a few of his own family photos on the credenza behind his desk. Her face was pallid, almost ghostly and the skin at the corner of her eyes tightened. She began to rub her hands together and he could see her chest heave.

"Did you see someone you know?" he asked taking up the photograph as he sat down. She looked at him and started to answer but then stopped. For a moment her eyes watered and she looked as though she might cry.

"No," she answered, pulling herself back together.

"Are you sure? It seemed like you were looking at this photograph," he said, placing it on his desk in front of her. "Do you recognize this person?"

"There's a shadow across her face. How could anybody recognize her?"

"On the back of the photo, it says: 'M.A.L. Freeport'. Does that mean anything to you? Are those your initials?"

"Yes, they are. So what? Are we through? You said the questions were over."

"Ms. Lewellen, yes, you are free to leave whenever you wish," he said. She stood, tucked the envelope under her arm and started toward the door. But then she stopped, paused and turned back toward him. She looked hurt and defiant.

"What is it that you think you know? What special part of the truth do you think you've uncovered? Do you think that you've somehow figured out that Michael wasn't a monster, that his threats weren't real, that I made it all up?"

"I think this is a picture of you. I think you've done some fishing, maybe in Freeport, the Bahamas. But you told the grand jury you've never fished and I don't know why you'd lie about that. You told the grand jury that you'd never been to that bar before, but if I'm right and this is a picture of you, then you have. Once again, I can't figure out why you'd lie. It makes me wonder if there's a bigger lie somewhere."

The color was back in her face, and when she spoke, he was surprised, maybe even impressed, by the calm, measured way in which she took him on.

"Before anything more is said, let me explain something." She pointed to the small law library that occupied one entire wall of his office, and said, "I don't know if there are tricks in those books that would allow you to drag me back through all of this again, and again, and again. But if there are, and they allow you do put me through it a hundred times over, you need to know one certain thing: My story will never change — not even a single word."

"There aren't tricks in those books, those are the laws we live by, not tricks."

"Laws, not tricks? Aren't you naive? Well, anyway, as I said, my story would never change, and the decision of the jury would be the same, over and over again. It would be because they believed, as I believed, that he was going to kill me and my daughters, period. They believed it, and that belief was what they needed to find their way to justice."

"It's not up to you to decide what the grand jury needs to make a just decision. You don't get to organize the evidence against you, it doesn't work that way."

"Mr. Hammer, I don't want to argue with you. Let me just repeat what I said a minute ago, my story will never change."

"I heard you the first time. As I said, you are free to go now."

"Before I do, let me tell you a few more things, things anybody could have found out, things they could have seen if they had looked. I'm doing this because you strike me as a good man, and I think you deserve to know as much as I can safely tell you. I'm a good person too, Mr. Hammer, but I have a sense that you aren't so sure about that right now. Decide later."

Roscoe sat back in the chair behind the desk and she resumed her position in the guest chair on the other side. As she started, she appeared calmer, less angry. It seemed that she had a story she needed to tell, if only she could find a way to do it without putting herself or her children back into danger. He was reminded of something he had observed throughout his career as a prosecutor; people really want to tell their story. They want to be understood.

"When I was one year old, my parents were killed in a car crash. I was adopted by two of the most beautiful people in the world, Paul and Mary Ann Lewis. They are both dead now — cancer. They, we, lived in a modest house on McPherson, only blocks from the Cathedral Basilica where we attended mass every week. When I was old enough, I went to Rosati Kain, just across the street from the Cathedral. No child was ever more loved than I, and never by any finer, harder-working, more decent people that Paulie and Midge Lewis, as everyone knew them. When I was two or three, they adopted another girl, a year older than me, named Maggie. We grew up together on McPherson Street, went to school together, adored our parents and came to adore each other. We became sisters."

"You testified you had only one relative, an aunt in California," he interjected.

"I said she was my only living *blood* relative, and she is. Please, let me go on. When my sister and I were grown, we both got married. I found a wonderful guy, the father of my two daughters who was killed in an accident. His name was, and my name still is Lewellen. My sister married a Jefferson County hick who had trouble finding his way home at night. She finally got tired of him and his girl friends and they broke up in a pretty nasty way. Paulie, who was a bricklayer with hands like mallets threatened to kill the guy if he didn't leave town, which, on account of him being a colossal coward, he did. After the divorce was final, my sister decided to drop her married name and reclaim the name of her parents, Lewis. And to make a completely fresh start, she dropped her first name, Maggie, Margret really, and began to use her middle name instead. Her middle name is Ann."

Three blocks down, a friend named Ann Lewis. The words staggered him. He drew a breath, but it was insufficient and he gasped again. Had they — he, Janet, the system — had gotten it wrong? His original instincts, for all they were worth, came rushing back. Do we know who did this? Do we have the right suspect?

"And so," Lewellen continued, "if you are a normal person, not a person of means, not a person of power or privilege, not a lawyer with a wall of books — like I say, a normal person — and you see someone you love, someone like a little sister, threatened again and again, and you know something awful is going to happen soon, and you have a chance, a slim chance to do something, do you take that chance, or do you wait.....wait until God knows what happens? What would *you* do?"

"I, I would…"

"I know," she said, "you think you know what you would do. You have trained all your life to be sure what you would do. You know what the books on the wall would have you do. But let me tell you something, Mr. Hammer, you do not know what you would do. I swear to God, you do not know for sure."

"And so, you made a bet, a bet that you were less likely to go to jail than she. If you stipulate to the act of killing him, then the jury's focus shifts away from 'who' to 'why'. And the 'why' is obvious, and compelling."

"I've said as much as I can, Mr. Hammer. If, as you said earlier, I'm free to go now, then I think I should. I should go."

"Wait, Ms Lewellen, a man is dead. Doesn't that bother you?"

"Mr. Hammer, there are no perfect people in this story. But the one truly bad person in the story is dead. People make mistakes. I made an awful mistake when I let him into our lives. I have scars that will never go away and I have two little girls who will probably never be as happy and carefree as two little girls should be. They may never be completely all right, and I'll have to live with that for the rest of my life. But I'm going to do the best I can to create a normal life for the three of us, the best I know how."

"So you get to decide who is truly bad? You know I could still pursue this?"

"With what? With that photograph? If you think that you and your books can make all of this better, then I guess you will have to do what you think is right. Good bye, Mr. Hammer."

Roscoe followed her to the door, and before she left, he extended the photograph. "Would you like to have this?" he asked.

"Like I told you, Mr. Hammer, I don't recognize that person. But thank you."

And with that, she was gone. He went back to his desk and put both his hands on the back of his neck. His head was down when Maxine came into the office.

"Are you all right, sir?" she asked. "You said earlier you wanted to see me when Ms. Lewellen left. Should I come back later?"

"No, no, Maxine, please sit down. You're right, I need you to take care of a couple of things for me. That's why I wanted to see you."

"Yes, sir, what can I do?"

"When you go out to lunch I need you to pick up a box of cigars for me to take to the Judge's birthday party tomorrow night. I've written down the kind he likes," he said, handing her a piece of paper. "And, here's my credit card, just sign my name."

"Anything else?" she asked.

"Oh, yes, I almost forgot. Call the florist and order some flowers to be sent to my daughter Kit. You have her address I believe. Something cheery, maybe some daisies?"

"Is everything all right?" Maxine asked with a concerned look.

"Yes, yes, Kit is just fine, and so is the baby. But she's a week overdue and she's a little down in the dumps. She really wants to get on with the process. This is just to cheer her up, that's all."

"A week? That isn't bad really, especially with her first."

"That's right. And if nothing happens this weekend, they plan on inducing labor next week. So one way or another, she doesn't have long to wait."

"Good, then, I'll take care of it. As you say, something cheery."

"Thank you, Maxine," he said, thinking to himself how much he would miss her. "You're a life-saver."

"Don't mention it, sir."

When Maxine got back to her desk, the phone rang. She used the intercom to let Roscoe know it was Judge McElroy calling.

"I'll pick up," he told her. "Judge, how are you?"

"Not great, laddie, not great at all. I just finished eating a shit sandwich and it's not even lunchtime yet."

"Davenport?"

"That's correct. I spent an hour and a half trying to reason with him. He's out. Says he's got a couple of candidates in mind who he is certain will sell better than Janet. He won't budge."

"Did he say who?"

"Hell no. Said he wasn't ready to unveil them, he actually used that word, *unveil*, for Christ-sakes. Said his thinking was still *in flux*, which is a lie. His mind has been made up for weeks. Said he was just informing me because he didn't want me to get myself too committed to Janet. Didn't want me to get embarrassed."

"What did you tell him?"

"I told him to kiss my Irish ass, that's what."

"Good answer," Roscoe said with a chuckle. "Is the governor going to be at your party?"

"Yes, I'm told he will be. Why, what are you thinking?" the Judge asked, intrigued by the question.

"Oh, nothing important. Don't worry about it. Just stick with me on this Janet business Judge, I need you on my side."

"There's nothing that would un-stick me, laddie."

"You still smoke Cohiba's?"

"Love them!"

"I'll have a little surprise for you tomorrow night."

"I'll look forward to that. See you then."

Roscoe hung up and saw Maxine standing in the doorway.

"The flowers will be delivered this afternoon. They had fresh daisies. I took the liberty of providing the message: 'Thinking of you, love Mother and Dad'".

"Perfect, Maxine. Thank you. Would you shred this for me?" he asked handing her the photograph from bar.

"Of course."

"And, Maxine, get the governor's office on the phone, please."

CHAPTER 37

For Roscoe, one of the county's two top elected officials, and his wife of more than thirty years, being on the social circuit was familiar. She, he readily acknowledged and genuinely appreciated, was better at it than he. Naturally gregarious, good-looking, smart and pretty good on the dance floor, she was his secret weapon. She got him through things.

But the night of Judge McElroy's birthday party was different. Roscoe wanted to be there. He wanted to have a few drinks, a few laughs with his old friend, and dance badly with his gorgeous wife. Change was afoot and he wanted to have some fun.

When they came through the double doors leading into the St. Louis Club's main ballroom, what awaited was a stunning reflection of how much the Judge was adored and revered and by how many. There was a sea of people, at least two hundred, Roscoe guessed, all laughing, smiling, greeting one another. A dozen tuxedoed waiters moved amongst them like silent acrobats, with trays of champagne in tall crystal flutes, and canapés on white doilies. At one end of the room, as advertised, there was a long, well-stocked bar managed by three handsome, very busy bartenders and adjacent to the bar, there was a replica of an Anheuser-Busch beer wagon with seven or eight beer taps on the side, where guests could draw their own frosty Budweiser. The beer wagon was a gift from the Busch family, represented by Mike O'Mara, the brewer's longtime marketing vice-president and a close Irish friend of the Judge. In the middle of the room there was a twenty-foot dining table groaning under the weight of the most colossal buffet they had ever seen, enough food, Roscoe speculated, to feed two college football teams for three days. Finally, toward the back there was a ten-piece orchestra capable of everything from Benny Goodman to Bruce Springsteen.

"Have you ever seen anything like this?" Roscoe whispered.

"Never. Look, back there, that's Governor Patterson. Who's he talking to?"

"Stan Musial and Bob Gibson," he answered, sounding like a breathless fourteen year-old boy.

"Hey," Amy reported cheerfully, "there's Janet Preston headed our way."

"Hi Amy," Janet said. "You look fabulous. I love your dress!"

"Thank you, Janet." Amy replied with a big smile.

"You look great yourself," Roscoe told Janet, silently wishing he'd had his suit pressed. "Where's your date?"

"He's over there trying to work up the courage to shake hands with Bob Gibson and Stan Musial. See him circling?"

"What about the governor, doesn't he want to shake his hand?" Roscoe asked with a grin.

"Not even close to the same thing," she answered, laughing. "You two are seated next to us at the Judge's table," she said excitedly. "Isn't this fabulous? All the people!"

"The publisher of the Post-Dispatch is here along with several of his section editors," Roscoe said. "And the paper's society columnist is here I'd bet. Janet, he's a short, fat, charming, absolutely lethal guy. Stay away from him."

"He never stops supervising, Janet," Amy warned, with a grin and a wink. "Show me where our table is, will you? Roscoe needs to go hobnob and make small talk, don't you dear?"

"It's part of the job description. Janet, don't let Amy have too much champagne. She'll start dancing to a song the orchestra isn't playing." They all laughed and the ladies went off toward the tables while he waded into the crowd.

And from that point on, at least for a while, the evening moved magically. Roscoe went from one old friend to another in what seemed like a secret farewell tour. He found Rusty Solich in the men's room.

"Roscoe, old friend," the red-head from south city asked, "are you sure this is what you want? There's no turning back you know? Are you certain?" Then he found Chief Hoskins at the AB Budweiser fountain, and he had the same question. These men were all close friends of roughly the same age, and so each knew what they were facing. But he was first, and so the questions came.

Finally, back at the table, Roscoe found himself with the Judge and his wife, Janet Preston and her date, a tall, handsome guy who had managed to shake hands with Stan Musial and Bob Gibson and who might never quite get over it, Rusty Solich and his wife, and an empty seat assigned to Governor Pete Patterson whose wife had not made the trip and who was busy all night working the room, as only he could. At the table, instead of boy-girl-boy seating, the guys had bunched together and the ladies had been more than happy to do the same.

"Is that Peter Davenport over there, at the bar?" Janet asked.

"It is indeed," answered Cassandra McElroy.

"What is that he is wearing?" Amy asked, whispering.

"It's a turtleneck," answered Janet. "I saw him at lunch the other day and he had one on then. I didn't even know they made them anymore."

"At his age, my dear," started Cassandra McElroy, "it could be considered a compression garment. A neck corset, you might say. When he removes it at night, God knows what jumps out."

"Oh, Mrs. McElroy!" Janet said, trying not to laugh.

"It's Cassie, please, Janet. We're going to know each other a long time, and so it is just Cassie, if you please."

"Yes ma'am," she answered with a smile.

Roscoe announced that after only two Budweisers, he was ready for something more substantial. "Can I get anyone anything?" he asked.

On his way to the bar, Roscoe passed Ray Hoskins.

"Can I buy you a drink?" the chief asked.

"You mean for free, over there?"

"Whatever."

And the two of them had a drink together. And they remembered, and they laughed, and they made predictions. Hoskins did not try to hide the fact that he felt Roscoe had gotten a bad deal at the hands of Peter Davenport. "He's a son-of-a-bitch, Roscoe, we both know it, a god-damned vampire," the chief muttered.

And then, as if on cue, Davenport found his way to the bar. "Roscoe and Ray, law and order, as it were," he said with mock cheerfulness, "how are we doing?"

"Who are *we*?" Hoskins asked, turning firm.

"All of us, of course, all of us happy Republicans," Davenport answered.

"You may recall that I'm apolitical, Peter," Hoskins said.

"Pity, we need all the good Republicans we can find."

"Well, find this up your sorry ass, Peter," Hoskins said, with a curious gesture. He was getting a little drunk. "I'll take leave of you now, lest things go sour."

"My goodness," Davenport said. "The chief is a little cranky, isn't he?"

"You have an effect on people, Peter, I don't know if you've ever heard that before."

"Oh well, police chiefs come and go."

"As we all do, right?"

"I suppose that's right, yes."

"Peter," he said, pausing, "I hear you've decided against Janet Preston, you and your group."

"I'm afraid so," Davenport answered, scratching his forehead like some intellectual. "She is just not ...."

"White? That's the word you're looking for, Peter, isn't it? She's not white enough for you and your courageous friends, the ones we never see. What, do they live under the streets?"

"You listen to me, Mr. Prosecutor, I do not have a racial bias in this matter. What I have is a bias for winning, and yes, regrettably, race factors into winning. There are people, people you may not like, but people who are willing to fund political campaigns, and some of them, not all but some, still think of this state as part of the South. My candidates are hard-working, ambitious, and well-known to the people who contribute money to politicians. If you could swallow your pride for a moment and consider their positive attributes, you might come to favor them — even over your Ms. Preston."

"Maybe you should have your candidates, whoever they are, ready for a Republican primary race," Roscoe said, sipping a whiskey and turning to face the ballroom.

"Well, now there we are! Expensive, but maybe you have a point. Ms. Preston versus one of our picks, may the best man or woman win, so to speak. This may be a very good idea, my friend."

Roscoe had an answer he was eager to give, but suddenly, from nowhere, the governor of Missouri, Pete Patterson appeared.

Patterson, who grew up in the middle of the state and somehow found his way to Harvard Law was able to kick dirt and talk like Andy from Mayberry, and at the same time be the smartest guy in the room.

"Roscoe," the governor said, smiling. "How the hell are you? Crime is down. Missouri is safe. Shit, you should run for governor."

"Thank you, Pete," Roscoe replied. "I think that job is in good hands. It is good to see you. I know the Judge appreciates you being here."

"Good evening, governor," Davenport said anxiously, as if he was feeling left out.

"Peter," the governor said, "and how are you? New shopping malls, coop apartments, lofts? That damned word, *lofts,* so pretentious, don't you think? We don't have any lofts in Jeff City, yet."

"It's great to see you again," Davenport said, with the mistaken belief that the governor could remember the last time they met. "I was hoping to have a private word with you this evening. Whenever it's convenient of course."

"Peter," the governor said, exhaling, "I'm staying at the Raddison tonight. Come by for breakfast in the morning; we can talk business then. Tonight is for old times and friends and fun. How about that?"

"Of course, governor, seven a.m.?"

"Make it eight, in case I have a couple of extra drinks tonight."

"Eight it is, sir." Davenport said, struggling to hide his distain. He was being batted around like a beach ball by some civil servant and he didn't much like it.

"Okay then, boys, I must go see some more of the glitterati. You two play nicely now." And with a smile, the governor was off.

"Roscoe, I wish you'd cool down and give my ideas a little..."

"Peter," he said interrupting. "When I said that you should have your boys ready for a primary challenge, I meant a challenge with an *incumbent.*"

Davenport's face went chalky. "That would be a very big disappointment, Roscoe. We thought you were with us. That would be an embarrassment. We would have to do all we could to beat you, you know that? We thought you had committed to do what was right, to make this your last term."

"I was not part of your deal, Peter. You came to me after it was already done. Nonetheless, I was committed to doing what was right. Let's just say that my idea of what is right is *in flux.*"

"I think we should talk about this tomorrow, when heads are clearer, cooler. You could be making a big mistake."

"I think, Peter, that we should not talk again, ever, that I should go have a dance with my beautiful wife, and you should go find something at the buffet table to choke on. Take big bites."

As Roscoe made his way back to the table, the orchestra began to play *Come Rain or Come Shine*, one of his favorites, especially when performed by Sinatra. How appropriate, he thought to himself.

"Amy, come dance with me. I'm feeling graceful."

"Oh, sure," she laughed. "You mean you're feeling *grateful.*"

"That too."

On the dance floor she made him look considerably better than he was. It was the same thing she did for him in almost any situation. What she got in return was someone who loved her conspicuously, without reserve.

As they danced, he pulled her into him tightly and whispered in her ear. "I need to tell you something."

"Yes, go ahead," she whispered back, smiling.

And they danced on and Roscoe told his wife about his plan. As he did, her eyes grew bright and her smile widened. At one point, she pulled her head back off his shoulder, looked him in the eye and asked, "Really?"

He nodded his head and continued with his story. When the song ended, they stood on the dance floor staring at each other like love-struck kids. She kissed him on the cheek, and said simply, "We'll figure it out together, just like always."

When they got back to the table, Cassie McElroy told Amy that the phone in her purse had been ringing.

"Twice, I think," she said. "I thought about trying to answer it, but I wasn't comfortable digging into your purse."

"Oh, thank you, Cassie," Amy said, as she pulled the phone out and flipped it open. "They were calls from Jamie," she said, turning to Roscoe with an excited look.

"The baby?" Roscoe asked.

"I don't know, I'm going to step out and call him right back."

As Amy left the room, Roscoe explained things to Cassie McElroy who looked concerned. "The calls were from Jamie, my son-in-law in Chicago. Our daughter Kit is expecting and is a week overdue. We may be having a baby!"

"Oh my, how exciting!" Cassie answered.

"Roscoe! It's started!" Amy said, literally shaking.

"Is everyone all right?" Rosoce asked.

"Oh yes! Kit's fine, the baby is doing fine. It's started! We need to go, Roscoe. If we pack and leave first thing in the morning we can be there by noon. We've got get home and pack. Cassie, will you forgive us, we've just got to go? It's been a beautiful night. I'm sorry to rush out on this special evening."

"Nonsense, Amy. You get to Chicago, get to that daughter and grandchild. I'm so excited for you. This makes the night even more special."

"Amy," Roscoe said, "go have them bring the car around. I need to catch the Judge for just one minute. I'll be right behind you."

By about 10:30 p.m. they were home, flinging clothes at two suitcases opened on the bed.

"I don't think I can sleep, I'm so excited," Amy said, trying not to cry.

That's when he noticed the blinking light on the cordless telephone by on the nightstand. He looked up nervously.

"You think Jamie called the house when you didn't answer your cell?"

"Probably," she answered, folding a light sweater. "Check it."

He dialed in the code, held the phone to his ear and listened as the recorded message began to play. Suddenly, the joy that was in his eyes just moments earlier vanished. His face went blank and his shoulders slumped. He sat on the edge of the bed and put one hand over his mouth while the recording came to an end. He turned to Amy.

"Roscoe! What is it?"

"Dad."

The call had come from the doctor, Frank Hammer's doctor, who was at the house with Adella and Frank. He had talked with Frank, who instructed him to stop anything that might prolong the process, a request he had honored. Frank was not in any pain, something the doctor simply could not explain. But the end was near, very near, and Frank had been asking for his son. The doctor promised he would stay with Adella and Frank until Roscoe could get there. But hurry, please. It was now a matter of hours.

"Sweetheart," Roscoe said sadly, "I'm so sorry. I've got to try and get to him. I hate this more than anything. You know I want to be in the car with you tomorrow, headed to Kit and the baby, but I've got to try to get to him."

"Of course you do, Roscoe. I understand that and so will Kit. I've driven to Chicago alone many times. Go to your Dad. Do what you can for him and then come see me and our grandchild. It's going to be all right, Roscoe. It's all going to be fine."

They finished packing, her for one trip, him for another. He phoned Ray Hoskins.

"Ray, I know it's late, and I know it's a lot to ask, but I need another favor. It's my Dad this time, Ray. Can you help me out?"

"When do you need to leave?"

"As soon as possible; I've already packed. I hate to do this…"

"I'll have a patrol car in front of your house in thirty minutes. We'll have you in the air in forty-five."

"Ray," Roscoe said, with a knot in his throat, "thank you."

"What about Amy, will she be going with you?"

"No. Believe it or not, Kit is in labor. Amy is headed to Chicago first thing tomorrow morning. Can you believe the timing of all this?"

"Let me get off the phone and get the ball rolling. Sit tight."

Twenty-five minutes later, Roscoe kissed his wife, admonished her to leave only after sunrise and to drive carefully. And to kiss his first grandchild for him. And to kiss his own baby, Kit. Bag in hand, he went out door and into the dark where, at the end of his front walk he found a St. Louis County patrol car, with a patrolman at the wheel and Ray Hoskins in the front passenger seat.

"Ray," Roscoe started, "what are you doing? You didn't have to.."

"I was getting tired of the party. Wanted to make sure we got you launched as fast as possible."

"You know, Ray," Roscoe said as the patrol car pulled away, "you've been a real friend for a long time. It means a lot to me."

"You want to talk about friendship? The police aren't perfect. We make mistakes. In what, twenty-five or more years, you've had a lot of opportunities to throw me or my guys under the bus. And never, ever once did you. You and Solich, there's not a thing I wouldn't do for either one of you guys. Now, go get in the helicopter. Go take care of your dad. I'm going back to the party and give Davenport some more shit."

Sitting in the helicopter, Roscoe looked out into the dark night sky. The pilot told him through the earphones that they would lift off in three minutes.

"Thank you, officer."

Against the solid blue sky his mind went to the seeming asymmetry of events. In five or six hours, his wife would be headed north, to the suburbs of south Chicago and the start of a new life, and in three minutes he would be flying south, toward the end of another. Soon that thought gave way to a clearer one. These two lives, the one struggling to start and the other, they were part of the same life. They were two plot points on a magical continuum. It reminded him of something he had read in a book as a child. We are life and life is like the tide, without beginning or end. Heaven, with her sun and moon and stars, pulls and pushes, and life ebbs and flows. The tide rises in one place as it recedes in another. There are no beginnings or endings, there is only the tide. As the helicopter lifted off, Roscoe looked at the stars.

"We'll be there in forty minutes sir," the pilot reported.

CHAPTER 38

Judge McElroy found Janet Preston on the dance floor cuddling with her date, winked at the young man, and tapped in.

"Janet," the Judge said, "out the doors and to the right, down the hall, there's a smaller banquet room, which is empty. I wish you would meet me there in a few minutes. I have something important to tell you."

"Of course, Judge," she answered, looking bewildered.

In the smaller banquet room, there was light, but only a little. There was only one table, a round one without a tablecloth, and that's where she found him, smoking one of the Cohiba cigars Roscoe had given him as a birthday gift.

"Sit down, Janet," he said, smiling. "Don't be anxious, this is not bad news."

"What is it, Judge?"

"What I am doing tonight, Janet, is something that Roscoe Hammer preferred to do himself, had his on-the-way grandchild not disrupted the plan."

"His grandchild is on the way, how wonderful!"

"Yes, yes it is," he said, blowing a puff of cigar smoke over his shoulder. "Janet, I don't suppose you've ever read the St. Louis County charter, have you?"

"I am ashamed to say I have not."

"Don't be. Very dull material, trust me. But, it explains some things that may become very important to you."

"Yes, how so?"

"Well, setting aside judges, there are only three elected positions in county government, the county executive, Rusty Solich, the county

226

prosecuting attorney, your boss, and county councilmen, a term, for the record, I use to mean the men *and* women of the county council."

"Noted."

"All of these positions serve four-year terms. The county executive and prosecuting attorney's terms coincide. But half of the council members run for reelection every two years. It's a scheme designed to insure some continuity in county governance. This is why there is a general election every two years. Up to this point, I suspect I have told you what you already know, yes?"

"More or less, yes."

"So, here is the wrinkle that matters tonight. The charter stipulates that in the case of a vacancy in the county prosecutor's position, the county executive appoints a successor from the same political party, a successor who serves in that capacity until the next general election, at which time they run for election for the remainder of the original term."

"Yes?"

"Roscoe Hammer, one of the best prosecuting attorneys I have ever known, has resigned his position effective Monday morning, the day after tomorrow and County Executive Rusty Solich would like to appoint you to replace him. If you accept this appointment, you will be prosecuting attorney for two years, at which time you will, if you choose, run for election to serve the remainder of Roscoe's original term. You will be running as an incumbent."

"God, I don't know what to say."

"My dear, this is where you say yes or no."

"But what about Roscoe?"

"Roscoe has made his decision. It won't change, no matter what you decide. He wanted you to have the best possible chance at replacing him for a long time. But, if he was here tonight, he'd tell you to do what is best for you."

She drew a deep breath, and said, "My answer is yes, Judge, yes. What do we do now?"

"You stay here. In a few minutes Rusty Solich will be in and the governor of Missouri will be with him. You give Rusty your answer, and in the case of Governor Patterson, tell him something that will make him feel good about the personal time he's going to spend refereeing a little Republican family squabble. Don't worry, he's in your corner, Roscoe made sure of that. Just give the man a little reassurance, that's all."

"God, what a night?" she said. "Thank you so much Judge."

"Thank Roscoe Hammer, Janet, thank him."

CHAPTER 39

A t the house on Plum Street, he found the doctor, at the kitchen table with a cup of coffee. It was now creeping up on midnight.

"Doctor, I can't thank you enough for this," Roscoe said.

"Don't mention it. Your father's helper lady, Adella, she's asleep in the guest room. I tried to send her home, but she was having nothing to do with that. Your father has been in and out, but he seems to be sleeping soundly now. I don't mean to be abrupt, but you should know I'm not sure he'll make it through the night. I'm glad you are here."

"Still no pain?"

"None that I can discern. It's a mystery to me."

Roscoe thanked the young doctor again, showed him to the door, and then went to his father's side. Frank's breathing was scratchy and fitful, but he was asleep, and that somehow seemed a good thing. Roscoe pulled a straight chair alongside his father's bed and sat down, feeling the weight of the day and night through his every joint. He was reminded of the night, years before, when he and his faithful Ranger had prayed beside the crib of his little sister. Though he was determined not to, soon enough he drifted off.

When he awoke, he could barely move, crippled by five hours of sleep in a straight chair. He stood, finally, and then teetered. He steadied himself on the back of the chair and wiped sleep out of his eyes. He moved both legs, one at a time, to make sure they would, and only then had the presence of mind to take a good look at his father, still asleep. Frank's face was grey and yellow and stretched. No pain? How could anyone know? His breath was still scratchy, as if when he inhaled, his body did not want to take the breath in.

He sat back down in the chair and wondered about Amy. Was she on the road yet? Was everything still all right with Kit and the baby?

"Roscoe, is that you?" his father whispered, coming out of sleep.

"Dad, yes, it's me. I'm here. It's morning. You've been asleep."

And then, mysteriously, Frank went out. The scratchy breathing resumed, his eyelids fluttered, and he was asleep.

Roscoe staggered to the kitchen, where he found Adella making coffee.

"Adella, you're a saint," he said.

"Your daddy is a saint. I'm an assistant saint."

"May I have some coffee?"

"Absolutely."

She handed him a cup and his cellphone rang. He flipped it open. It was Amy.

"Are you on the road?"

"Yes....grandpa!"

"What?"

"The baby is here, a little girl, Roscoe. We are grandparents! I can't stop crying. People who pass me on the highway think I'm nuts. A little girl! Everybody is fine. Kit, the baby, everybody."

"Ten fingers, ten toes?"

"Since nothing otherwise was reported, I believe our granddaughter has all her parts."

"Oh, Jesus, I wish I was with you. Be careful, get there, hug them Amy. We're so lucky."

"Roscoe, they named her Laura. How about that?"

His throat tightened and he couldn't speak for a second. "Laura?"

"That's right. Tell your dad."

"Be careful. I love you."

"Wait, honey, what about your dad?"

"It's almost over, I think. I'll call you."

Roscoe took his coffee and went back to his father's room, where, surprisingly, he found Frank Hammer awake and fairly alert. Roscoe raised the shade on the south bedroom window and when the bright sun came through it seemed to bring with it new hope. Maybe Frank would recover somehow, get back on his feet, another few weeks, another few whiskeys. But when Roscoe looked into his father's eyes, he saw resolve, acceptance. A sunny one yes, but this day would be the last one, so said his eyes.

"Dad, is everything all right? Are you all right?"

"We're fine, son."

"Kit had her baby, Dad, a little girl."

Frank's eyes, now only half opened, became moist and moved from right to left in unison, like searchlights in a prison yard. And he raised his right hand, no more than eight inches above the bed and extended a crooked index finger, as if preparing to make a point. Finally, having found what they were looking for, his eyes locked.

"The wagon?" he whispered. "The wagon?"

"Amy is on her way to Chicago. She has the wagon. It will be there today. Are you in any pain, Dad?"

"Pain? No pain. The baby's name?"

"They named her Laura, Dad, Laura. How about that?"

Frank smiled and paused for what seemed several seconds. "You and I know how tricky family names can be, don't we?"

"Yes, we do," Roscoe chuckled.

"If she is like Laura, she'll be pretty and smart," he said with tears at the corner of his eyes.

"You're right, dad. You're right about that."

"And everybody is all right?"

"Yes."

"You know how much I enjoy our visits, don't you? Thank you for coming today, Roscoe. I always look forward to these visits." Frank paused for a moment and then said, "Son, would you go and get me some orange juice? I have a taste for some orange juice. Would you mind?"

What Roscoe heard was different from the words that had been spoken to him. *Would you leave me alone now, for just a little while. No son should witness his father's last breath. Because I love you, I wish you would leave me now.*

"Coming right up Pop, coming right up."

Roscoe went to the kitchen, poured a small glass of orange juice and braced himself. He went back to his father's room where the door was only slightly cracked. He stood perfectly still for a moment, hoping for a sound, any sound. In a room, any room, there is no greater silence than the silence made by death. Air doesn't move, cars don't drive by, the trains at the edge of town don't whistle, dogs don't bark. He opened the door and found his father dead. He sat the glass of orange juice on the nightstand. His father was gone. He went to the side of the bed and raised his father's hand up against his own cheek. It was still warm and smelled of Ivory soap. He hoped he would never forget that smell.

CHAPTER 40

In two days, everything was done. He had talked with Hannah and Andy, and though sad, they felt some relief, at least that was his sense of it. Frank's last wishes were not as difficult for Hannah as he had suspected. Colorado had made her less churchy and more spiritual. Andy, as he had anticipated, was agreeable. Amy and Kit and baby Laura were all doing well in Chicago, and he couldn't wait to join them. The tide rises in one place and recedes in another. Consistent with Frank's and the family's wishes, Roscoe had offered Adella the house on Plum Street for as long as she might wish to stay, but she wanted to move to Louisiana to be near what little family she had left. To her, Mitchell, Missouri was Frank Hammer, nothing more, and he was gone now.

And so he came to the last day. Before leaving town, he went to Gertie's, looking, he supposed, for some last shred of his childhood. He went through the door and announced to the young woman in an apron that he had come in search of the perfect apple.

"Well," she said with a smile, "you have a lot to choose from."

"It's a hard choice."

He gazed out the window above the bin of apples, at the old potting shed, still shrouded in honeysuckle and caked with moss. And while he stared, it became like the white center of a kaleidoscope. All the people he had known, Fatty, and Tommy Corks, and Bobby Cato, and Doak Posey, and JL Woodson, George Mabry, and all the rest, all the things he had done and seen, they became like tiny bits of broken colored glass, dancing around the white center, shaping and reshaping themselves into beautiful mosaics, each one more majestic than the one before it.

"The lady we bought this place from, she said the best apple was always in the middle."

"Althea Woodson?" he asked.

"Yes, that's right. How'd you know? Are you from around here?"

"I am. Althea Woodson saved me from monsters when I was a child."

"It's hard to see, I know," the young woman said.

"What?"

"The window, it's so dirty. I'm embarrassed."

"I can see enough," he said.

"If you grew up around here, maybe you can give me a little history, fill in some of the missing pieces."

"There are always some missing pieces, aren't there?" he replied.

"There are around here, yes sir. But, you know what, I guess missing pieces, they are what make life…."

"Magical," Roscoe said, finishing her thought.

"Magical? Well, I'm not sure that was what I was thinking, but okay, magical, I suppose that's right. What was it like growing up around here?"

"Nothing special, I suppose. But then again, I guess that anything really important, I learned it growing up here."

"Like?"

What could he tell her? What had he learned? That there is always something we cannot see, a part of the truth we cannot know? It's the same with magic and life. It's not what you see so much as what you can't. You sit at the bus stop beside the same man every day for one hundred days. You notice things because you are the type of person who notices things. You notice if his shirt is starched, how he combs his hair, if his shoes are shined, if the laces are frayed, you notice all of this. And after a while you begin to talk and before you know it he tells you his story, about his wife and children, and what he did in the war. And after all of this, you think you know about him. But, you don't. You don't because there are always things we cannot see, things we do not know. An old love lost or bargained away. A wound that will not heal. An ancient dream, buried deep but glowing still. The warm memory of a baby's birth. An anonymous act of kindness. These are the things, so often unseen, that shape our lives and the lives of the people we pass on the street every day, the people we stand in line with at the grocery store, the people we love who sleep down the hall. How could he tell her all that?

"That things are never exactly what they seem to be," he answered. "Maybe that's what I learned."

"I suppose that's right," she said. "Take for instance this place. Me and my husband, we had no idea what we were getting into. Kids in and out of here all the time. You can't make any kind of decent life for yourself selling penny candy to school kids. But we didn't know."

He just smiled at the young woman. Would we wish it to be any different, he wondered? If granted perfect knowledge, would be want it? If we could see everything, would we dare look? After all, who has a heart big enough to hold all the world's love and joy, and strong enough to shoulder the sum of its sorrow and suffering? Who has such a heart?

"I think I've got it," he pronounced.

"Sir?" she asked.

"The perfect apple, I've found it," he said, holding up a big red beauty. "How much?"

"For a native like yourself, I think it is on the house."

"Thank you, you're very kind. Can you see that Mercury out at the curb? Do you think she can make it to St. Louis?"

"I don't see why not. Is that where you are headed?"

"I'm going there to catch a flight to Chicago."

"Sounds exciting. Enjoy the apple."

"A last question if you don't mind? Do you imagine yourself ever selling this place?"

"Absolutely! My husband and I want to move to Florida and retire at the water's edge. Warmer weather. First good chance we get."

"Well, then, my best to you," he said with a smile. "So long."

When he turned toward the front screen door a cool dry breeze came through and it carried with it a chorus of angels, the voices of children on their way to Masonhall Elementary. And he felt lucky.

The End

CPSIA information can be obtained
at www.ICGtesting.com
Printed in the USA
LVHW041558130619
621125LV00002B/310